ESSENTIALISM

a Life. Destiny. Fate. *novel*

The Story of Bridgette and Troy

LK COLLINS

Print Edition

Cover Design by Allie Brennan, B Designs
Edited by Lisa Christman, Adept Edits
Formatting by Paul Salvette, BB eBooks
Photography by Pawel Sierakowski

Table of Contents

Dedication

To my mother, for giving me the strength to be the woman I am today. I love you.

Prologue

-Bridgette-

On the drive over to Drain Café, I call Troy. That's where he told me to meet him when he sent the flowers. I know I'll be there in a few minutes, but I can't seem to get enough of him; he is sex on a motherfucking stick. His eyes, they mesmerize me, combined with his messy hair, and ludicrous body. I just become a flustered mess when he's around.

Regardless of his looks – he's real. That's what I like most about him. I've met and been involved with a lot of fake people, so being around him and his genuineness feels so right. Pulling into a parking spot, I look for his Jeep. It's nowhere in sight, so I decide to head in and order for us.

My heels hit the ground, and the moment my car door closes, a hand clamps over my mouth. "Don't make a fucking sound."

Fear takes over my body as I instantly recognize the voice. Standing behind me, holding me against my will, is a monster. My worst fears are coming true. "Did you get my flowers?"

Tears fill my eyes as he removes his hand from my mouth and I stand frozen…petrified. "Answer the goddamn question, Bridgette."

I nod my head trying to pull myself out of the daze I am in. I know I have to do something. I have to fight. There's anger in his voice, and the repercussions terrify me. I begin to kick and scream, attempting to lunge out of his arms. But physically, I don't stand a chance and I quickly find that out.

Suddenly my body begins to burn, everything hurts, and I shake violently until…blackness.

Chapter 1

Boyfriend

Jesus Christ, I hate moving. *Note to self, find a good enough job to afford movers for the next go around.* Honestly, I didn't realize how much shit I had until I started to load it all into the U-Haul. A light rap on my door takes my attention away from organizing. "Come in," I say.

My roommate, Cara, comes in and sits on the bench at the end of my bed. "Are you getting all settled in?" she asks.

"Yeah, I am. Thanks for letting me move in."

She shakes her head. "Don't thank me; this is your sister's place. I'm as lucky as you are to be living here, rent-free."

Cara is so sweet. She's newly pregnant and glowing. I know we are going to get along beautifully. From the moment I met her we clicked. "Well then, we're both lucky."

"So tell me what you've been up to."

"Honestly, school. I'm so glad it's over. It felt like I

was never going to graduate."

She laughs as my phone beeps on my nightstand. I grab it checking the message, and Cara asks, "Who's that?"

"Uhh. My…boyfriend."

"Are you serious?"

I nod my head.

"Since when?"

"I don't know, a month or so."

"You really should've told me this earlier," she says.

"Why?" I ask, confused.

"Ummm. I may or may not have given your number to Troy."

My stomach knots up thinking about him. I push away those feelings because I know they're wrong. I'm with David. "I've been meaning to tell you, I really have. It's just…things are new and I've been so busy getting ready to move down here."

"It's all right. I know all about being busy. So what's his name?"

"David."

"Are you going to tell me anything else about him?" she asks jokingly.

"Yeah, of course. He graduated last year from CSU. I met him when I was at a party a few months ago. We became good friends and then it evolved into more. He lives in Fort Collins for now, but is planning on moving down."

"And he's good to you?"

I nod my head and Cara says, "Oh Bridgette, that's great. I'm really happy for you."

"Thanks," I respond grabbing a stack of hangers to use on my last pile of clothes.

"Well, I'll let you finish getting settled. I'm gonna run and grab some dinner from The Cherry Cricket; I'm craving their fries. Do you want anything?"

"Yeah, I'll take a cheeseburger and some fries."

"Cool. I'll be back soon."

As she walks off I plop down on my bed with my phone and reread David's text. *Sorry I couldn't make it to help with the move, love. I had a tournament that ran all day. I made a G so it was worth it.*

Thinking about his text, I'm unsure how to respond. Inside, I'm sad that he wasn't here to help me and meet everyone. I know he's always been into poker, more so now than ever. It's how he makes his living. However, it's starting to interfere with *us*. It used to not bother me, but now it takes all of his time. It's not just that; I feel like there is something else going on. ***It's okay. I missed you. But Cara got some friends to help, so it went smoothly. I'm about done unpacking now.***

Who???? he immediately texts back.

Her boyfriend, my sister's boyfriend, Alexa, me, and a friend of theirs. I make sure that I give everyone a title so he knows that two of the three guys are taken. He has recently become possessive against – or rather jealous of – other men.

Who's the friend?

Troy, he works with Cara's boyfriend.

Does he have a girlfriend?

I don't know, David. Does it matter?

Yeah, it does. I don't like you hanging out with single guys.

I don't even know how to respond to his text. It's honestly crazy that I have to think about those kinds of things, but I do. Thinking back through our relationship, I never saw any of this coming. It's like he hid behind a well-placed mask, until he had me right where he wanted me. Now, I guess he's letting his true colors show. Since I don't know how to respond to him, I don't, hoping he lets this one go.

I decide to shower before I eat dinner with Cara; wash away the grime that accompanies moving. Turning on the water, I faintly hear my phone beep. *Damn it.* I go to check it and to my surprise, it's not David.

I hope you don't mind me texting you. I asked Cara for your number. I know I should've asked you, but…I'm a pussy. Now that we have that out of the way, I guess I should tell you who this is. It's Troy. Am I rambling? I feel like I am. Okay, foot in mouth. I'll shut up.

I can't help but giggle at his words as my fingers move over the keyboard. ***First of all, I DON'T mind. Secondly, you're not a pussy. I watched you move all my stuff; that's the last word I would use to describe you. And lastly, I don't mind rambling. Please don't shut up – I need a distraction.***

I hit send and then reread my words. Crap, why did I tell him I watched him move all of my stuff?

I've been told I'm a good distraction. LOL.

Really?

Yeah, by my sixth grade teacher. She said I interrupted the class more than any other student in her 27 years of teaching.

I can't help but laugh again. ***Well, I just laughed out loud so I think you've succeeded again.***

As I contemplate what to say next, another text from him comes in. *I gotta run, we just got dispatched on a call. TTYL.*

Go figure, that's my luck. Well, he is a firefighter, so I'm sure this kind of thing happens to him all the time. That brings me back to David. It's really not like him to drop something, although I'm thankful for the reprieve. I know I probably shouldn't be texting with Troy, but it felt good to just have fun with someone. I mean, the guy's hilarious – how could I resist?

Chapter 2

Secrets

Staring at myself in the mirror, I'm not sure of my outfit. David's coming down from Fort Collins and invited me out to dinner. He's particular about style. Looking in the mirror I don't think my shorts are that short and I don't want to change what I feel comfortable in. I stick to my black shorts and silver, sequined tank. I go against throwing on a pair of heels because David is short, and wear flats instead.

Emerging from my room, Cara is posted up on the couch wrapped in a blanket with her iPad. "Are you sure you don't want to come out with me?" I ask.

"Thanks, but I'm not feeling well. You go and have fun. Abel's bringing a movie over when he gets off, so we're gonna relax."

"Works for me. Besides, it's just David and I going to dinner. So it might be a little awkward if you came. Don't wait up for me; it might be a long night."

"You're so silly, why did you even ask?" she questions

me laughing.

"I didn't wanna be rude."

"Whatever. Just be safe and call me if you need a ride."

"Yes, ma'am," I say nodding my head before I turn and walk out.

Getting in my car, I text David to let him know I'm on my way and buckle up. The restaurant is close to my condo and within five minutes, I've arrived. I know this area well, and parking is always a bitch, so I valet and walk into the upscale eatery. It's small and intimate, yet modern. The lighting is dim and the décor is black.

Looking for David, I'm not seeing him, so I decide to head to the bar. As I wait for my drink, I catch a glimpse of him entering the front doors. He looks even better than I remember, with his dark hair and retro fashion. "Hey, love," he says with an ear-to-ear smile.

I turn and slide off of the barstool, looking into his large, brown eyes – they're so dark, they're almost black. He smiles at me. "Hey to you," I respond, and kiss him on the lips. All we get in is a quick peck before we're interrupted. "Yo, Dave, the table's ready," Xavier, one of his obnoxious friends, says.

"Miss, your drink's ready," the bartender calls from behind me.

I turn and grab my seven and seven. "We'll be right there," David says with irritation in his voice. "What's with the outfit?" he questions me.

I look at him confused. "I thought it was only going to be us for dinner."

"Does that matter? I just saw the bottom of your ass and your tits are hanging out."

"David, it's only shorts and a tank top."

"Exactly, that's all it is. You need to wear more clothing and cover yourself up."

I don't respond; I just stare into his eyes trying to fathom where this is coming from. He never used to care what I wore. Then he grabs my hand and leads me in the direction his friends went. "There's a tournament that popped up tonight; that's why the guys came."

Approaching the table, it's loud. His friends are by far the loudest in the place. As we sit, David joins in on the conversation with them. Glancing over the menu, I honestly don't have an appetite. After the way he's acted, there is no way I can stomach anything. I decide on a salad so I have something to pick at.

Listening in on their exchange, it's all about how David won the tournament last night and they know he will have a victory tonight. I sit back observing, getting pissed that David is acting like I'm not even here. I send Cara a text in frustration. ***Guess what? David invited about ten of his friends along to dinner. This is so romantic.***

What? No, he didn't! Why would he do that?

You got me, and here I was actually thinking he missed me.

I'm so sorry. What are you gonna do?

I don't know… ☹

"Are you okay?" David asks me.

"Uh-huh."

"You sure?" he asks creasing his brows at me.

"I just thought tonight was going to be the two of us, and since we sat down, you haven't said a word to me. Why did you even invite me?"

"Come on, Bridgette, it was supposed to be the two of us. Then this tournament came up, and you know how I roll. I can't go in alone. You understand, don't you?" he says holding the back of my head. I nod my head, because it's not worth the fight, when what I should do is walk out on him. He kisses my cheek and turns back to his friends.

I sit back against my chair frustrated. That is until a message comes through from Troy and my insides turn to mush reading it. *Sorry I had to run the other night. Where were we?*

I think I was in need of a good distraction. Can you help a sister out?

For you, I can do anything.

That simple statement provokes me. He's such a charmer and knows exactly what he's doing.

Anything?

Yes. I think you would be surprised what I'm capable of.

Thinking of my response, David interrupts me and asks, "What are you going to order?"

I set my phone facedown on the table and glance at

the waiter. "Uhhh, I'll have the Mediterranean salad please." I'd been completely unaware that he was waiting for me. I'm here for David and that's what matters, right? So I try and ignore my phone "What have you been up to?" I ask him.

But he continues to talk to his friends and I see no point in trying to get his attention. My phone vibrates and as I check it, David asks, "Who are you texting?"

"Oh, it's just Cara."

"Hmm," he says staring into my eyes. "Can I see?"

"What, you mean check my phone? No, you can't. I'm not your fucking property to do what you please with. I've sat here like your puppy dog and been ignored long enough." I stand and throw my napkin on the table and with everyone staring at me I say, "Goodnight, David!" Leaving him stunned.

Once I reach the fresh air, I breathe it in filling my deprived lungs. Getting upset always causes my breathing to spiral out of control. Handing my ticket to the valet, I wait and hope he hurries, but he's not fast enough. "Bridgette, don't go. I'm sorry, love. I shouldn't have questioned you."

"You're damn right you shouldn't have. David, I sat there for our *entire* date while you ignored me, and then you have the audacity to question me."

"I know, but I swear the name on your phone said Troy. I can be insecure, and that's not your fault. I'm really sorry. Please don't go," he says, pulling me against him and looking in my eyes. "Will you stay?"

"David, I don't get you. It's like you want me, then when you have me, you don't."

"I do want you, trust me, I do. I'll work on being a better boyfriend. I'm sorry I invited the guys. I'll make it up to you. I promise. Just come back in and eat dinner with me, okay?"

I want to leave, but guilt is eating me up for lying to him. The screen on my phone did say Troy and he saw it. Feeling bad, I agree to eat my meal in order to calm the waters. The valet pulls up and hops out, holding my door open for me. "Can you repark it?" I ask.

"Sure thing, you can grab another ticket from Jeremy."

David and I turn to head back in. He grabs the new valet ticket, wrapping his arm around me.

We reach the table and his friends don't even acknowledge us as we sit back down. "Thank you," David says.

"Of course. I'm sorry I got upset and left."

"Don't mention it. I'm really glad you came back." During our meal we laugh and talk, and David makes sure to keep his attention on me so I know he's trying. My phone keeps vibrating in my purse, but I'm scared to look at it. I'm sure it's Troy, so I leave it be. It doesn't take us long to finish our food and David's posse to make their game plan for getting to the tournament. "Are you sure you don't want to come?" David asks.

"Yeah, I'm sure. Thank you, though."

David has a firm grip on my hand as everyone stands and starts to head out. Xavier stops us, "Here's to good luck, D." He shakes David's hand and passes him something. "Don't take it all at once."

"Cool, thanks, dawg."

We walk out and David puts whatever he gave him in his pocket. "What was that?" I ask.

"Nothing, love. Thank you for dinner. I'll call you after I'm done and let you know how I did, okay?"

I shake my head, puzzled by what just happened. *What did Xavier give him?* My gut tells me that it was nothing good. The David I know is not that kind of person…or is he? Thinking back to how he snapped and how he's recently changed, maybe there is something bigger going on. For the time being I let it go. I'm not one to be prying regarding someone's secrets, especially when I have one of my own buzzing in my purse.

Chapter 3

Cut

I'm officially exhausted. I took my resume everywhere today and no one seems to be hiring, at least not for what I have my degree in. As I walk to my car to head back home, my cell phone rings. "Hello?" I answer, fishing my keys out of my purse.

"Oh my God, please tell me you're on your way home," Cara says in an exhausted tone.

I can't help but titter at her. "Yeah, I am. Are you okay?"

"I'm fine, I just need your help."

"All you have to do is ask."

"Thank you. Hurry home and we'll talk then. I'm carrying in groceries."

The line goes silent and I don't think I want to know what she is up to. The day is hot and my car is even hotter as I get behind the wheel. My legs instantly stick to the leather interior. Immediately, I start the engine and blast the A/C. On the drive home I call David; I haven't talked to him since dinner. He never called like he said he would and that was over a week ago. He answers on the fifth ring and I say, "Hey there, stranger."

"Who's this?"

"Are you kidding me? It's Bridgette, your girlfriend!"

"Oh shit…I'm sorry, love. I didn't recognize your voice. What's up?"

"Nothing!" I snap. "What's up with you?"

He proceeds to ramble on for the next fifteen minutes about himself and his poker games. He never asks how I am, or what I have been doing. Instead, he talks a mile a minute. I finally lose track of what he is saying, thinking about Troy. "Does that work for you?" he asks.

"Huh?" I respond, a little lost, bringing myself out of the cloud I'm currently in.

"I wanna see you. Can you come up here tonight?"

Automatically I lie. If he's not even going to know my voice when he answers the phone, I'm not about to give him my time. "I can't. I have plans with Cara and the rest of the week depends on what happens with the resumes I dropped off today. There were some really promising places. Hopefully, I'll have some interviews coming up soon."

"But I miss you, love. I need you."

"I miss you too."

"Soon?

"Yes, soon."

"Are you behaving without me?"

"Of course, are you?"

"What?"

"Nothing. Listen, I gotta run. Cara's bringing groceries in and needs my help."

"Behave, Bridgette."

I hang up completely and utterly…frustrated. Where did that come from? One second he doesn't recognize my voice, then he's sweet and misses me, then he's being possessive and telling me to *behave.* I thought we'd moved passed the controlling shit the other night after I walked out on him at dinner. Irritated, I push away all thoughts of him and focus on hanging out with Cara. She needs my help and I want to be there to help her any way I can.

Walking into the house, her iPod is blasting and she is feverishly working away in the kitchen. I turn it down and look over her shoulder. "Whatcha making?" I ask.

"A cake. Thank God you're here."

I bust out laughing at her when I see she has flour on her face and looks exhausted. "I'm all yours, but you have to tell me what has you in such a tizzy."

"It's Matt's birthday and Abel forgot to tell me about it. The poor guy doesn't have any family here, so Abel agreed to have a party for him at the station and asked me to cook. When Abel asked what he wanted for his birthday, the only thing he said he wanted was a cake like his mom used to make."

"That's not a big deal. We can totally do this."

"Bridgette, there are going to be almost twenty

firefighters there."

"It's okay. Take a deep breath. Let me change and I'll help you."

She nods her head and I go into my room unzipping my dress and stepping out of it. I grab a pair of jean shorts and go in search of a tank top in my dresser. My phone interrupts me, like it always does.

I hear I get to see you tonight. Now I have something to look forward to.

That you do, although I might be cooking, I'll be there.

Works for me, I'm glad we'll get to talk more. I'm at the liquor store now, do you want me to grab you anything?

A bottle of Tuaca! LOL.

That's my kind of girl. See you soon.

I was joking, I text back, but I get no response. Oh well, there's nothing wrong with taking a shot. Or two. Or three.

"All right, girl. How can I help?" I ask Cara.

"Can you wash and cut all the veggies?"

"Sure thing. What are we making?"

"Italian subs. I've made them for the guys before and they *loved* them, especially Matt."

"Why don't we set everything out buffet style and let them add what they want to their subs? It would be easier on us and that way everyone gets what they want."

"You're a genius."

"Nah, just thinking outside the box."

Cara and I work feverishly in the kitchen preparing all the fixings for the sandwiches. Then I watch her decorate the cake. She really is quite talented at it, not to mention her writing is perfect and looks professional. After we load everything into the shiny new white Tesla my brother-in-law, Vincent, bought for her, she drives us to the station. Glancing at my phone, I see a text from Troy. I open it to see he sent me a picture of the Tuaca bottle and two shot glasses. "What's that?" Cara asks as we approach a stoplight, glancing over.

I show it to her. "Troy sent it to me."

"So you've been texting him?"

"Yeah."

"Does he know about David?"

I shake my head unable to speak the words. I hate lying. "Are you going to tell him?" she asks.

"I don't know. I mean, should I? Troy and I are only friends. I don't see the point of telling one about the other."

"You sure that's a smart move, girl? I'd be worried that it would come back to bite me in the ass."

"Ugh, that would be awful," I say and glance out the window hoping she's not right.

Pulling up to the station, there are a ton of vehicles. A good amount of people are standing around outside watching a group of guys playing basketball. As I get out of the car, I can't help but join in on the gawking. I lean back watching the sweaty men battle back and forth. I don't recognize any of them except for Abel. He sees us and shoots the ball, scoring.

"God, isn't he so yummy?" Cara says, as she slides up next to me and leans against her car watching the show. Abel jogs away from the game and Cara immediately goes towards him. I continue staring, but am pulled out of my daydream by Troy saying, "I don't know what's so interesting over there, considering I'm not in the game and all."

I can't help but laugh at him. "I was just looking for you."

"Sure you were. Come give me a hug, you naughty, little thing." He wraps his arms around me and instinctively I cling to him, resting my head on his chest. "You know, you really are small," he says looking down at me.

I look up into his mesmerizing eyes and respond, "You know, you're really tall." He's wearing a hat, but I can still see his brown hair. It's normally a mess and I would love to feel it in my fingers.

"Eh, I've been told that in my day."

"In your day? How old are you?"

"Twenty-six. How 'bout you?"

"Twenty-two."

"See, I do have you by a few years. So I can say 'in my day.'"

I slap his chest and he releases me placing his hand over the place I hit. "Did you really just hit me? You've got some anger issues, girl."

"I don't have anger issues; you're the one—"

Cara and Abel interrupt our banter and look between us. We each point at the other placing the blame on one another. "All righty," Cara says. "Let's get all this food inside and feed these beasts."

She pops the trunk open and the guys grab everything, taking it inside. Cara and I walk behind and she asks me, "What was all that about?"

"He was being annoying. I was only picking on him."

"Uh-huh," she says rolling her eyes.

I ignore her comment and focus on getting everything set up. As we empty all the bags and work together getting the food laid out, I can't keep my eyes off of Troy, and every time I look at him he is looking at me. Finally, I move to the opposite counter and start slicing the bread. This way my eyes can only stare at the wall in front of me. I turn my focus onto deep-breathing exercises for a distraction. That is until I feel Troy behind me. I look to my left and he is reaching in a cabinet above me, pressing his pelvis into my behind. I can't help but smile as he squeezes my hip before he turns around and works at the island. Great, there is no hope in calming my erratic breathing now.

Fuck. My finger.

I yelp in pain and stick it in my mouth. "Are you okay?" Cara asks.

I nod my head as I fight back the tears. *It hurts so bad.* I can feel my pulse throbbing in the tip of it. I decide to take it out of my mouth and I wish I hadn't. Blood runs down my finger and Troy grabs a towel.

"All right, let's get it wrapped up. You need to keep pressure on it to stop the bleeding."

"Mmm-hmm," I say nodding my head.

"Troy, why don't you take her downstairs and clean her finger up," Abel says.

"Of course. Follow me, Bridge, and I'll fix you up." I smile and follow him downstairs. "Normally, I would take you down the pole, but seeing as you're injured, that's going to have to wait 'til next time."

"Thanks."

As we get downstairs, Troy directs me to sit on a bench between the ambulance and fire truck while he grabs what he needs out of a supply cabinet. "Are you okay?" he asks me.

"Yeah. It just hurts."

"I'm sure it does. This isn't going to feel any better. Let me look at it; I won't do anything without telling you first, okay?"

Removing the towel, I place my hand in his. He looks at the wound and then at me. "Jesus, Bridge, that's a deep cut. No wonder it hurts."

"I can't look at it."

"That's okay. I'm going to pour some peroxide on it. This may sting a little, but not for long."

"I trust you," I say and feel the cool liquid run over

my finger. Then he gently pats it dry.

"You probably could use a stitch or two, but if you can keep it dry I can use surgical glue instead."

"Whatever you think is fine with me."

"It's gonna burn, so take my hand, I want you to squeeze the shit out of it."

I glance at him as he places my hand in his lap. Instantly my finger begins to burn when he starts to apply glue. *Sonofabitch, it fucking hurts.* I bite my bottom lip and squeeze his hand as hard as I can. After a few moments, the pain subsides, soothed by him blowing on it. I look at him and watch the care he takes with repairing my injured finger.

"Are you this good with all of your patients?" I ask.

"Nope, only you."

I glance at my finger. The cut is closed and the bleeding has stopped. I watch as he applies another coat and blows again, this time he looks into my eyes. After a minute he rubs my finger on his bottom lip and then tenderly kisses it. All the while his eyes never leave mine. I realize then that we're still holding hands as he intertwines our fingers.

My heart is pounding and my mouth is dry with wantonness. "Bridge, are you okay?" Cara asks as she comes down the wooden stairs with her heels clanking.

Troy places one more kiss on my finger before letting go of both of my hands. "Yeah, I'm good," I say to her as she rounds the corner and comes into view.

"Nothing a little surgical glue couldn't fix," Troy says as he wraps a Hello Kitty Band-Aid around my wounded finger.

"Seriously, Troy?" I ask.

"What? It's all we have."

"That's such a lie; there are other Band-Aids right there." I point into the first aid kit he's closing.

"Now you are going delusional, woman. Let's get you some food and I believe you ordered Tuaca for tonight."

We all laugh and head upstairs. I can't help but smile looking at the pink Band-Aid covering my finger. And then thinking of his lips, when they delicately kissed my finger, and the look in his eyes – there's something about that look. I can't pinpoint what it is, but it's there.

Chapter 4

Piggy Back Rides

"Troy, maybe you should just carry her to the car," Cara says, as I try to focus on looking between the two of them.

"I'm fine," I interject and push myself off of the kitchen counter. As soon as I move, I regret it, losing my balance. Troy steadies me.

"You, my lady, are most definitely *not* fine. Hop on," he says and turns his back to me.

I hesitate for half a second and then wrap my arms around his neck and my legs around his body. As he stands, I can't help noticing how hard his muscles are, and how his warm hands wrapped so possessively around the sensitive skin of my thighs feels…so right.

"Hold on tight, Bridge."

"I told you I'm fine," I argue back, resting my cheek on his back as we begin to move. Each stair bounces us and he carries me as if I'm weightless.

We make it down before Cara and Abel. They're still at the top of the stairs wrapped up in one another.

Approaching Cara's car, Troy sets me down and then stands turning to look at me. "Are you sure you're okay?" he asks.

I nod my head, feeling everything begin to spin. *Focus, Bridgette.* "Thank you for the ride."

"The first one's free, but I'll have to charge you next time," he jokes.

"How much?" I slur, trying to concentrate on his face.

"Let's get to next time and I'll tell you," he says pulling me into a tight bear hug. I breathe him in and sigh heavily. Mixed emotions run through me; unbidden, David pops in my mind. I haven't thought about him all night, why now?

Cara approaches the car and unlocks it. Troy opens the passenger door and I plop down. He leans his head on his forearm and looks at me. "Buckle up," he orders.

I glare at him and reach for the belt, fumbling to get it clicked. Chuckling, he leans over me and clicks it in place. I swat at him and say, "I told you I'm fine."

"I know you are, but safety first. Good night, Bridge," he says inches from my face and kisses my forehead, leaving me stunned – speechless.

My door closes and Cara starts the car. "Oh, girl, you're playing with fire."

I place my head in my hands; she's so right. "Cara, tell me what to do."

"I wish I could, but I can't. What I do know is some-one is going to end up hurt. You need to decide if you want that to be Troy or David."

I contemplate Cara's words. As much as I don't want to believe her, I know she's right. Closing my eyes, I let the alcohol set in and drift off to sleep; it feels better than beating myself up.

I wake to a knock on my door. *Jesus, it's way too early to be awake.* I'm in bed and faintly remember Cara helping me in here. "Go away," I moan into my pillow. The door opens and speaking into my pillow I say, "Cara, you better have a damn good excuse for waking me up." She doesn't respond, but turns the light on. "Cara," I snap, pulling the covers over my head.

She sits on the bed and takes the covers, gently pulling them off of my face. I look over at her with one eye opened and gasp when I see Troy sitting there.

"How are you feeling?" he asks.

I shake my head, completely mortified. "What are you doing here?"

"I came to check on you."

"You snuck in here?"

"No, Cara let me in. How are you feeling?"

"I don't know. I'm cold and tired."

"I'm sorry, but you did drink *a lot.* I brought you a Starbucks. Maybe that will help?" I smile at him and can't help the shiver that courses through my body. "You're adorable in the morning."

"Thank you," I whisper, and he lies down next to me. We're facing each other; he's on top of the covers while I'm huddled underneath. Taking his right arm, he pulls me to him. I nuzzle myself against his chest and close my eyes, knowing deep down this is so wrong. *I shouldn't be doing this, I shouldn't be doing this, I shouldn't be doing this.* I repeat the words in my head, but the truth is he comforts me. He doesn't push me to do anything more. I know he came here with good intentions. He really just wanted to check on me and make sure I was okay. I've never met a guy like him. Hell, I never even knew they existed.

He takes his fingers and runs them through my hair while we lay in silence and he lets me just be. Radiating heat disburses off of his body and engulfs me, lulling me to drift back to sleep.

…My dreams are consumed with him and we are doing bad things – very bad things. I'm locked in a basement, tied to a bed and blindfolded. Everything is dark and it's a bit scary until I feel his lips on my forehead and then slowly he moves them to mine and the rest of the way down my body.

Once he reaches my breasts, he attacks them, growling while he does so. My body moves and bows beneath him. He pulls up hard on a nipple before he lays down on me. His naked, hot body is pressed onto mine, his pulse is hard moving through his groin.

Sliding the blindfold up, he looks into my eyes. Like always, he mesmerizes me. Giving me a cocky smirk, his mouth consumes mine, taking full control. I pull on the rope wanting to touch him – but I can't.

He looks at me and says, "You know the rules, Bridge. Behave or I'll spank you."

"But I want to touch you."

"Not yet; let me indulge in you first."

Closing my eyes I lean my head back. Troy pulls himself up off of me and lets his mouth take over, kissing everywhere. He takes particular time with each of my ankles, kissing the sides before moving his way up.

Once he has drenched both of my legs from top to bottom, he pulls my body down, giving no slack on the restraints, and spreads my legs wide. "Jesus, you're beautiful."

I smile at him, watching his eyes roam every bit of my naked body. Gently, he nudges his cock against my awaiting pussy, teasing and tantalizing me, taking a great amount of pleasure in doing so. I whimper waiting for him to fill me…

Gasping awake I'm short of breath and look next to me. *Dammit, he's gone.* On my nightstand sits the Starbucks and a pink Hello Kitty Band-Aid. *Shit, how long did I sleep for?* Feeling bad for falling asleep, I text him.

You left me…

You needed to rest. Trust me I could've stayed and watched you all day. You're breathtaking while you sleep.

Chapter 5

Preparation

I'm sitting at the table waiting for Lex, and I can't help but anxiously tap my fingers. We're meeting for lunch and she said she has a surprise for me. I'm not the biggest fan of surprises. I push away the anxiety and enjoy the view from the table. It overlooks the interstate and all of the cars bustling by, with the Rocky Mountains in the background.

"Hey, doll," Alexa says, pulling me away from my thoughts.

Promptly I stand and hug her, holding her tightly against me. "Hi. You look amazing, have you lost weight?" I ask.

We separate and both take our seats. "Yeah, about ten pounds. Vince and I have been doing hot yoga. It's a killer workout. You should come with us sometime."

I chuckle at her comment and glance at my phone noticing David is calling. I ignore it. "Well, if it promises I'll look as good as you, sign me up."

"Whatever," she says. "You're gorgeous, Bridgette.

You always have been and always will be."

"Thanks, sweets. So you have to tell me, what's the surprise? It's killing me."

The waiter comes by interrupting us and takes her drink order. I can't help but get lost in his hands, thinking of Troy's holding mine.

"Uhhh...earth to Bridgette. Did you hear me?"

"Hear what?" I ask.

"I said if you think he's cute, you should get his number. Aren't things with David kind of rocky anyways?"

Propping my elbows on the table I rest my chin in my hands. "I don't know what's going on with him."

"Care to tell me what's going on with Troy then?" she asks, with one eyebrow raised.

"Damn Cara. If she weren't pregnant I would punch her. She's the worst at blabbing everyone's business."

Alexa grins and says, "Calm down, it wasn't Cara who told me anything. It was Vince. Troy told Abel and Abel told Vince."

"Oh God, what did he say?"

"Well, for starters that you got drunk the other night at the station and Troy had to give you a piggyback ride to the car and buckle you in. Then I know there was some early morning cuddling, and that's about all. So spill the beans – what's going on with you two?"

"Jesus, hearing you say it out loud makes it sound so much worse. I mean, since I have a boyfriend and all."

"Hey, it's me you're talking to. You know I won't

judge you."

"I know. David's just changed, not to mention that he's practically ignored me since I moved. Then I met Troy – it's been a breath of fresh air. He's so real and funny and genuine. He gets me and lets me be myself, not who he wants me to be. With David, I always feel like I'm putting on a persona of someone I'm not. With Troy, it's not like that at all."

The waiter brings her drink and as I look at him, Troy's face flashes before my eyes. I can't help but smile and know no one compares to Troy with looks. My phone rings again; it's David and I decline his call. Christ, I just want to have lunch with my sister. I'm not about to drop what I'm doing because he decides to finally call me.

"Thank you," Alexa says to the waiter.

"What can I get you ladies?"

We both order and he looks back at me as he walks off. "Well, you just poured your heart out, and if I heard you right, it sounds like it's pulling you towards Troy."

"Yeah, I think it is. I guess I have some soul-searching to do. Anyways, can we not talk about my love life anymore? I *need* you to tell me about the surprise."

"I guess that's the reason we're having lunch. So I know you've been looking for a job and have applied just about everywhere. Well, I brought an idea up to Vince a while ago. I told him we need an office manager. He agreed and then it dawned on me, with your degree and all, you'd be great for the job."

"Are you serious?" I ask excitedly.

"Yes. So he talked to Liam and C.J. and they agreed to interview you. And this stays between you and me. Vince said they are all onboard, if the meeting goes well."

"Lex, that's amazing."

"Well, you deserve it. Think of how cool it would be if we worked together?"

"Oh my God, it would be the best. So when can I meet with them?"

"Tomorrow at 9:00am."

"That's perfect. I can't wait."

I finish my lunch with a perma-grin on my face. This is what I've been waiting for. All I have to do is knock their socks off. Alexa was kind enough to help get me this far, now it's all me.

I spend the rest of our lunch grilling my sister, asking any and all questions I can think of, about the firm. I really wanna be prepared. As I leave the restaurant, I decide to call David back, since he called me four times, and never left a message. I want to know what's so urgent. He doesn't answer either so I leave him a voicemail. On the drive, I think about my clothing options for the morning and decide to swing by the mall. My work attire is lacking. I know in order to knock 'em dead in my interview, I'm going to need the right clothes to get the job done.

I make quick work of my time at Macy's and once I've settled on the perfect outfit, I check out and take the escalator down to the exit. On my way out I stop at the perfume counter, smelling each delicious fragrance until I reach my favorite – Juicy Couture. As I spray a few squirts on my wrist and neck, I indulge in the scent and wish I had enough money to buy this for myself. However, I stay optimistic and know after I land this job, I will. Turning away from the counter I run smack dab into Troy. "Oomph," I yelp as I hit his hard body.

He laughs at me. "Sorry, I thought you knew I was behind you."

"No! I didn't know you were there. Were you watching me?"

"Maybe."

"Okay, now that's just creepy. Did you follow me here too?"

"As much as I wish I did, I didn't. I got lucky. I'm here with my mom and sister. What about you, what brings you here?"

"You're not going to believe it. My sister got me an interview tomorrow at the law firm where she works. You know how hard I've been looking for a job."

He hugs me tight and says, "Congrats, Bridge. I'm so happy for you. You're going to do awesome."

"Thanks," I say as we separate.

His phone rings and he pulls it out of his pocket. "Do you mind if I grab this really quick?"

"No, of course not. Go ahead."

He smiles as he answers and I try not to listen, but honestly I can't take my eyes off him. *God, he's tall.* My eyes scan down his body. He's wearing dark jeans, a black t-shirt, and some bright purple Nikes. I love his style; I can tell he's confident and doesn't care what others think.

"Sorry," he says. "That was my mom, I have to meet her and my sister for lunch. I'm really glad I ran into you though."

"Me too."

"When can I see you again?"

My phone rings saving me from answering his question. "I gotta take this," I say answering it.

"Good luck tomorrow," he whispers and kisses my forehead, before walking away.

"Who was that?" David questions.

"I'm at the mall; it was the cashier. What's up?"

"I've been trying to get a hold of you all day," David says with urgency in his tone.

"I know and I called you back. Is everything okay?"

"Yeah. I had a tournament pop up in Denver tonight and wanted to see if we could meet up."

"It depends what time it is. I have a really important job interview tomorrow morning and I want to get to bed early."

"That's fine. I'm cool getting to bed with you as well."

"David," I snap.

"What?" he laughs.

"I don't know, how about we have dinner and catch up before we jump back in bed? I've barely talked to you lately."

"Okay, okay. But my tournament starts at six and you know how long those things can go, I might not have time for dinner."

"Whatever, just call me when you're done."

"I will."

We hang up and I honestly can't believe his brazenness. He truly has some balls, suggesting that we sleep together considering we have barely spoken in the last few weeks. I'm not going to let him get in my head or take over my thoughts. I have to focus on this interview. Getting in my car, I call Cara in hopes she will be home tonight so I can pick her brain for some interviewing tips. Lex gave me a lot of info on the firm, but I've never had a *real* interview.

Unfortunately, I get her voicemail and ramble on about the day's events. It's not long 'til I'm home. I park my car and head inside with my new clothes. Hanging them on my closet door I admire my new purchases. They are *so* perfect. I decide to try the whole outfit on again to make sure the shoes will look as good as I've imagined. I search my closet for my Mary Janes. I can't find them so I pull out two other pairs of heels. One is a black, patent leather pair and the other is a red, pointed toe pair. I put one on each foot and look in the mirror.

I try and decide which pair looks best, but the doorbell interrupts me. Pulling the shoes off I make my way into the living room. When I open the door, I'm shocked – it's Troy.

"Wow, you look amazing," he says, rubbing the back of his neck.

"Thanks. Come in," I say and move out of his way. He steps in and I notice the small Macy's bag in his hand.

"Is this what you're wearing to your interview tomorrow?"

"Yeah, do you think it looks okay?"

"Uh, yeah. I would say it looks more than okay. I would hire you based solely on the outfit."

"Whatever, Troy. People don't get hired based solely on their attire. But since you're here, wanna help me decide which shoes?"

He chuckles. "Sure."

I start to put a shoe on and get a little off balance. He steadies me and I look at him as his hand grips my arm – he has such a firm grip. Once I have both shoes on, I take a step back and look at him questioningly.

"Which ones look better?"

"The man in me says the red, but for an interview I would go with the black."

"Really?"

"Yeah."

"Thank you. I can't find the shoes I planned on wearing so I was a bit perplexed. What brings you here anyways?" I ask as I take them off.

Outstretching his long arm, he hands me the Macy's bag. "I got this for you."

"Troy, you didn't need to buy me anything."

"I know I didn't; I wanted to."

Smiling at him, I take the bag and pull out the box. I can't contain my excitement when I see what he's bought me. "Holy shit! You did not buy me Juicy perfume."

"Yup, I did. Now I have no doubt you'll get the job."

"Thank you so much," I exclaim throwing my arms around his neck.

"No problem. You're gonna do great. I know it."

"Thanks for saying that. I don't know why, but I'm really nervous."

"That's normal. This is a great opportunity, with a huge firm. Can I help with anything?"

"You've done enough; I don't want to bother you with my worries and self-doubt."

Stepping closer to me, he takes my hands in his and looks down at me. "If anyone knows about self-doubt, it's me. You gotta let it go. Tell me what's on your mind."

Giving him a half smile, I agree, nodding my head. "Do you mind if I change real quick?"

"Go right on ahead. I'll wait out here for you."

"Thanks. There are some beers in the fridge if you want one," I say entering my room.

"Do you want one?" he yells in at me.

"No, thanks."

Quickly, I remove my new clothes and hang them back up. I slide on my jean capris and yellow tank top from earlier. As I emerge from my room, Troy is on the couch checking his phone. I sit next to him and he sets it in front of him saying, "I got you a water since you didn't want a beer."

Opening it, I take a sip and pull my feet underneath me. "Thank you."

"No problem. Now talk to me," he says. "Tell me what's stressing you."

"I don't know. I'm worried the minute they ask me a question, I'm gonna clam up."

"It's probably because you want the job so much. All you can do is take some deep breaths and have a game plan."

"I can take deep breaths, but the game plan…that's a whole other story."

"Hey, I'm all yours tonight. Let's make a game plan together. I'm pretty good at interviewing myself, so between the two of us we got this in the bag."

I smile at him and lie back on the armrest of the couch. Lying there, I look at the ceiling, and he grabs my feet, placing them in his lap. I tense at his touch, contemplating letting him do this. But it's only my feet, there's no harm in that.

"Tell me what you know about the position," he says, beginning to rub them.

Mmmm, that feels good. His hands are big and strong. He definitely knows what he's doing and the pressure…it's just right. I close my eyes and begin to speak. Troy listens attentively, giving me his opinion and advice at all the right times. He's extremely smart and the little tips he adds here and there give me that much more confidence. Things like making eye contact, connecting with each interviewer.

Glancing at the clock, it's after nine. Troy and I talked forever. We got off the interviewing subject and talked about everything else instead. I learned he's from Colorado as am I. He's huge into snowboarding, like I am, and we promised to go up to Loveland Ski Basin the day it opens. He has a younger sister and his parents are still married. From what he said, it sounds like he gets along great with his mom, but the relationship with his dad is a bit strained.

"Will you call me as soon as you're done tomorrow?" he asks.

"Of course. Are you working?"

"Yeah."

We get up and head to the door. "Good-bye," I say and hug him. I don't want him to leave. Hanging out with him feels so good and is easy.

"Good luck tomorrow and sleep well, Bridge," he says, pressing his warm lips against my forehead. I squeeze him tightly and then let go. As we separate, he grabs my hand and holds it until we are too far apart to stay connected. I watch as he closes the door and I lock it behind him.

God, I need to figure out what the hell I'm doing. My feelings for Troy are growing and I can't stop them. It's like they are on a roller coaster and the bar's locked; there's no getting off the ride for me now. Even if I wanted to, I couldn't. This is all a mess, and I'm so worried that at any moment this is all going to blow up in my face. As I set my alarm clock for the morning, I notice David hasn't called. After tonight with Troy, I have to do something. I need to talk to David and be honest. I love hanging out with Troy and I don't want to stop. He's become such a good friend and I think he wants more, or at least I hope he does. I don't know if I should ask him where his head is. I don't want to assume that he wants to be with me, if he doesn't. He might just enjoy being friends. He's never pushed himself on me, always being such a gentleman.

Jesus, this is such a clusterfuck. I guess I can only handle one thing at a time. Next up is my interview and I need to do extremely well. I need this job not only because of my finances, but also for my sanity. I can't live on my student loans and handouts from my sister forever. I already live here rent-free.

Chapter 6

Interview

I wake excited, refreshed, and ready for what the day holds. I check my phone as I roll out of bed and notice a text from Cara.

Good luck today. I crashed at Abel's because it was close to the hospital. Can you believe my ankles are already starting to swell?

I giggle at her message, unable to imagine her with any part of her body swollen. I'm sure she's exaggerating. ***Thanks, sweetie. I'm sure your feet are fine. Will I see you tonight?***

Yup, I'll be home around 7:30. I'm working a twelve-hour shift today.

Good, 'cause Troy stopped by last night and we talked and he rubbed my feet and… I need some advice.

OMG, I want details tonight!

I laugh at her and begin getting ready for the day. I decide to flat iron my hair, to keep it all tame. Normally, I wear it curly or messy, but I want a clean, polished look. I put on more make-up than I usually do and decide to pull my bangs back as they keep hanging in my eyes.

I dress and do one last lookover of myself in the mirror. My grey pencil skirt and black blouse complete the look. *You got this, Bridge,* I say to myself before heading out of my room. Grabbing my resumes and purse, I lock up and leave. Once I'm behind the wheel of my car, I plug my phone in and pick an upbeat song for my drive. There's nothing like a little Ellie Goulding to start the day off right. My phone beeps, interrupting the song. I glance down at it and read the message from Troy.

Good luck today. You got this, Bridge.

I can't help but smile; that's what I just said to myself. Pulling onto the freeway, traffic is stopped. I'm thankful I gave myself extra time. As I creep along, Ellie sings about chasing love and I wonder if that's what I'm doing with Troy.

Turning into the parking lot of the high-rise that I hope will be my new workplace, I park and head in.

On the elevator ride up, I check my phone one last time and put it on silent. There are no new text messages, but I quickly respond to Troy's earlier one. *Thank you, I'll call you when I'm done.*

The doors open to the twenty-ninth floor. Behind an oval desk is a red-haired receptionist, and her nameplate reads "Autumn." She smiles at me as I approach. "Welcome to Smith, Brown, and Mileski. How may I help you?"

"I have a nine o'clock interview with Liam, C.J., and Vincent."

"Your name?" she asks, and I suddenly sense a bit of an attitude coming from her.

"Bridgette Schaefer."

"Have a seat," she says.

I do so and text Alexa. ***What's up with the wicked witch in reception?***

She doesn't respond, instead she emerges from the back. "Bridgette. You can come on in."

I get up and walk towards her and she tells Autumn, "Don't bother calling the guys. I'll take her back."

As we walk I give her a side hug. "You look adorable," she says.

"Thank you." She leads me into a huge corner conference room. "Take a seat and I'll grab everyone. Just be yourself, okay?"

I smile and nod my head, sitting down. While I wait, I take some of Troy's advice and run through my mental notes. I begin to go over my resume, remembering which key points to hit on when Liam, C.J., and Vincent enter the room. I stand shaking all of their hands, well, all except for Vincent who gives me a hug.

As I sit across from the three men, I'm baffled by their appearance. All of them are gorgeous; they are absolutely to die for. No wonder their law firm does so well – I'm sure when they go up against someone in court all the opposing party can focus on is keeping their libido under control. Honestly, I don't think it matters if it is a male or a female these three are up against because their looks are lethal.

C.J. starts first with the typical 'tell us about your background, schooling, and previous experience.' Just like Troy said he would. Then Liam leads in with a bit more of a difficult question about why they should hire me over other candidates.

As the interview gets going and the questions are thrown at me, I'm unstoppable. Mainly because of Troy; he really helped me get into the right mindset. They laugh at some of the funny stuff I say and all around they seem captivated by my words. Leaving, I feel like I did a great job. I know deep down, I gave it my all.

I call Troy on my drive home, but he doesn't answer so I leave him a message. I decide to call David too. I need to see him and be honest with him. What Troy and I are doing is not innocent and it's not okay.

"Hello," David answers in a groggy tone.

"Hey. There you are. You never called me last night."

"Oh yeah, sorry about that. I won my tournament and was on such a high I spaced it."

"Uh, okay. Well, listen I need to see you. Do you have time tonight?"

"Probably, I'm still in Denver. Can I call you later?" he asks yawning. "I'm going to go back to sleep, I didn't get to bed 'til seven this morning."

"Okay—" He hangs up before I can get in another

word. I pull off the highway and head towards the condo. My phone rings, and it's Cara. I can't wait to talk to her. "Oh my God, Cara, you're—"

"Where are you?" she questions.

"Driving home. Why? Is everything okay?"

"Can you come to the hospital?"

My heart races and I turn around to get back on the freeway. "Of course, is the baby okay?" my voice quavers.

"Yeah, we're fine, it's…it's Troy. He was brought in from a fire. I don't really know what's going on. Abel's a mess and the ER is slammed. I really need you."

"Oh God, what happened? Is he okay?"

"I don't have all the details, honey. Just get here, please."

"I'm on my way."

I hang up and try to blink back the tears. I need to pay attention to the road. However, it's too late; they're already streaming down my cheeks. *Lord, please let Troy be okay.* I can't believe something has happened to him. Whatever it is, just don't let it be serious; he's so young. Speeding through traffic, I feel like a maniac and am thankful that there are no cops around to see me.

I park in front of the gigantic hospital and jog inside looking for Abel. He is nowhere in sight. I spot Cara behind the check-in desk and she points to the right. I head to the doors and when they open, she's there to greet me. "Thank God you're here," she says, embracing me.

Hugging her back, I see Abel on the phone with his

head hung low, leaning on the nurses' station. "Cara, what happened?" Before she can speak, her name gets called over the intercom. "Talk to Abel, sweetie." And she's gone. I watch her run away from me and through the double doors.

Approaching Abel, I hesitantly rub his arm and he looks up at me with worry in his eyes. Switching the phone to his other ear, he wraps an arm around my shoulders and hugs me close to him. He scribbles down a phone number on a pad of paper and hangs up. "Are you okay?" I ask him.

Running his fingers through his hair, he says, "Fuck if I know."

"What happened?"

"That fucker didn't evacuate when I ordered everyone out. This is the second time in six months he has done this and each time he's ended up in the hospital. I swear to God, he's like a fucking child."

"Calm down, Abel. I'm sure he had good reason. What happened to him? Is he okay?"

"I'm not sure. A stairway gave way and he was trapped inside. Thank God we were able to get a few guys in there and get him out. Had he been inaccessible, I don't even want to think about it. If he'd listened when I ordered everyone out, he wouldn't have been caught."

"Jesus. I'm sorry, Abel. Where is he now?"

"They took him back for a CT scan."

"Have you called his parents?" I ask.

"No, I just got the number from the station when you walked up. What do I say to them?"

"I wouldn't call yet and jump ahead of yourself, okay? Let's see exactly what is going on and then call. We need all of the details. I know Troy's relationship with his dad is strained and I don't want to make it worse. If he finds this out and Troy doesn't want him to know, it could make things awkward."

"Hey," Cara interrupts us. "I just got an update. He's being brought back down. They said everything looks normal minus a few cracked ribs and a concussion. The attending said it appears the way Troy fell limited his injuries, which is a good thing. Any other way and it might have been much worse."

"Oh thank God," I say.

Abel inhales sharply as Troy is wheeled by us. His eyes are closed and you can see the exhaustion on his face. Before I can watch him any longer, he is gone and in a room. "Go ahead," I tell Abel.

"Are you sure?"

"Yes, just be nice to him. I'm sure he had good intentions."

"I'll try."

"Abel," Cara snaps.

He nods his head and walks away. "Are you okay?" she asks.

"Yeah. I was just so worried. I'm glad he's going to be okay. Thank you for calling me."

"Of course. I care about you both, but I think you need to be honest with him and end things with David."

"I am ending things with David tonight. We have plans to see each other."

"Good girl," she says. Another nurse comes up behind her and starts asking questions about a patient. She tilts her head and mouths *sorry* to me as they walk off. I keep my post at the nurses' station, as there's no seating back here. Checking my phone, I notice a text from Alexa. *I think you have good news coming your way.*

I hope so. Is my response. I'm going to need a little luck, not only to land this job, but also to handle David. I don't know how he is going to take the news I have to give him, but I guess I'll find out.

Abel emerges another ten minutes later. "He wants to see you."

I nod my head and walk towards his room, stopping at his door to calm my nerves. Quietly, I enter and Troy is as he was earlier, resting with his eyes closed. I smile to myself, absorbing his perfection, and stand next to his bed. He doesn't move and I wonder how he went from telling Abel he wanted to see me to this? Grabbing his hand I wrap my tiny one around his and watch his breathing. "Troy," I softly whisper.

Moving my hand in his I begin to tickle the inside of his palm and a smile spreads across his face. I keep doing it and his smile gets bigger. "You better not be faking it," I say.

He shakes his head and I smack his arm. Squeezing his eyes tightly he grunts in pain and rolls to the side. "Oh my God, I'm so sorry. I didn't mean to hurt you." My hands move manically wanting to calm him, but at the same time I'm afraid to touch him.

Finally, he opens his eyes and looks at me. "I take back everything I ever said about you being small, because that hurt like hell."

"I'm so sorry, I didn't mean to."

"It's okay. I probably deserved it considering I was messing with you."

"So you were awake?"

"Mmm-hmm."

"Why were you pretending then?"

"I was hoping you would have been so worried that you would've kissed me. Instead you find the one spot I'm ticklish and use it against me."

"Fine, close your eyes," I tell him.

He smiles like a Cheshire cat and complies. Staring at his soft lips as his smile softens I'm extremely tempted, but I won't touch his lips until I end things with David. So instead I gingerly kiss his cheek and he looks at me.

"That's all I get?"

"Yup."

"You're cruel, woman."

"Well, you should've listened to Abel when he ordered you out of the building. I mean, really, Troy, what were you thinking?"

"I swear I heard a kid. Last time I didn't evacuate it was for the same reason, only it was too late and the kid died. I can't leave someone in a fire, Bridge. I can't."

"That's brave of you, but what if neither of you make it out? You have to think about that. Imagine what that would do to your family and Abel. You didn't see him; he was a wreck when I got here. Please don't do that again, okay?"

He nods his head and I take a seat in the chair next to his bed. We spend the next few hours visiting and he decides he doesn't want his family to know. I'm so glad I spoke up; my gut was telling me to not let Abel call them. As much as I want to stay all day with him, I can't. I have plans with David – I need to end things. If Troy and I are going to have a chance at a future, then I need to do this first.

We agreed to meet at a local sushi restaurant. It's bright and they have large booths. I figure the break up will be less conspicuous in a place like this. As I sit here and sip on my water, my stomach is a jumbled mess of knots.

Checking the clock, it's quarter after seven, and David's fifteen minutes late. I shoot him a text asking where he is. The waiter stops back by. "Ma'am, would you like any edamame while you wait?"

"No, thanks, he'll be here any minute."

My phone vibrates as the waiter walks off. *Finally*, I think to myself. I check the message, but it's not David.

It's from Troy. *I don't think I can eat this food.*

Uhhh, I bet. I'm sorry. What did they serve for dinner?

Salisbury steak, at least that's what they said it was.

Hey, look at the bigger picture. At least you're going home tomorrow.

That's true. What are you doing?

Fuck. I don't want to lie to him. I decide not to respond rather than lie. Checking the clock again, it's twenty after seven. I call David in a last-ditch attempt – I'm not going to sit here all night. The phone rings and rings, but he doesn't answer. I leave a message. "Hey, it's me. I'm not sure where you are, or if you're coming, but I've been here for almost thirty minutes. I'm going home. At this point don't bother calling me."

Hanging up, I actually feel good that he hasn't shown up. As much as I know I need to end things with him in person, I also know him bailing makes doing that so much easier. Walking to my car, I text Troy back. ***Bringing you dinner, what do you want?***

Chapter 7

Got It

I pull out of the neighborhood and my phone rings. Anticipating it's Troy, I answer in a chipper tone. He was released yesterday from the hospital with a clean bill of health minus his ribs and ordered a few days of bed rest. He promised Abel from now on he'd always listen to evacuation orders. We have lunch plans today since he's bored and bumming at home. To my surprise, when I answer, it's Lex, and I'm a bit thrown off because she's whispering. "Hey, I can't talk long, but keep an eye on your phone, I think you're going to be getting the call today."

"Okay, that's good news, right?"

"Mmm-hmm. I'll have those documents couriered over to the courthouse right away, Susanna. Thanks for calling and letting me know they were missing. Bye." And she hangs up. *Damn it.* One of the guys must have walked up on her. Oh God, please let it be good news. I park in front of Chipotle and run in to grab our lunch order, since

Troy was nice enough to place the order online so I don't have to wait. I'm thankful because this place is slammed. Bypassing the line, I walk around to the check out and am greeted by an Abel look alike. *Who knew he had a twin.* "How can I help ya?"

"I'm picking up a to-go order."

"Sure, what's the name?"

"It should be under Bridgette."

He scrolls through the computer and then looks at the orders on the back of the line. Coming back over to me, he shakes his head saying, "Sorry, but I don't have an order under that name."

"What about Troy?"

He looks again. "Ah ha. Troy and Bridge?"

I smile. "Yeah, that's us."

"Cool, here you go. It's all paid for."

"What? How?"

"It was done online. I'm sorry, we're kinda getting backed up."

I turn to see a couple scowling at me. Taking our food, I stop and grab a few utensils and then head out. That fucker said I could buy him lunch. Now I know why he wanted to place the order online. He wasn't trying to be nice – he wanted to pay. Sitting in my car, I contemplate what to text him, then my fingers move of their own accord. ***What happened to ME buying YOU lunch?***

Oh good, you got the food. You didn't really think I would let you do that, did you? What kind of guy do you think I am?

I ignore his text and drive to his house. It's not a long trip; he lives between the fire station and my house. Pulling down his street, it's an older neighborhood. A lot of the homes have been remodeled while others are still run down. Parking on the street in front of his, I see it's cute. I would say it's just what I imagined. It's two stories, constructed of dark red brick, with a long walkway leading up to the front porch. I love the porch – it's long with a built-in swing. Earlier, Troy told me to just come in, so he wouldn't have to get up.

Suddenly, I'm nervous and questioning even doing this. I mean, what am I thinking? Then I remind myself that David is the one who was a no-show on me and I haven't heard from him since. In my mind, he and I are done. Over. I take a deep breath – it's too late now…I'm already here. Closing my eyes, I search for the strength to be honest with Troy. I need to tell him about David, and I pray that he understands. Troy interrupts my thoughts by opening the door. Standing before him, I melt again. He's too hot for his own good.

"Are you okay?" he asks, smiling so big a dimple I've never noticed, is exposed.

"Yeah, of course. Why are you up?"

"I used the bathroom and saw your car, so I thought I would come see you. Come in," he says gesturing me inside.

When I walk inside, I immediately notice the floors are a dark wood, and the walls are all neutrals. His home has definitely been remodeled. It's a little bit bland, but it's nice. "Where do you want to eat?" I ask.

"The living room, if that's cool with you?"

"Sure."

I set the bag down, and we sit next to each other. Troy takes his time sitting down and I feel bad for him. I can tell he's still sore. "Thanks for coming over," he says.

"Of course. How are you feeling?"

"Sore. Really sore and I can't sleep for shit."

"That sucks," I say taking our food out of the bag. "Can the doctors give you anything for the pain and to sleep?"

"They have, but I really hate taking that shit. I'll be good; I'm better now that you're here.

"I'm happy to be here. Your place is really cute."

"Thanks, it's kinda growing on me."

"What, you don't like it?

"I don't know, it's a little plain."

"All you need to do is decorate a little. Some accessories would do wonders here; add a few rugs, pillows, and pictures."

"Bridge, don't forget I'm a guy."

"Trust me, I haven't. Just go to Pier One."

"I have a better idea – why don't you come with me?"

"Fine, as soon as you're feeling better."

"Deal," he says.

Swallowing hard I take a sip of my tea and say, "Listen, I want to talk to you about something."

"Shoot," he responds with a mouthful of food.

Trying to think of where to start, I feel out of breath. I remind myself that I'm with Troy and he'll understand. "You—" My phone rings interrupting me. Fishing it out of my purse, I see the number is blocked. This might be the firm. "Can I take this?" I ask.

"Of course."

"Hello," I answer nervously.

"Hey Bridgette, it's Vincent. Sorry to bother you, do you have a quick second?"

I laugh, "Vincent, you're never a bother. Of course, what's going on?"

"I'm going to put you on speaker. I'm with Liam and C.J. and we have one more question to ask you, if that's all right?"

"You can ask me anything."

"Good answer." I hear – I think – C.J. say.

"Bridgette, this is Liam. In order to work at this firm, I need you to tell me how *you* make a peanut butter and jelly sandwich."

I stifle the laugh, because these are potentially my three new bosses and simply give an answer. It might not make sense why he's asking, but I assume that's the point. "I don't know about you guys, but I like to use honey-wheat bread. I take two slices out and spread the jelly first. I don't have a preference on the kind; it really depends on my mood. Then spread the peanut butter. I like to do this last so it doesn't mix in with my jelly. Then I slap it together, cut it in half diagonally, and voilà, you've got yourself a yummy PB&J."

I look over at Troy as he's smiling at me and I shrug my shoulders like this is a normal conversation.

"Well, that was spot on and to the point. Thank you for answering and not questioning our motives behind it. Congratulations, Bridgette. On behalf of all of us, I would like to officially welcome you to Smith, Brown, and Mileski. You got the job!" Liam says.

"Oh my God, thank you all so much. I promise you won't be disappointed."

"We know that, or we wouldn't have hired you," C.J. says.

"How does Monday at 8:00am sound to start?"

"That's absolutely perfect, thank you again."

"No, thank you – thank you," they all say and hang up.

Sitting next to Troy I'm flabbergasted. *I got the freaking job.* Holy hell, I can't believe it!

"You got the job?" he questions.

I nod my head and Troy says, "Congrats Bridge," while taking his good arm and wrapping it around me, hugging me tight. "What did they say and what was up with that question?" he asks. Clinging to him, I truly can't even process all of this, or fathom that they gave it to me! "Well, are you going to say anything?" Troy asks, looking down at me.

"I…I'm speechless."

"Come on, did you really doubt yourself? I knew all

along you were going to get it."

"I've wished and wished for this to happen. This is like my dream job. I thought after years and years of working I would be doing something like this. But to be starting out at this level, it's crazy."

"Well, you did it!"

"I don't think I could have done it without your help." I squeeze him and he groans. "Shit, I'm sorry. I didn't mean to hurt you."

"It's all good, but eventually you're going to have to stop being so rough with me."

Chapter 8

Trepidation

My mind is fuzzy as my sweet dream is interrupted by the sound of my phone buzzing. I reach for it and look at the screen. It's David calling. *Jesus Christ, it's the middle of the fucking night.* "Hello," I answer rolling over and brushing the hair out of my face.

"Hey, what are you doing?"

I glance at my clock, "I'm sleeping. Didn't you get my message? I told you to not bother calling me."

"I know I fucked up and I'm sorry. Let me come see you and I'll make it up to you. I'm coming down to Denver now."

"You more than fucked up, you blew me off."

There are people laughing in the background and it makes it hard for me to hear him clearly. "I'm sorry, love. Come out with us. Joey knows of a sick party, that's why we're headed down."

"Is that the only reason?"

I hear someone call his name in the background.

"That and you. I wanna see you."

This time I hear a girl call him and I snap. "You know what, David? Don't fucking call me again. I don't even know why I wasted my time answering your phone call. You seriously called me when you're hanging out with a bunch of girls and try and tell me that you're coming here for me? You're not coming here at all – we're done."

"Bridgette, please. Text me your address and I'll come right now. Don't say things like that. We're not done!"

"Yes, we are. Leave me the fuck alone. Maybe if you would've helped me move, you would know where I live," I yell and hang up.

What an absolute asshole. Who does he think he is? The nerve. I roll over and try to fall back asleep, but I can't. I shouldn't have answered his phone call. I should've known better, considering I hadn't heard from him for a few days. I sit up frustrated and grab my laptop off of my nightstand. Maybe some meaningless Internet surfing will make me tired. As I check my Facebook account and scroll through my newsfeed, my phone rings again and I answer it yelling, "What the fuck do you want, David?"

"Uh…Bridge, it's me, Troy. Are you okay?"

"Jesus, I'm sorry. I thought you were someone else."

"Yeah, I got that. Who's David?"

"Listen, Troy, I'm sorry. I'm really sorry; I should've been upfront with you from the beginning. I've wanted to tell you for a long time and even tried to today. He is…he *was* my dumbass boyfriend."

Troy sighs into the phone. "That was the last thing I expected you to say. I'll let you go."

"No, please don't."

"Why? You're with somebody else. Bridgette, why wouldn't you have told me something like that?"

"I'm not with him anymore. I don't know why I didn't tell you. I tried, I really did, but the time never seemed right."

"I just don't get it. Can't you tell that I have feelings for you?"

I stay silent. *Fuck, what am I supposed to say?* How am I supposed to respond to him?

"Don't answer that. Have you been with him since I met you?"

"Uh-huh."

"I really gotta go. I can't do this."

"Please don't go. Let me come over and I'll explain everything."

"Five minutes ago I would've done anything to have you here, but you're with someone else, or at least you were. You weren't honest with me, Bridge. I can't do this. Goodnight," he says and hangs up.

My heart wrenches – I hurt Troy and I feel horrible for doing so. All along I did everything I could to ensure he was the one that *didn't* end up getting hurt. He's been so amazing to me, every interaction we've had has been perfect. I never should've kept this from him, I owed him that much. I should've told him about David from the day we met. I wish more than anything that I could go back. If there was something I could do, I would, but it's too late. I've made my bed, now I have to lay in it.

I go to Troy's Facebook page and stare at his profile picture. It's him and a few of the guys from the station playing basketball – shirtless. Troy is shooting the ball and looks so hot. I can't believe I answered the phone the way I did, but maybe it's better this way. At least he knows the truth now and we didn't start a relationship based on a lie.

There I go again getting ahead of myself. Who's to say he ever wanted a relationship? Although he did say he had feelings for me. I close my laptop and roll over. I have to get to sleep. Maybe I'll wake up and this will all have been a bad dream.

Waking up, the house is quiet. Cara stayed at Abel's last night, so I'm alone. Pouring myself my second cup of coffee, my cell phone rings. I grab it and contemplate answering David's phone call. I told him to leave me alone; then again, I want to chew his ass out.

"Yes," I say, as I head out front to enjoy the warm summer morning.

"Hey, love. How are you?"

"Don't call me that. What do you want?"

"Just hear me out. I'm sorry about last night and for how I've acted lately. I shouldn't have called you in the middle of the night, demanding that you see me. Lately I've taken you for granted and I'm really sorry. I'll change, but please don't end things with us. Bridgette, you mean so much to me. I want you to know that. Let me see you today; we can talk through this."

I'm a little taken offguard by his change in attitude and sudden sweetness. This is the David I know, the one I first met and have desperately missed. This is the David who was my best friend. Clearly he's not going to let this go easily and I've ruined things with Troy, so what do I have to lose? My heart aches for the budding relationship I had with Troy, but my head reminds me how lonely it gets without someone there to share life with. If only Troy could forgive me, but I have a feeling he doesn't forgive these things easily; I'm the same way. Whether it's a mistake or not, I decide that I will hear David out. Worst thing that can happen is I end things in person with him like I originally planned.

"Where are you?"

"In Denver, we crashed at Joey's friend's. I think it's close to you."

I give him my address and directions. Then call him through the gate before I run into the bathroom and pull myself together. Hastily, I comb my thick, brown hair and apply a thin, natural layer of makeup. Then I dress in a pair of yoga pants and a teal tank top. As I walk out of my room the doorbell rings. I take a deep breath and answer it.

Standing before me, David looks exhausted, strung out even. He has flowers in his hand and hugs me tight. As he releases me, I look into his eyes and he says, "Thank you for seeing me. You look beautiful."

I smile and lead him into the condo. I walk to the couch and sit down in the corner, putting as much distance as I can between us. I don't really know what it is, but I know any doubts I had about us making things work are gone now. Just seeing him in person is enough to harden the last bit of softness my heart had for him. Regardless of how things work out with Troy, I need to break this off with David, for me. He sets the flowers down, taking the hint that I'm not going to take them from him, and sits next to me.

I stare at him with wide eyes waiting for him to say something. "Don't look at me like that," he says.

"I don't know what you want from me. You had to have seen this coming. We barely talk anymore. You don't have time for me, we never see each other, and quite frankly, you've changed. I go days on end without hearing a peep from you and then you get all manic trying to get ahold of me. What's going on with you?"

"I don't know, love! I know I haven't been myself, but I can change for you. I'll stop playing poker if you want. I'm going to move down here and from this day forward you'll be my number one priority."

I shake my head vigorously. "NO! That's not what I want. That's what you want!"

"Please, Bridgette."

"David, stop! Just stop. Things aren't going to work out with us. Whether you are here or there, my feelings aren't the same. You're not the same guy I met all those months ago. I can see it in your eyes – something's different, something's going on with you."

"Nothing's going on with me. I'm the same guy! I love you, Bridgette." He takes my hand in his and I pull it away.

"Don't make this any harder than it needs to be. There are plenty of girls out there who would kill to be with you."

"I don't want them. I want you," he says with tears in his eyes.

"I…my feelings have changed."

"It's that Troy guy, isn't it? You're with him now, aren't you?" he accuses in a harsh tone.

"Not that it's any of your business, but NO, I'm not with Troy. This has nothing to do with anyone except you. Please, David, just go." I keep my voice firm to let him know I'm serious. I'm *not* backing down.

"I'll leave, Bridgette, but only because you're mine and I love you. I don't care what you say, but this isn't finished. You'll see that we belong together," he says, leaning over me. Resting his hand on the arm of the couch, he's inches from my face. I watch as anger blazes in his eyes and he grabs my cheeks with his other hand and holds my face in place. His grip is hard and he's hurting me. I try and move to shake him off, but I can't. He presses his lips hard against mine. I squirm and whimper fighting against his kiss. He's now straddling me and has both of my hands in his. "Kiss me back," he demands.

I shake my head and he squeezes both my face and wrists. *Fuck, it hurts.* Tears prick my eyes and his tongue enters my mouth. I gasp in repulsion, giving him access to deepen the kiss. He tastes disgusting, and if I had any way to fight him off of me, I would. I know I can't, so I have no choice, but to let his snakelike tongue invade me. Finally, he stops and stands up looking down at me. "We're not finished." he growls, his voice low and menacing.

I sit back into the couch, frozen, watching the demon of a man I once thought of as my friend-turned-lover walk away from me. Once he is gone, my instincts move me to the door and I scramble to lock it. Remembering the look in his eyes – I shiver.

Going into my room, I grab my phone and call Lex. She answers, "Hel—"

I cut her off. "Are you home?"

"Yeah, why?"

"Can I come over?"

"Of course. Are you okay?"

"Just stay on the phone with me, I'll explain everything when I get there."

Grabbing my purse I look out the kitchen window and don't see David's car, so I lock up and head straight for my car.

"Talk to me, Bridge, you're scaring me."

Getting in, I lock the doors and take off as soon as it starts. "Sorry, I had to get out of my house. I'm on my way over now."

"What happened?"

"David happened. I ended things with him. Let's just say he didn't take it very well and he scared the shit out of me. The look in his eyes was…it was like he was possessed."

"Take deep breaths, sweetie, and get here safely. Vince is here so we'll be safe. Please focus on driving. I'll stay on the line, okay?"

"Okay," I say, checking my rearview mirror to ensure he's not behind me. I never in a million years thought David would react the way he did. Why can't he just accept that my feelings have changed and let me go? I've never had a break-up go so wrong. Most of my break-ups have been amicable, so there were no worries with having an ex. I don't know what is wrong with David, but I call bullshit that nothing is going on with him.

Chapter 9

Troy

I wake gasping for air. *It was only a dream. Thank God, it was only a dream.* I was back in my living room with David, only this time he was holding my neck instead of my face and I couldn't breathe. Looking around Alexa and Vincent's spare room, I'm safe. He's not here and doesn't know where I am. I have to keep reminding myself of that. It's crazy how quickly I've changed from a confident, brave woman to one that is hiding out at her sister's because I'm terrified that my ex will come back.

Grabbing my cell phone I check the time. It's four in the morning and way too early to be awake. Closing my eyes I try desperately to fall back asleep. Thankfully this time when I close them my thoughts are flooded with images of Troy. God, he's so fucking sexy, with his messy, brown hair and thin stubble that I want to drag my tongue across.

Going against my better judgment, I grab my phone and text him. ***I hope you're feeling okay. I'm sorry***

again for not being honest with you. If I could only go back and change things, I would.

Laying my phone against my chest, I take a deep breath and pray he responds. After another thirty minutes of unsuccessful sleep and no response from Troy, I get up. Walking into the kitchen, I'm surprised to see Vincent sitting at the island. He's on his laptop sipping a cup of coffee.

"Hey, you're up early," he says.

"I could say the same about you."

"I'm up because of work. What's your excuse?"

"I had a dream that woke me. After David kept calling me last night, over and over, my mind was consumed with thoughts of him. I guess that turned into a nightmare that scared the shit out of me."

"I'm sorry. What time did he finally give up on calling?"

"About twelve."

"Has he called since?" he asks getting up to refill his coffee.

"No."

"Would you like a cup?"

"Please," I say getting up and grabbing the creamer out of the fridge. "What would you do if you were me?"

"Honestly, I don't know him. However, if it were me, I would give it a little time and let things die down. I'm sure he'll back off. My gut tells me he acted out in the heat of the moment."

"I hope so. Can I ask you another question?"

"Of course," he says, as we both sit back down at the island.

"I know you're aware I like Troy. Well, he found out about David the other night before I could explain things to him. I'd planned on telling him the day you called and offered me the job. But after the news, I was way too excited to go into all of that. Anyways, I broke up with David and then when Troy found out, it was too late. He knew I'd been lying to him since the beginning and I haven't heard from him since."

Resting his elbows on the granite counter he looks at me. "I don't know if I am the best person to be giving you advice, but don't give up on him. See if he's willing to meet with you. You need to tell him your side of things and explain why you lied. He might not forgive you, but you owe him that much."

"Okay, I can do that. Thank you, Vincent."

"Of course. Try not to stress about all of this, okay? You're only going to make yourself sick."

"I'll try. Thank you for your honesty. I'm gonna shower, if you don't mind?"

"Go right on ahead. Lex will be asleep for a while, I'm sure of it. Make yourself at home and let me know if you need anything."

"Thanks, I will." Walking back into the spare room, I check my phone before heading into the bathroom.

Troy texted me back, and his response is cold. *I'm*

feeling okay.

My throat tightens looking at his words. He didn't even acknowledge my apology. But I don't really deserve him to…do I? Thinking of Vincent's advice, I figure what do I have to lose?

Can I see you?

No response. I'm not surprised though. I tried and that's all I can do. I walk into the bathroom and peel off the pajamas that Alexa let me borrow, then stand under the hot water, allowing it to cascade down my body. I'm not sure how long I let the water soothe me, as I'm lost in my own thoughts. I know that everything changes when David's face flashes in my mind and I tremble. Pulling myself out of the clouded trance, filled with illusions of daydreams turned to nightmares, I wash, rinse, and get out of the shower. Suddenly I feel tired…or more like exhausted. After I'm dry, I dress and back into bed I crawl, rereading Troy's text, wishing he would respond. I clutch my phone to my chest and drift off to sleep.

"…Troy, please," I plead with him.

"Please what, Bridge?" he growls hovering above my body.

"I…I want…Ahhh," I cry out as his thick shaft fills me.

"You want me to fuck you?"

"Mmm-hmm."

Moving he says, "But, you've been bad, so I'm going to fuck you hard. Tell me how much you want my cock."

"Please, Troy, fuck me. Make me come."

"Oh, you're so naughty." He grips my hips holding me tightly in

place, pleasing me like I want. Oh fuck, it feels so good. My chest begins to buzz…

Waking up, my breathing is heavy and I'm damp between my legs. I glance at my phone – that's what woke me – and read Troy's text. It hurts. The words are not what I'd hoped for. *I don't think there's any point to that… It would just be harder on both of us.*

Sitting up I rub my eyes and pull my hair over to one shoulder. ***I'm sorry that you feel that way. But I need to see you. If you ever had any feelings for me, please do this. I'm so fucking sorry.***

I'll be home all day.

Thank God he agreed. *Now what the hell do I say to him?* I think on the way out. I grab my wallet, making a stop in the kitchen where Vincent is still hard at work. "Hey Vincent, I'm gonna run to Troy's. Will you let Lex know when she wakes up?"

He smiles at me. "Sure, aren't you gonna change?"

"My clothes are in the wash and I don't want to wake Alexa. This will have to do." I smile and turn around.

"Hey, Bridge," he calls out after me.

"Yeah?" I say stopping to look back at him.

"Speak from your heart. Don't let any words go unspoken."

"Thanks."

Driving to Troy's, I keep repeating what I'm going to say to him, over and over in my head. Vincent's words replay in my mind and I feel like I have a good game plan.

All of my thoughts seem to be in order and I hope they all come out the way I've planned. Before I know it, I'm sitting in front of his house, thankful to be here, so I don't let another minute pass me by and walk up to the front door. Knocking lightly, I wait and turn, looking around the neighborhood. It's an awkward few moments and my heart begins to race. *Fuck, maybe I should…just go.*

Then the door behind me opens and I look to see Troy standing there – shirtless, with sleepy eyes and messy hair. "Hey," he says running his hands through his hair and looking at my pajamas. Inwardly I feel self-conscious. Why didn't I just sneak into Alexa's room and change, or at least put some make-up on? My hair's huge from sleeping with it wet.

"Hey," I say back, suddenly at a loss for words.

"Come in," he says moving out of the way for me.

"Thanks. I didn't mean to wake you. I can come back later if you want. I should have texted you and told you I was on my way. I don't know what I was thinking. I guess since you said you were gonna be home all day, I—"

He cuts me off, "Calm down, Bridge. It's fine."

"What? I mean…okay. How have you been?" I ask. *Damn it, brain, work.*

He rubs his face with his hands and then looks down at me longingly. "Are you nervous or something?"

"I don't know what I am. I… I'm sorry I fucked up."

Troy moves to the couch and sits down. I follow and sit next to him. "I don't know if I can do this," he says.

"Do what?" I ask.

"This," he says gesturing between the two of us.

I didn't realize how close I had sat to him. My knee is against his leg. "I'm sorry," I say and begin to scoot away, but he grabs me and grips my thigh. Looking into his eyes, there's a need there – and I want to fulfill it. He's fighting this and I don't want him too.

"Don't be sorry. I want to hear what you have to say."

I swallow hard and chew on my lip. I remind myself to speak from my heart. "It was shitty of me to lie to you. I should've told you the truth from the first moment that we started texting. I know that, but honestly, I kept lying to myself and saying what we were doing was innocent, that we were *just friends*. I made myself believe the lie, so in turn I guess I was okay with it."

"But you—"

I cut him off. "Please let me finish. Then you can yell at me or say whatever you want and then I'll go." He nods his head, loosening the grip he has on my thigh. I hadn't realized he was still clinging to me, but he was. My heart wrenches as he pulls away and sits against the back of the couch. "I wasn't happy in my relationship. If I was being honest with myself, I'd never been happy with David. He didn't accept me for who I was, who I am. That's one of the things I like most about you. Since the moment we met, you haven't judged me; you've always taken me for who I am. Like right now, me sitting here in pajamas with giant hair, you don't judge me. I admire you for that."

"Can I say something now?" he asks.

"Not yet. I'm almost finished." I remember Vincent's words and they give me strength. "It all comes down to the simple fact that I like you. I have since the day you grabbed my hand and helped me into the back of the U-Haul. I would be lying if I said otherwise. I want us to get back to where we were. I want to see where this can go."

He looks up at the ceiling and takes a deep breath, contemplating what I'm asking. As the seconds tick by, it feels like minutes. "Please, say something," I whisper, unable to sit in silence. Troy doesn't move or speak. He's very still, staring with calm even breaths. Reaching out, I touch his face and the moment my fingers graze his coarse morning stubble, he looks at me, leaning into my touch. Moving my other hand, I touch the other side of his face and crawl over his lap, straddling him. His breathing stays even. With my knees on either side of his hips, I rest my forehead against his to try and regain some composure.

He doesn't look at me right away; he's staring down. Then finally his eyes meet mine, and they are as entrancing as ever. Slowly he brings his hands to my face and cradles mine like I am his. Moving my hands off of his face, I rest them gently on his chest. Even though his breathing is calm, his heartbeat is erratic, pumping like that of a scared animal. Every pound is firm and wild. Slowly he touches our lips together. I should melt into him, but I can't close my eyes – he's forgiven me. *Thank God.* I watch him as his eyes are tightly shut, and his expression is that of pain. It's almost like he's hurting. But he keeps moving his lips, so I give in to him and indulge – in his taste, his touch, his scent. The room around me spins, and as I try to part his lips with my tongue, he stops.

Looking down at him, that look of pain is as prevalent as ever. He shakes his head and says, "See what you ruined, Bridge? We could've been so good together." I can't believe the words that come out of his mouth. I sit motionlessly on his lap and look at his agony-stricken face.

"No. No. No. No. No. We can. We are."

Moving my mouth again I go to kiss him, but he places his thumb over my lips and stops me. Still in his hold with his hands braced on my face, I sit there stunned. Blinking back tears, I fight them away with everything I have, but they are too strong – he's breaking me. "Please," I plead in a whispered tone and kiss his thumb as it covers my mouth. He just shakes his head. *Is this really happening?* Is this what my reality has come to?

"I'm sorry, Bridge, trust me I am. But I won't start another relationship based on a lie. I did it with my last girlfriend and I can't do it again. Nothing good will come of it."

He is serious, and as much as I don't want him to be, there's nothing I can do to wager with him – I know that. *Speak from your heart. Don't let any words go unspoken.* "I know you feel what's going on between us. Please don't fight it. I fucked up – I'm not perfect, but who is? Haven't you ever made a mistake? Trust me, I'll never do it again."

He ponders my words, and I can't stop the tears as they spill out of my eyes. My instincts move my lips to his and I crash our mouths together. This might be my last time. Although I'm small, I take everything I have and put it into this kiss. Hugging him tightly, I securely wrap my arms around his neck and press my body as close to him as I can get. Moving my lips with need, I caress his – and he does the same. I try again to part his lips, and this time he accepts. The moment we intensify the kiss, I whimper, threading my fingers into his hair. God, it's soft, exactly how I imagined it would be.

Please don't let this be the end for us. Troy takes his hands off of my face and glides them down my body, running them over my neck, collarbone, breasts, and stomach until he finally lands on my hips and lifts me off of him. I stand before him not only mortified, but also utterly shocked when I see the expression on his face. As the tears begin to flow and wash down my cheeks he says, "Trust me, this is harder on me than you could imagine."

I shake my head as numbness takes over my body. "Then don't do it."

"Don't blame this on me, Bridge."

I fight back the tears. Is he seriously not going to forgive me? "Troy, I made a mistake. I get that. Are you really going to hold it against me forever."

"Don't make this harder than it has to be."

I place my hand over my chest and search for the right words to say. I'm shocked. I listened to Vincent and followed my heart, what more can I do? I'm at a loss for words so I step towards him and he retracts away from me. With that cold blow to my ego and heart, I snatch my keys and wallet off of the table and bolt. I walk outside and leave the door open on my way. As I drive off, I look at his house and he's nowhere to be seen. The door is shut. We are finished, before we even started.

The tears won't stop. I'm completely dumbfounded. *What the fuck just happened?* I can't pinpoint where it went wrong. I mean, I know I made a mistake. But why in the world would he agree to see me and kiss me like he did, if it was just going to be like this?

At this point, I'm unsure where to go. Part of me feels like going home and curling up in a ball where I can sulk in my sorrows 'til Monday when I start work. The other logical part is telling me to go to my sister's. Maybe she can help me find my way out of this rabbit hole I've fallen down.

It's not long before my reason makes the right decision and I'm shutting my car off in front of Alexa and Vincent's sprawling, gorgeous home. When I walk in, I immediately spot them on the couch in the front room. Lex is in Vincent's arms and they are both laughing.

"Hey, guys," I say in a somber tone and flop down on the love seat.

"Didn't go so well?" Vincent asks.

I shake my head and the tears that just stopped, show up again. Dammit, perfect timing.

"I'm sorry, honey," Alexa says. "Do you want to talk

about it?"

I swallow and push away my wounded ego the best I can. "I don't know what to say, besides he's the best fucking kisser in the world and he's not gonna forgive me. I fucked up too badly. I shouldn't have lied."

"Whoa, whoa, whoa. Slow down," Vincent interjects. "He kissed you?"

"Yeah. Well, I kissed him."

"But he kissed you back?"

"Yeah, and I was dumb enough to believe he'd forgiven me."

Alexa looks at me with concern in her eyes and says, "Jesus, Bridge. I'm so sorry."

"Lex, don't be sorry," Vincent says. "Coming from a guy, if he kissed you then he's into you. He needs to make his point. We might act tough, but we're sensitive creatures. Don't give up on him. I promise he won't be able to stay away from you for long."

I think about Vincent's words and hope to God that he's right. "Baby, not every guy is like you." Alexa says, leaving a soft kiss on his neck.

He brushes the hair out of her face and says, "I know, but I promise I'm right on this. We can even call my douche of a brother and I guarantee he'll agree."

"No," I blurt out. "Don't do that. Abel is Troy's boss and I don't want to be spreading his business, even if it's to your brother."

"Fine. But I know I'm not wrong on this one, and remember, ladies, I've never lost a case."

Chapter 10

Rescue

I decide to go home. I mean, I am a grown woman after all, and Cara lives here, well, most of the time she does. Vincent and Lex follow me and check the place out with me to be sure. I don't think David's going to show up here or do anything. He acted in the heat of the moment and he'll get over it.

Plus, I can't live scared of him forever. I mean, he would never actually hurt me. All he wants is to get back together, so it's more of an annoyance than anything – right? I decide that a bath will relax my mind. I've felt on edge since leaving Troy's and I need to calm down. I turn the water on and leave the room to add a little soft, relaxing music. My brain needs it and I know it. Flipping through the stations of the TV, I decide on the soundscapes channel. The cool ocean waves crash through the speakers as I undress.

When I return to the steamed-filled bathroom, I slide into the hot water. It burns my skin and is so refreshing.

I've always loved the sting of a hot bath. Closing my eyes, I can feel Troy's lips on mine. The passion he showed me was not something you do with someone you're letting go of. Vincent's words make sense. He had to be proving a point. I pray that he is.

Keeping my eyes shut, I take even breaths to clear my mind, focusing on thinking of nothing. I soak for a while longer and then decide to wash myself. Finally I feel tired enough to sleep and drag myself to my bed. As I climb in, I leave the music on and check my phone. There's a missed text from Cara. *Would you mind if I crashed at Abel's? I'm exhausted and just want to sleep.*

Of course not, get some rest. Call me tomorrow.

Before I close my eyes for the night, I text Troy. I'm not going to give up on him. I stare at the blank screen, thinking of what to say. He knows I'm sorry; I don't want to repeat myself and start to sound like a broken record. So I simply decide on – ***I miss you.***

He doesn't respond and I hold out hope that he's busy. It takes everything I have to keep my eyes open. Soon the blackness soothes away my fears and takes me back to this morning…

…Rocking my hips against his, I'm rewarded with his erection – it's hard and hot underneath me. Suddenly he hoists himself off of the couch and engulfs me in his arms. Brushing my bangs out of my eyes, he asks, "Come to bed with me?"

I nod my head at him and he grabs my hand walking us out of his living room. I follow as he leads us upstairs, driving me absolutely mad watching his ass as we move. His thin pants barely hang on his hips and I want to just pull them down. Troy walks with purpose and doesn't hesitate. His confidence lets me know we made the right decision.

Entering his room, he says, "I have one rule. No shirts allowed in my bed."

Looking at him, his expression is serious. I swallow hard and grab the hem of my grey t-shirt, pulling it above my head. Troy's eyes never leave mine and I love how he respects me. "After you."

I climb in, and he's right behind me. Right away we get comfy and lay facing each other. Then I say, "You have really silly rules."

"It's not really a rule, just a way I could get your shirt off."

"You could always do it without asking."

"Really?"

"Yeah. I trust you."

"Then you won't mind if I do this?" he asks, removing the covers and scooting down, placing his lips on my neck, then my chest, each breast, and nipple. God, I wish I didn't have a bra on. He moves further, kissing my stomach and ribs, stopping along my right side, staring at the script tattoo that falls down my body. "So sexy," he murmurs. Moving to my left side he kisses another tattoo. As his mouth grazes the top of my shorts, he pulls them down a little bit. Not exposing me but allowing himself more access to my skin and the spot of an additional tattoo. This one is a heart with two angel wings.

"Fuck, Bridge. You're killing me. These are so hot."

"Mm-hm." I can't get out any words. I'm lost in the pleasure of his lips.

"Do you have more?"

"Uh-huh."

"Where?" he demands suddenly.

I roll over moving my hair to one shoulder. As I lay down, Troy presses his long body along mine and then his lips touch my back as he unhooks my bra. He sits up studying my art. My back piece is by far my biggest tattoo and the newest one I've been working on since I lost my mom. It represents everyone I've ever loved and lost. It's the one thing I can always count on to never leave me. I've lost a lot of people in my life and this wraps them all together. This one is of a seated fairy, surrounded by tons of sparrows and the wind from their wings swirling about. The large birds each represent a person. I'm the fairy seated in the midst of it all. Most of my tattoos are black and grey, minus the one I got with Lex, of an orchid with half of a butterfly perched on it.

After Troy drenches my back with his kisses he lies down next to me tickling my skin and is mere inches from my face. "Thank you for that," he says placing a gentle kiss on my forehead and covers us back up…

I wake to a loud bang, instantly jolting upright. Clutching the covers to me, I glance around my room. It's dark and quiet. I don't hear anything except for the noise from the birds chirping in the rainforest on my TV. It must have been the music on the TV that woke me. I turn it off and lay back down. Checking my phone, I smile as Troy did indeed text me back. I stare at the words for a few minutes, trying to make sense of what he said. ***I miss you too.*** Am I still dreaming? There is no way he meant to send that to me, did he?

Another loud bang shakes me and I panic. *What the fuck?* The noise almost sounds like it's coming from the roof. My hands begin to tremble and I don't know what to do. The moment I hear the noise again, I dial Troy's number. I'm huddled on the top of my bed, shaking. It rings and I pray he will answer.

"Hey," he answers in a cool, crisp tone.

"Troy," I whisper and there's a crackle in my voice. "I…I…" I can't get the words out.

"Bridge, what's wrong?"

"I…I don't know."

"Talk to me, Bridgette. What's wrong?"

"Something's…" is the only coherent word I can get out.

"Dammit, you're freaking me out."

I hear the bang again and scream. I swear my bed just shook. "Shit, where are you?"

"Home," I whisper.

"Stay on the phone with me. I'm on my way. Whatever you do, don't hang up, okay?"

"Mmm-hmm," I say and shake my head clutching my knees to my chest.

"Is Cara or Abel there?"

"Nuh-uh."

"I know you're freaking out, but I need you to talk to me. Can you do that for me?"

"Uh-huh."

I hear wind in the background and I know he's on his

way. "Where are you?"

"My room."

"Why did you scream?"

"I…I keep hearing—" I stop talking when I hear voices outside. "Fuck. Someone's outside, I can hear them."

"Look out the window."

"No, I don't want them to see me."

"Okay. Okay. Good point."

"Please just get here."

"I'm hurrying. Bridge, it'll be okay. I'm almost there."

I hear whoever it is outside shouting. "I think they're leaving. I just heard tires screech."

"What's the gate code?"

"Four, two, seven, seven."

"I don't see anyone leaving the neighborhood."

"There's another exit, separate from the entrance."

"Go to the front door. I'm almost there."

I scramble out of bed. Knowing Troy is close gives me the courage to look out the kitchen window. I see him pull up and my heart settles a little. "Stay inside. Someone was definitely here. They egged the shit out of your house. I'm gonna walk around and make sure they're gone."

"Okay."

He's quiet for a minute and I stay by the front door. "Let me in."

As quickly as I can, I unlock the door. He slides in relocking it, and instinctively I drop my phone clinging to him. He shrouds his warm arms around my shivering body. It must be the adrenaline that has me so worked up. "Shhh, it's all right. I got you."

I nod my head, trying to absorb his words.

"Come on, let's sit down."

We walk to the couch and sit. He still has his arm around me and I nestle in his warmth, feeling safe. "Thank you for coming over," I murmur.

"Of course. Bridge, who do you think did this?"

I nod my head, feeling sick imagining David stooping to such a low, childish level. "The only person I can think of is David."

"Are you kidding me?"

I shake my head. "There's no one else that would do something like this."

"Bridge, I think he's a bigger problem than you imagined. There are M80 shells all over outside. That's the noise you kept hearing."

"Are you serious?"

"I wish I wasn't. I hope he and some friends just thought it would be funny to scare you. But those things are loud and they're not shit to fuck with. What if one of those caught fire to your grass or something? I'm sure they were just lighting them and then tossing 'em, but still…" He trails off and I can't believe David would do something like that because I broke up with him.

I'm stricken with disbelief. "Who does something like that?"

"Someone that's fucked up."

"I know he didn't take the break-up well, but seriously? I kept telling myself he would get over it. God was I wrong."

"What the fuck did he do?" he asks in anger.

"It's hard to explain. He just wouldn't accept the fact that it was over." Troy traces his fingers over my arm making it hard for me to concentrate.

"What did he do, Bridge?" He says my name like silk, letting it roll off of his tongue and I'm pissed we're talking about David. Troy's finally here, at my house, and we have to waste it discussing some piece of shit.

"He pleaded with me. He said he would change. I kept telling him that's not what I wanted, that's what he wanted. Then he accused me of being with you."

"What did you tell him?

"The truth. You and I aren't together, although it was none of his business. He told me he and I belong together. Then he pinned me down, holding my face and hands while he kissed me aggressively. I tried to fight him off, but I couldn't. Before he walked away, he said we're not finished."

"What the fuck – who does he think he is? Did he not hear you clearly? He held you against your will and fucking kissed you?"

I nod my head a little uncertain of Troy's tone. I've never seen him this worked up before. Tears fill my eyes and I search for the strength to speak – but it's lost.

"Give me your phone. I wanna call the asshole."

"It's not going to help, especially now. Something's clearly wrong with him. He's gotta be on drugs or something."

"Jesus, are you serious?" I nod my head. "Well, that explains why he did what he did tonight. He's not thinking clearly."

"I know and a pissing contest is only going to make things worse."

"I hate seeing you upset, especially over him. I want him to know that I'm going to protect you."

"We're not together, you made that pretty clear. It's not your job to protect me, Troy."

"I want it to be." His words catch me off guard and I move my face from the comfort of his chest. We stare at one another staying silent. "Don't look at me like that," he says.

"What are you talking about?" I ask.

"That look in your eyes with your lips all pouty."

"But you said—"

He cuts me off, "I don't give a fuck what I said. I was being a complete asshole. I want you, Bridgette, there's no denying that." His words increase my heart rate. I watch his mouth and can't help, but want it on me. His breath is sweet as it washes over mine. I won't make the first move, not this time. I did that last time and was mortified when he turned me down. He knows I want him. I fucked up and can't change the past, so it's all on him now if we move forward or not. Taking his time, he connects our mouths. This time I move slowly, getting to know every bit of him. It doesn't take Troy long before he's holding my face again, and controlling not only my mouth but my movements. *Fuck, he's a good kisser, even better than I remember.*

We go on like this for God only knows how long. I'm scared to stop, scared that he'll leave. But as he slows the kiss, he doesn't move. Instead, he holds me, looking through heavy lids. "If we do this, you have to promise me one thing."

"Anything," I say breathlessly.

"Be honest with me, no matter what."

"I promise."

"Never lie to me."

"Never."

He exhales loudly "Do you have any idea how much you turn me on? I've been dying to kiss you like that for almost a month."

"You sure didn't act like it."

"I mean it. I've been imagining what your lips would feel like since the day I first met you."

"Then don't stop," I say kissing him again. He indulges in me and I in him. We both pick up right where we left off. Jesus, I've never kissed anyone like this. He's so slow and patient, but domineering all at the same time. I feel so small next to him as he drags his hands down my body and lies back, pulling me on top of him. I spread my legs wide, grinding my core against his already very apparent erection.

A growl escapes him and I move my hands to his chest, bracing my weight. Troy stops kissing me and pulls away.

The look in his eyes tells me he's in pain. Suddenly I remember his ribs. "Oh fuck. I'm sorry, I'm so, so sorry!" I say removing my hands. "Are you all right?" I ask.

Opening his eyes he murmurs, "Mmm-hmm."

"I can't believe I forgot."

"It's all right; it was worth it."

"Don't say that. You should be resting, not lying on the couch making out with me. Come on." I get up and hold my hand out to him.

He takes it and follows me into my room. The bed is messy from my earlier sleep. "You don't have to stay all night if you don't want to," I say with a yawn.

"I want to. You're not staying alone."

We both get comfy under the comforter. Moving my arms, I enclose them around Troy. He intertwines our legs and lets out a deep breath. "Sleep well, Bridge."

"You too, Troy."

Chapter 11

Patience

I wake to the sound of my phone ringing, but it's so far away I can barely hear it. Glancing around the room, the sun is bright, and next to me, Troy is comfortable and fast asleep. I lay there and watch him, as if nothing else matters. I almost lost him a week ago when he was in the hospital and then again yesterday when I thought I'd totally blown it. Going forward, I'm going to make sure that doesn't happen. After last night, who knows what the future holds. David is clearly out of his mind and I don't know how far he's willing to go. I really hope last night was all a dumb prank.

I go to touch Troy's cheek, but my phone rings again. I slide out of bed, padding quietly across the room and find it on the floor by the front door. My throat tightens as I begin to scroll through my missed text messages. *Please don't let any of these be from David.* Thank God, they are just from Cara, Lex, and Vincent.

As I start to text Alexa back, she calls, interrupting me.

I answer walking away from my room and towards the back of the house. "Hey, doll."

"Hey. Are you all right? You never called me last night."

"Yeah, I'm good. I'm sorry. I fell asleep. Listen there was a bit of an incident here at the condo."

"What happened?"

"Someone egged the house and threw M80's at it. I think it was David."

"Jesus, are you serious?"

"Yeah. I panicked and called Troy. He came over and stayed the night."

"Do you really think it was David?"

"Yeah, I do."

"Dammit. I'll call security and let the patrol and the gate know about the incident. What kind of car does he drive?"

"Thanks, Lex. It's a newer, black Toyota 4-Runner."

"Of course. I'm glad you're all right. So what happened with Troy?"

"It's a long story; a really long story. I'll fill you in later when he's not here, but we're going to give things a chance."

"Oh, sweetie, I'm happy for you."

"Thanks."

"I actually called to see if you wanted to have breakfast. Do you want to ask Troy if he wants to join?"

"Sure, I'll ask him when he wakes up, then I'll text

you. Thanks for checking on me and I'm sorry about the condo."

"Don't be sorry. If you can make it, head over in about an hour. I'm glad you guys worked things out. Oh, and Bridge, don't bother cleaning up the condo, I'll call and get someone out there."

We hang up and I turn to see Troy standing staring at me. "Ask me what?" he says walking over to me.

"If you want to have breakfast at my sister's?"

"I would love to."

"Good."

He walks over to me with purpose and poise, placing his cool hands on my sides under my shirt.

"You look really good without a shirt on," I say.

"I bet you would too," he says removing my shirt and throwing it to the floor.

I can't help but giggle. Troy licks his lips and grabs my breasts, caressing them through the fabric of my bra. "What color are your nipples, Bridge? You know I've thought about them a lot."

"Why don't you look?"

"Mmm. Someone's eager."

Reaching behind me, I unclasp my bra, allowing the straps to fall down my arms. Troy stands still, holding each of my hardened mounds in his hands. I can tell he can't believe what I just did. The ball's in his court, all he has to do is move his hands. "You really do what you want, huh?"

I nod my head, "When I've been waiting for it for far too long, then yes, yes, I do."

"Let me ask you this. Do we have to make it to breakfast at your sister's?"

"Yup."

"Fuck," he gripes and pulls me to him. As our chests touch, I'm stunned that he re-clasps my bra. Separating from me, he stares at me longingly and then suddenly pinches both of my nipples, provoking me that much more. I whimper as he squeezes down on them and leans into my neck sucking harshly on my skin. Pulling away he says, "I can see you're feisty as fuck and love to disobey."

"Mmm-hmm."

"Then let this be a lesson. Now you'll have to wait. Trust me, Bridge, this isn't something I want to do. I want to know what your nipples look like, taste like, and feel like. I wanna know what my mouth wrapped around them does to your body. But *you* made breakfast plans that we *have* to go to, so this is your fault."

"It's not for like an hour," I dispute.

"Dammit, Bridgette, I'm gonna need far more than an hour with you. You might as well pencil me in for a full day and I don't even know if that's enough."

I stare back at him with uncertainty, trying to comprehend his words. "A full day?" I ask baffled. I couldn't imagine having sex with someone more than once a day. I've certainly never done so.

"Yes, a full day. Maybe more, I don't know. Once I

start, it's hard to stop. Since I've met you, you've clouded my mind. You're all I think about. I don't know how many times it's gonna take to satisfy this craving."

"Wait…you what?"

"You heard me. My cock's been hard for weeks; I need to be able to take my time."

"So when can I pencil you in?"

"God, you're bad and I love it," he says squeezing my ass.

"You're bad," I counter back.

"Let's change the subject before I fuck you on the floor and we miss breakfast, okay?" he orders.

I pout and walk into my room to change. He follows me in and asks, "So is Alexa your only sibling?"

"No. I have a younger brother too. His name is Lincoln. What about you? Just your sister?"

"Uh-huh. So tell me who is Bridgette?"

"I'm simple. I'm who you see."

"You're more than simple."

"I don't know, I guess I'm a bit more complicated," I say, taking a deep breath.

"You don't like to talk about yourself do you?"

My phone rings interrupting our conversation. I glance down at it and see David's picture on the screen. Instinctively I ignore the call and toss it on the bed. I don't know what to say, so I search through my clothes for something to wear.

"Was that David?" he asks.

Nodding my head I pull my eyes up and connect them with Troy's. He stands and pulls my chin up to face him.

"Let me answer his call next time."

"I don't think that's a good idea. We talked about it last night; I think it'll make him even more crazy."

"Bridge, it's gotta be better than seeing you upset like this. Look at the effect he has on you."

"Trust me, I don't want him calling me."

"Just think about it, okay? I'll even call him on my own, if you want." I contemplate Troy's words and am a little caught off by his persistence to want to talk to David. Maybe I should hand him my phone the next time David calls. God, this is not what I want to be thinking about as I stand next to the sex god himself.

I decided to push away all thoughts of David. I turned my phone off and am not going to think about him. What I am going to think about is Troy, and what we are going to do later. I can't help, but be turned on as I watch him maneuver his silver four-door Jeep Wrangler. I love how he controls it – he's so patient, yet every move he makes is dynamically calculated to get us quickly and safely to my sister's. Then you add how he's dressed in a pair of dark jeans and a white linen shirt with the sleeves rolled up, and don't even get me started with how good he smells. We stopped by his place so he could get changed and I about died when he walked downstairs.

"Do you think we should stop and grab a bottle of champagne or something?" he asks, as his left hand tightly grips the wheel and turns a corner.

"If we were going anywhere else other than my sister's I would say yes, but they have a full bar."

"Ahh, I see. My kind of people," he jokes.

Troy glances over at me momentarily as we stop at a light and glides his right hand off of the center console and directly between my legs. He clutches my left thigh, holding it tightly. His grip is firm and so high on the inside of my leg that his hand is resting against my sex. I love that he's content with the simple things, like cuddling and making out. Don't get me wrong – I want more, so much more – but it's nice that he appreciates the small things too. I have to keep the conversation platonic in order to keep my crazy, sex-filled mind under control. "I love your Jeep. Have you had it long?"

"Thanks. About six months. We should take it up four-wheeling. Have you ever been?"

"No, but it sounds fun."

He begins rubbing his fingers deftly on my sensitive skin and grazes my underwear. "It is. I think the best part is the view once you reach the top. You can see all the snow-capped mountains. I know a trail that no one else goes to. It's on my family's property."

Stay calm, Bridgette. "I…I would love that. Maybe you

could schedule me in for twenty-four hours?"

He shakes his head with a huge smirk on his face and says, "Since they do have a cabin, why not?"

"It's a date," I say, with a giggle and glance over at his jeans. His erection is ever present and straining the dark fabric. *Fuck, why do we have to wait?* Leaning over, I grip his thigh like he has mine and squeeze. Troy squeezes my leg in return. Making my next move I cover his package and press my small hand against him. I'm rewarded when he bucks his hips into my hand. I push again and he cups my sex, holding it tightly. I push against his hand as we come to a stop. He looks over at me while we wait at the light and says, "Goddamn you for making plans. I hope your wet, little cunt aches for me all morning, the same way I am for you."

"It will, trust me. I wish more than anything we were in bed."

"You're a very bad girl. You've teased my cock for weeks and now that I can finally be with you, I have to wait."

"Don't wait," I say breathlessly with my heart beating so fast I can barely speak. "Touch me."

"I…I won't be able to stop. Trust me, I know my limits and what I can handle. You're a drug I've never had and my body has been craving you. I need to take my time with you to satisfy us both. I'm not going to get you off in my car like some prick, especially not the first time. You'll come in my bed, under my control, when I say you can.

Understand?"

I nod my head and adjust my hand back to his thigh. He does the same, my mind still fogged by his words. Who is this man next to me? He has a totally different side to him when it comes to sex. This is something I never saw coming. Fuck, the word 'coming' makes me tremble just thinking about it. Pulling up to my sister's, I'm sad to let go of Troy and that he has to do the same to me. As he removes his hand, he cups my chin and looks into my eyes.

"Kiss me, before I'm deprived of your lips for far too long."

I give him a half smile that fades away the moment he touches me. I don't know what it is about this man and his mouth, but I love it. He kisses me with more passion than anyone I've ever known. I melt into him when he brings both of his hands to hold my face and really controls me, controls us. My insides flame with desire. I've never wanted someone the way I want him. Maybe it's because we are waiting. Regardless, it's hot as hell. Unfortunately, we can't kiss all day and he stops. I continue to peck his lips, wanting more and he holds my head just chuckling at me.

"Ready?" he asks.

"I guess."

"Patience, Bridge. I promise it'll be worth the wait."

I titter at his comment and hop out of the Jeep. Walking around to me, Troy says, "There you go misbehaving again."

"What did I do?" I ask, surprised.

"Well, for one, you laughed at me, and then I told you at my place to wait for me and I would get your door."

"I didn't think that meant every time."

"Well, it does," he says kissing my neck. I grab his hand and we walk up to the front door. I never knock and as we walk in, Troy and I are greeted by a very excited Blair, my sister and Vincent's dog. I pet his head and Troy leans down giving him extra attention as Alexa and Vincent round the corner. "Hey, guys," I say embracing them both.

"Troy, it's good to see you man," Vincent says, shaking his hand. Troy hugs Alexa and kisses her on the cheek. "It's good to see you too. Thanks for having us."

I love the way he says *us*. I never imagined I would hear those words come from his mouth and there they are. With a smile on my face, we all head into the kitchen which smells delicious. Of course, Vincent goes to the oven while Alexa gets us each a drink. We both decide on coffee and then everyone settles around the island.

"So what have you guys been up to?" Alexa asks us.

I look at Troy for his response and he pulls me to him. "Well, after I saved your sister, we just slept and talked a lot."

Vincent laughs under his breath. He's in the fridge and I hear him clearly, so I throw a biscuit at his head. He turns and looks at me with a sly smile on his face. "On a serious note, thank you, Troy, for protecting Bridgette,"

Vincent says.

I smile at him. He's such a shit. He always picks on me then plays the big brother card, like he is right now. He walks past us heading to the dining room table and the doorbell rings. "Oh shoot, I forgot to tell you Cara and Abel are joining us," Alexa says.

I look at Troy and ask, "Is that okay?"

"Yeah, why wouldn't it be?"

"Uh, I don't know, maybe because Abel's your boss?"

He smirks at me. "Please, he's more like a really good friend."

"Oh," I respond back a little thrown off. I guess it shouldn't have come as a surprise considering Lex said Troy told Abel who told Vincent about our piggyback ride and early morning cuddling. That's really not something you tell your boss, but a friend, yep. Slim arms wrap around me from behind and a small bump presses into my back. "Hey, honey," Cara says.

"Hey, girl. I'm so glad you guys are here."

The guys exchange a goofy high-five and start to talk about the station. It sounds like Troy has missed a lot since being out after he got hurt. "There's my beautiful sister-in-law," Vincent says kissing Cara's cheek and rubbing her tummy.

"Get your paws off of her, douche," Abel snaps.

"Suck it, asshole. I can say hello to my niece or nephew whenever I want."

"Niece," Cara exclaims and we all look at her shocked

and then break out in congratulations. Everyone hugs Cara and Abel and then starts asking a million questions. Before any of them get answered, Vincent orders us into the dining room. As we begin to move, Alexa asks them, "How did you guys find out the sex of the baby so soon?"

"We did one of those 4-D ultrasounds this morning."

"No shit, that's awesome," I say.

We all get seated comfortably around the massive square table that's meant to seat kings and queens with its oversized chairs. Then Troy moves his hand under my skirt gripping my thigh like he did in the car. As soon as he touches me, I whip my head and stare at him, giving him the not-here look. He smiles and leans over, gently kissing me. As our lips stay connected, I hear the table silence and upon opening my eyes I look to see everyone staring at us. "So what have *you two* been up to?" Abel asks us.

"Napping and talking," Vincent retorts jokingly.

Snatching a strawberry off of the fruit tray, I launch it at him. He dodges it just in time as it barely flies by his head. "What's with you throwing food at me?" he snaps.

"I don't like your snarky comments."

"Snarky?" he repeats.

"Yes, snarky," I repeat and cross my arms over my chest glaring at Vincent. Troy places his forefinger and thumb on my chin directing me to look at him. Leaning down again he kisses me and I melt, his lips are as soft as heaven.

"Anyways," Abel says sparking up conversation about

his and Vincent's dad, thankfully taking the conversation off of us.

When Troy pulls away, I look at him through heavy lids. I have no clue how I'm going to make it through this meal. He simply captivates me, and his words from earlier consume me. *You'll come in my bed, under my control, when I say you can. Understand?* "You okay?" he asks, handing me the fruit tray.

"Yeah, I'm great."

"Good. Eat. You'll need the energy," he whispers.

I fill my plate and as hard as it is to not think about what we are going to embark on later, I focus on our friends. It feels so good for all of us to hang out and have such a good time. As we all sit together, I'm grateful that the conversation stays off of Troy and I.

"Thanks for having us, guys. Cara and I do have an announcement." Abel says.

We all look to him confused, a bit perplexed, I guess. She's already pregnant and I don't see a ring on her finger. "Tell us already," Alexa says excitedly.

"We bought a house," Cara blurts out.

"No shit, congratulations, bro," Vincent says patting his older brother on the back.

"Congrats, you guys," Troy and I say almost in unison.

"Where is it?" Lex asks.

As Cara and Abel take turns explaining the house, the location, and all the little details, I can't help but feel uneasy. Cara's not going to be there anymore and David knows where I live. He's already overstepped his boundaries once; what's going to stop him next time? I think Troy was right. I might have a bigger problem than I realized and living alone makes me see that. His words haunt me; I can hear them as clear as the moment he said them to me: *We're not finished.* I shake my head, reminding myself I'm not going to think about David today. Nothing's going to happen. It just can't.

"To Cara and Abel," Vincent announces raising his glass. We all follow suit and congratulate the happy couple. Abel leans over, kissing Cara behind the ear and she smiles, leaning into him. Looking at them, as well as my sister and Vincent, I'm envious. I hope one day I can be as happy.

Chapter 12

Endurance

Pulling away from my sister's house there is a strange silence in the car. Maybe it's just me because I had a few too many mimosas, although I'm not drunk. I made sure of it. Troy just seems…distant. Staring over at him, he's focused on the road, gripping the wheel with both hands. His brows are creased and I can tell he's deep in thought. "Are you all right?" I ask him.

"Are you on birth control?"

Whoa, excuse me? Way to start off a conversation. "Uh…yeah. Why?"

"I don't want us to use protection. I haven't slept with anyone for almost four months, so I promise I'm clean."

"Okay," I respond with a little smirk on my face.

"What's so funny?" he asks, tightening his hold on the wheel.

"Nothing, well, you are. I asked if you were all right and you blurt out 'Are you on birth control?'"

"Sorry about that. I'm fine, Bridge, trust me. That's

been bothering me for a while. I had to ask."

Troy parks in his driveway and looks over at me grabbing one of my breasts, pinching my nipple through my bra. "Stay put."

I chuckle at him and do so, all the while watching his every move, trying to contain my drool. He opens my door oozing confidence. He's a cocky fucker and knows damn well that he is. But being the gentleman that he is, he helps me out and quickly changes moods. Pinning me against his car, he crashes his mouth to mine. I whimper and brace myself on his forearms. Troy's as eager as ever and starts to grind himself against me. Since we are outside, I pull away. "Lets go inside," I say quickly.

"After you," he responds. "Just so you know, I would carry you to my bed if my ribs weren't still sore. Besides, I need to save my strength so I can fuck you all day."

"I can walk," I say trotting up to his front door.

He unlocks it and ushers me in first. I hear the lock click and look at his mouthwatering face. His dark hair is a mess and his hands are fists at his sides. His expression is carnal and ambiguous as we stare at one another, like two wild animals about to take each other down. I make the first move by taking a step closer to Troy, sliding my hand under his shirt, and grabbing the top of his jeans. Looking down at me, he takes his hands and begins to rove them all over my body, pulling me close to him while exploring my every curve. Leaning up on my tiptoes, I press my lips to his neck and move my fingers to the soft fabric of his white shirt, deftly unbuttoning it. As it hangs open, Troy is clearly letting me take the lead, letting me do what I want, so I meander my hands over his body, exploring every bit of his sculpted physique. He's lean yet muscular; his svelte stomach has a very nice six-pack. Each ridge sparks something inside of me as I get to know it. Moving my hands to his shoulders, I push the shirt off, watching Troy's breathing stop as I do.

Reaching for his jeans, I start to unbutton them, but he stops me and grabs my hand, pulling me up the stairs. I almost have to run to keep up with his long strides. My short legs have nothing on his as he takes the stairs three at a time.

"My turn," he says as we enter his bedroom.

"But I wasn't finished," I pout.

"Oh, but we have all day, baby. You'll get your turn." His words remind me of his earlier statement. *I know my limits, and what I can handle. You're a drug I've never had and my body has been craving you.* I wonder if that's really how he feels. Has he been craving me? Troy lifts my shirt above my head and suddenly my skin is clammy with anticipation. "You know, Bridge, I didn't take you for a skirt kind of girl." And he's kneeling before me.

Looking at him guiltily, I say, "I'm not, but it was easy access and a girl can always hope, can't she?"

"Jesus, you surprise me sometimes. I can't wait to see how far you'll let me push you."

He stands up and I reach for his jeans again. This time

I get them unbuttoned and slide the zipper down. Troy's notable erection is waiting for me, straining against his black Hugo Boss boxer briefs. I slide his jeans down and he steps out of them. Both of us are watching one another, our eyes never faltering although our breathing is ragged. "Take your bra off," he commands.

Reaching behind me, I unclasp the cream and black lace bra, my favorite, and let it fall to the floor. The moment Troy's eyes leave mine, he pursues me, walking me backwards to the bed and guiding me down onto the soft fabric. It's messy, but it's not what's underneath me that matters. It's what's on top of me.

He doesn't waste a moment becoming acquainted with my body. Touching everywhere, and then grabbing each of my breasts with his hands, moving them to his mouth to kiss and suck on them. *Oh fuck.* His mouth causes my sex to tighten in zeal. I can't help my hands as they explore his body. He has no chest hair, and as I reach into the back of his boxer briefs, he looks at me. Jesus, his ass is something else – it's so firm, yet soft. I grip and massage him trying to keep things slow, but I can't. I need to feel him. I want more of him, so I snake my hands around to the front and clutch his shaft with one hand. *God, it's velvety soft.* I take his balls in my other hand and begin playing with him, stroking his shaft and massaging in unison. "Oh…Fuck…Touch me just like that," he says biting his bottom lip and moving his hips in the rhythm of my hand.

"So soft," I murmur.

Troy removes his boxers so he's now completely naked and I lean up to get a better look at him. "You wanna see my cock, Bridge?"

Nodding my head, I lay back down as Troy moves on his knees and comes to my face. He presents me with his throbbing dick and I look over his size. I'm completely satisfied with what I see and I need to know it better, so I lean up wrapping my plump lips around the stiff end. Taking my time, I kiss and suck, teasing only the tip. Troy moans once I start moving. Threading his fingers into my hair, he helps to guide me up and down him; he's so gentle, yet he's not. I'm trapped below him; his knees are on either side of my shoulders. Just as I get in my rhythm and really begin to move, he snakes his hand inside my panties, separating my wet folds, and begins pleasuring me.

His touch is too much and I stop, spreading my legs wide, relishing in the feeling of his expert fingers. "Mmm, you're nice and wet. Is it for me, baby?"

"Uh-huh."

"Good. Why don't you suck my cock some more?"

I follow his command, keeping our eyes linked, but Troy only lets me get about three more good sucks in before he pulls out of my mouth. "You know, I've never come in anyone's mouth. With lips likes yours, you might be my first."

Excuse me? How has he never come from oral sex? I'm definitely making it my mission to be his first. Before I can fantasize any longer, he's removing my underwear, taking his time, letting me feel every one of his fingers as they skim down my legs. As he glides his warm hands back up, he's focusing on one thing and one thing only. "Motherfucker," he murmurs under his breath.

Smirking up at him I ask, "You like?"

"Oh fuck, yes. I can't wait to taste you."

Watching Troy go down on me has to be one of the sexiest things I've ever seen. He kisses everywhere he can, before placing his tongue in my slit, moving it up and down from top to bottom again and again. I run my fingers through his hair, loving the feeling. As Troy gets a good grip on my legs, he settles down on the bed and begins to move. There is a blissful suction holding him to me, and although my body writhes and I fight coming with everything I have…*goddamn he's*…quickly I let go, losing control and coming hard. Troy holds me to him as I spasm. My heart is racing in my chest so fast I swear he can feel it. I'm completely out of breath and it takes everything I have to try and regain my composure, but it's almost impossible with Troy still latched onto me. Squirming away from his hold, he looks up at me and says, "That was one. How many more times should I make you come today?"

I can tell that he is dead serious and wants an answer. Crawling up my body, he lays down on me, running his fingers through my hair. "How many times?"

I shrug my shoulders. "Answer me," he snaps and clamps down on my neck, sucking hard. He doesn't let up and it feels incredible, then I remember I have work Monday. If he doesn't stop it'll leave a mark. I wriggle trying to get him to, but it's useless. "Two!" I yell.

He stops and looks at me. "Two," he repeats.

I nod my head in agreement.

"We'll see." Before I can contemplate his words, he sinks inside of me, filling me with his thick cock. Once he's nestled balls deep, I tighten my pussy. Troy lets out a moan and begins to move. I love how close we are. Our bodies are pressed together and he keeps a hand on my face. As we move, I wrap my legs around him. Grabbing his face, I pull his lips to mine, kissing him with more passion than I ever have anyone else. I can't help but moan and whimper. His movements are made with pure precision, working both of us impeccably. Finally, Troy pulls away and says, "God, you're tight."

"Mmm," I respond.

"Do you want me to come inside of you?"

"Yes," I cry out grabbing his ass assisting him as he begins to pound me. "Put your arms above your head," he says.

I listen while endorphins take over my system. *What's happening? It's too soon.* He takes a hold of my arms and has a firm grip on my wrists, holding them together. The sensation of pleasure turns to ravenous need. "Oh fuck," I mumble. "Yes. Yes. Just like that."

Troy listens to my commands, stroking himself inside of me like I want. I'm unsure how he knows my body so well, but he does. A loud moan escapes him, followed by long, purposeful thrusts. Spurts of warm cum seep high inside of me. Watching his face as he lets go pushes me over the edge, and I throw my head back against the pillow. My world is upside down as my body is sprinkled with pure bliss and I fall into insensibility. Nothing else matters in this moment. All of my worries float away as I'm under his control. It doesn't last long, as it never does, and reality creeps back in. I feel my senses return and hear his sweet words. His movements don't falter as he keeps moving inside of me. "So beautiful."

Glancing up into his eyes, there is a clarity I haven't seen before. He looks refreshed and at peace. He let's go of my hands and grabs my hips, holding them as he kneels above me. With his bottom lip tucked into his teeth, Troy watches himself moving. "Wanna see?" he asks me.

"Yes," I respond and sit up, looking at what he's watching. *Jesus, it's hot.* I've never actually watched anyone move in and out of my body. His dick is so hard and slick; I love how effortlessly he moves. Leaning down, he takes a mouthful of one of my breasts, squeezing it hard and then nibbles on my nipple. As he pulls it between his teeth, I hold him to me. Once he pulls away, he touches my clit continuously rubbing slow, agonizing circles. "Are you sure you only wanna come twice?"

"You choose. I'll do whatever you want."

"That's right, you will. You're in my bed and I will do with you as I please."

"Ahhhh," I cry out as Troy slams into me, still tantalizing me with his fingers. I'm enjoying the pleasure too much to think of stopping, or anything else for that matter. I need him to keep moving. Heat radiates all the way to my toes. Opening my eyes, reality smacks me hard as I glance up at Troy. He's watching me, and smiles when we connect eyes. Sweat glistens on his body and his brow. He takes his free hand, running it through his hair, but his movements never cease. As he lifts his arm, I see the faint outline from the bruising on his ribs. I totally forgot about them; he's been working so hard to please us and fighting through that pain. I want to let him rest. I know he's far from finished and now's my turn to take control.

"Troy?" I ask out of breath, causing him to slow, but not completely stop. "Can I get on top?"

He shakes his head. "Not yet."

"But your ribs."

"I'm fine," he says breathlessly. "Fuck, Bridge, being inside your pussy makes everything better. Please don't make me stop."

"Trust me," I moan trying to control my voice. "I don't want you to. I only wanna help."

"Just lay there and let me savor this," he grunts, filling me. "Come for me again and again. Watching you let go is what I want."

Looking up at him I close my eyes and ask, "How can you keep going?"

"I told you I wouldn't be able to stop. This is nothing compared to what you're in for. I'm only getting started, baby."

Chapter 13

New Beginnings

Walking up to my new office is so surreal. I cannot believe I landed this job. Granted I have my sister and Vincent to thank, but deep down I know it was partly because of me. It wasn't just their decision after all. Liam and C.J. had a lot to do with it. Before I step inside, I look down at my black slacks, flats, and white dress shirt. *You got this.* I take the elevator up to the twenty-ninth floor and breeze right past Autumn in reception, saying a simple, "Good Morning," as I walk by. She glances up and I can see the shock on her face. Vincent told me to just come in and find Lex, that she would get me all set up. As I approach her desk, she's leaning over staring at her computer screen with a scowl on her face.

"Morning," I say, in a chipper tone.

"Hey, honey. Welcome. How was the rest of your weekend?"

"It was nice. Troy and I had a great time together."

"Oh good. Glad to hear. Wanna follow me to your

desk?"

"Yup, lead the way."

Alexa comes out from behind hers and I follow as we walk around the row of cubicles. "The guys' offices are all over there," she says pointing to the left-hand side of the office. As we reach the end of the row, she says, "Here's your desk, dear. Max is on the other side of the wall from you."

"Great. Thank you."

"Of course. Here are your keys. Inside is a binder with enough stuff to keep you busy for a few hours. Just getting logged on and setting up your e-mail and other accounts, voicemail, and blackberry…it'll take ya all morning."

"A what-a?"

"Blackberry. As office manager, be prepared to be on call whenever needed. Oh, and I think the guys wanted to meet with you at eleven, but check your Outlook calendar to be sure. Love ya," she says and walks off.

I set my stuff down on the desk and plop down in my chair. Oh God, am I going to be able to handle this? Is it going to be too much responsibility? My phone buzzes, interrupting my negative thoughts, and as I fish it out of my bag, it buzzes again. Once I have it in my hands, I glance at the screen to see two missed text messages, both from Troy. The first says. *How's my girl holding up so far?* The second is a picture of us in bed this morning. Both of us have huge smiles and you can see the happiness is pouring out of us like water from a spout.

Thanks for the text and the picture. I miss your face. I think this is going to be a lot to handle. I hope I can do it.

Baby, you can do anything you put your mind to. You're one of the strongest women I've ever met. Don't forget that, okay?

I hope so. You're so sweet. Thank you for saying that.

My pleasure, I'm just speaking the truth. Wanna have lunch?

I would love to. Let me see what my schedule looks like and I'll text you back.

I place my phone in the top drawer of my desk and glance around to make sure no one saw me texting. As I unlock all of the other drawers, I'm nervous about what's inside. Thankfully, it's clean and empty, and I'm sure I have Lex to thank for that. I pull out the binder and skim over the contents of what's in front of me.

As I read, I'm startled and look up to see a heavy set, red-haired guy with the cutest red, white, and blue checked bow tie on. He smiles at me and says, "Hi, cube buddy. I'm Max. It's nice to meet you."

I stand and shake his hand. "Hi. I'm Bridgette. It's nice to meet you too."

"Oh, I know who you are, darling. Lex has told me all about you."

"Oh God, I hope it's been good."

"You know it, sugar. Let me know if you need anything, I'm right on this side of the wall."

"Thanks. You know, I could use a cup of coffee."

"Oh girl, clearly you haven't seen our espresso machine. Let me show ya."

As I follow behind Max, he walks with such a sway in his hips. I can already tell that I'm going to like him.

"Ta-da," he announces, giving his best Vanna White impression. "What's your poison, honey?"

"Uhhh, coffee."

"No way, something else. How 'bout a Caramel Macchiato?"

I can't help but giggle. "As long as it has caffeine, that'll work."

He places a cup under the machine and presses a few buttons. I can't help the yawn that ensues and I'm happy he's giving me caffeine. "Tired?" he asks.

"Yeah, you could say that."

"Didn't sleep well?"

I blush remembering how little Troy and I slept. It must've been around three in the morning when he woke me. I was sleeping so well, but the way his fingers parted my pussy and entered my body – it was paradise. He was right when he said I was his to do what he pleased with in his bed. He made me come from his fingers, then his mouth, and then his—

"Hey, Bridgette!" Max says, holding my coffee. "Are you all right? You kind of left me there."

"Oh yeah, I'm good. Sorry, I got distracted. You were asking about how I slept. I was just excited for work today and my nerves kept me awake." *Ha, if he only knew.*

"Well, don't be nervous, I can tell already that you'll fit right in." We walk out of the kitchen and go our separate ways, going to our own desks. Alexa was right – it does take a while to get settled and up and running on the system, but it's nothing I can't handle. And my meeting with Liam, C.J., and Vincent goes well. I glance at the clock, and to my surprise it's about time to meet Troy for lunch.

My desk phones rings and the screen says it's Autumn from reception. "This is Bridgette," I answer in a professional tone.

"Bridgette, I have a Troy Sorano here in reception for you."

My heart rate jumps to Mach speed. "All right, I'll be right out."

I go to hang up and miss the base of the receiver. The phone clangs on my desk and Max asks, "Everything okay over there?"

"Uhh…yeah…no. I don't know." I get the damn phone hung up and Max is staring at me over the wall.

"What's wrong?" he asks.

"My boyfriend's early for lunch and he's *in* reception."

I don't know why I'm nervous, it's just Troy. Fuck, that's why I'm nervous, *it's Troy.* I pop a stick of gum in my mouth and stand brushing my fingers through my hair and over my clothes.

"You look beautiful, honey."

In the next moment, Troy's standing in front of me.

"Yes, I agree with the man, you look beautiful, babe."

He has a huge vase of lilies and is in his work clothes. Mmmm, I love him dressed in uniform. Although he's not in his full fire gear, it's close enough. "I hope you don't mind me bringing him back," Alexa says. "But I just came in from Starbucks and saw him waiting."

"Of course not," I say hugging him. He hands me the flowers and I set them on my desk. "These are for your first day."

"Thank you, baby. Troy, this is Max. He's my cube mate."

The two guys shake hands and I'm so grateful Max is gay. "Are you ready to go?" he asks.

"Yup, let me grab my purse."

As Troy and I walk out hand in hand, he makes a point to kiss me as we walk by Autumn's desk. As the elevator doors are closing, I can see her staring at us. He shows no mercy kissing me while he presses me against the wall. My eyes close and I forget everything except for him on our journey down the twenty-nine floors. As we emerge and walk to his Jeep, I ask, "What was that all about?"

"What? I miss you."

"Troy, be honest."

He growls a little and then says, "That chick in reception was eye fucking me; I wanted her to know that I wasn't interested. You would think the flowers were a clue, but some women are ruthless and she looked desperate."

I laugh out loud. "In that case, you can mark your

territory anytime. Thank you for surprising me by coming early and for the flowers."

"My pleasure. How's the day so far?"

"It's been amazing." I ramble on and Troy asks if Subway is all right for lunch. I'll eat anything at this point because I skipped my breakfast and Max got me zinging on two Caramel Macchiatos. Since there aren't many seats left inside, we grab our subs to-go and opt to eat them in his Jeep.

We find a nice little spot under a tree in the shade to enjoy our food. "So how's work for you?" I ask, enjoying my sandwich.

"Boring. Abel's babying me, like someone I know," he teases.

"Troy, I'm not babying you, I'm just worried; that's all. There's a big difference."

"I'm only joking, babe."

"I'm actually glad you asked about work. I talked to Abel about getting the entire weekend off so we could go four-wheeling and he agreed. What do you think?"

"Yeah, I would love to."

"Great, we can leave on Friday night if that works for you?"

"Yeah, that's perfect," I agree and move my hand over the center console. "You know what else is perfect?"

"Hmm?" he asks.

"This," I say massaging his cock through his pants.

"Yeah? You like him, don't you?"

"Mmm. You have no idea. I'm going to miss him tonight," I say unzipping his pants. Troy reaches over and caresses my breast through my shirt. Leaning in, I kiss him while I remove him from his underwear. He unbuttons my shirt and slides his hand into the cup of my bra pinching my nipple between two of his fingers, then uses his thumbs to tantalize it.

I whine and pull away from his mouth going straight for what I want – his cock. Taking my time I flick my tongue over the end and wrap my lips around his plump head. With my hand, I keep a firm grip on the base and continuously stroke him. I know to get him to come I'm going to have to work hard. As I sink all the way down, I keep my breathing even and begin to move. "Oh yeah, Bridge, you suck a good dick."

I moan in agreement and don't let up. I want this. I need this. I'm not going to have Troy for the next three days while he works and he deserves this. No man should ever go through life without experiencing oral sex to the fullest. "Baby, stop," he orders.

I pull away and look at him confused. "Why?"

"I don't want to come in your—"

I cut him off and begin to jerk his cock and sink my mouth around him. "Oh fuck." His words are barely a mumble and he weaves his hand into the back of my hair helping to guide me. Having him agree to this and let go of his worries is such a turn on. "Ahhh…baby…I'm…" He starts just before he explodes deep in my throat, repaying me with his warm cum. Jesus, he tastes good. I pull every last drop from his shaft and enjoy the satisfaction. I'm his first. "Christ, you're fucking talented."

"Why, thank you, and you, my dear, taste delicious."

"Thank you for that, Bridge, for real. I've never had a girl who could get me there and then when you just did, I didn't want to let go. You know how I am. I like to take my time. But fuck, babe, I think I just found my new favorite pastime."

"Anytime you need it, I'm your girl."

"And I'm one lucky son of a bitch. Let's get you back to work."

"Sounds good, same time tomorrow?"

"Sure thing, just wear a skirt so I can finger the fuck out of you and return the favor."

Chapter 14

Secure

"How has the week been so far?" Troy asks me, taking a swig of his beer.

"It's been great. How 'bout you?"

"Eh, Abel doesn't let me do shit so that kinda blows."

"Well, you do need to take better care of yourself."

Cocking his head to the side he says, "I have been, thank you very much."

"I mean it."

"What? I think I've been doing a damn good job of thoroughly enjoying being inside of you. It's the best medicine there is."

"Troy, you know what I mean," I argue back. "When are you going to the doctor anyways?"

"Tomorrow. Maybe after they clear me, Abel will let up a bit."

"What time?"

"You're not coming with me."

"Tell me or I won't have sex with you," I say dipping a

fry in ketchup.

"You wouldn't," he dares me.

"Oh, I would," I challenge back.

"Motherfucker! You're evil, you know that?" he says chewing a bite of his burger. "I think it's at nine."

"I'll see if I can go in late."

"No way! Not on your first week. I promise I'll do whatever the doctor says."

"You promise? Because I know you've been pushing yourself."

"I told you, baby, I'm fine. Honestly, I barely hurt. I guess I have a high pain tolerance or something."

"Please take care of yourself. I can't get another call that you're in the hospital, I mean it."

"Scouts honor, babe. Are you ready to get going?"

"Yep," I say, as Troy leaves some cash on the table and we head out into the warm sun. We decided to head up to Golden after I got off of work. It's an old historical town outside of Denver with a river running through it. Tons of people love to wade and tube in the river, but Troy and I went for a hike then grabbed a bite to eat. Now we're going to explore the small shops before heading back to my place.

Walking hand in hand with Troy makes me feel so secure. He has such a confidence about him; I can tell others quickly notice. He's always touching me and I love it. Looking into the window of an old antiques shop, his hands are in the back pockets of my shorts and his chin is resting on top of my head. "Wanna go in?" he asks.

"Nah. I'm just looking." We begin to move and my cell phone rings. I pull it out glancing at the screen. Right away my stomach knots and a queasy sensation creeps up my throat.

"Who is it?" he asks.

I show the phone to him and he sees David's name and picture. "Let me answer it; he's been calling a lot lately."

I don't know what to do. I'm not sure what's right or wrong. Unfortunately, there are no rulebooks or guides to follow in these kinds of situations. My instincts decide for me and I hand my phone to Troy. He hits the answer button and brings it to his ear. "Hello," he says in a cool, even tone. "Hello," he says again.

As I watch, his reaction is blank. "David, I know you're there. If you care about what's best for Bridgette you'll leave her alone."

He hands my phone back to me. "He hung up."

"Thank you for trying. Hopefully he'll stop calling."

"I hope so, babe. If he continues, let's get you another phone, okay?"

"Okay," I agree.

"Now are you going to go into one of these shops so I can buy you something?"

"I don't need anything."

"Oh yes, you do," he says grabbing my hand and dragging me into a toy shop.

"Troy, this place is for children." He waves me off and keeps pulling me through the aisles of toys. Finally he stops in the back corner in front of a huge shelf packed with an assortment of stuffed animals.

"Pick one," he requests.

"Troy."

"What? Pick one."

Scanning over the selection of soft and cuddly items, I'm a little unsure. I mean, I am a grown woman right, why do I have to pick one out? Nothing sticks out to me. Well, nothing except an ugly rhinoceros. "This one," I say, grabbing the sad, gray animal.

"I'll take that one, thank you very much," he says, snatching the animal out of my hand. "Now which one should I pick for you?" He doesn't take but half a second to skim over the items and hands me a tan lion with a huge mane of hair.

"This is what you picked for me?"

"Yeah, why? It reminds me of you."

"Uhh, I don't know about that and what's with the hair? It's a lot, don't—"

He cuts me off, "And so is yours. We're buying it! Come on, let's go."

Following Troy to the register I can't help but laugh. He's got his ugly, grey rhino in hand and I'm holding this ridiculous lion. "Just these two for today?" the cashier asks Troy as we set down our stuffed animals.

"Yup, unless my girl wants anything else?"

I don't know why my checks flush, but I feel all the blood rush to them and shake my head.

"Yup, just these."

Troy pays and we head outside. The walk to his Jeep is short since we parked close by. He took the doors and top off before he picked me up from work and driving it completely open like this is so much fun.

"In you go, baby," Troy says, handing me the bag with our stuffed animals.

Then he walks around and slides behind the wheel. "Do you need to stop anywhere on the way to your place?"

"Nope. Just get me home."

"That I can do," he says backing out of the parking spot. Once we're on the freeway, I close my eyes, letting the wind whip through me. I feel Troy's hand creep over and grip my thigh, holding it like he likes and I relax in that moment feeling so safe. I know being with him, he'll never let anything happen to me. He's shown me nothing, but care and protection since the day I met him. I wish I'd ended things with David when I moved. Something in my gut was telling me to, and I ignored it. Then when I showed up and Troy was waiting outside of the condo sitting on the steps, with his huge smile and sincerity, I should have followed my heart that very moment. Regardless of the past, I'm so thankful to be where I am now.

When we pull into my neighborhood, I can't believe

the sun is starting to set. *Where oh where has the day gone?* Troy enters the gate code and we drive through.

"I'm glad we get to stay together tonight. I've been tempted to make you stay at the station with me to ensure you're safe."

"David might be a little out there, but he would never hurt me."

"Bridge, he already forced himself on you. Please don't push it. I know how guys think. We're sick bastards, and now that I've answered your phone, he… I can't go there, I won't. I'm here to protect you, and I promise I will."

"I know you will, thank you."

I open the front door and notice a piece of mail hit the ground. The moment I see the handwriting on the envelope, I know it's not mail.

Troy picks it up and asks, "What's this?"

"It just fell out of the door. I think it's from David."

"Fuck, babe."

I shake my head and Troy hugs me, kissing me hard on the top of my hair. "Are you gonna open it?"

"No," I whisper. That's the last thing I want to do. "I don't care what David has to say, we are finished and he needs to accept that."

"I know, baby. Listen, it's just a note. Don't waste a second on it or him."

I nod my head staring into Troy's beautiful face and know I have to let this go. He's not going to let anything happen to me.

"What do you say we shower and then go to bed?"

I nod my head and follow him into the bathroom. We both get in the shower and stay until the water is cold. I love how attentive and gentle he is with me. He makes me forget everything bad in this world. I've never had a man treat me like Troy does. As I stand in my bathroom shivering, Troy removes his towel and helps me dry. "Thank you," I say.

"Of course. You feel better?"

"I do."

"Good. PJs and bed, babe."

I walk out of the bathroom and throw on an old faded t-shirt and a soft, cotton pair of underwear. Troy walks out naked and slides on a pair of shorts from the bag he packed. We both climb into bed and lie facing one another.

"Thank you for everything lately and for forgiving me."

"I wouldn't have lasted long staying away from you. I just wanted to make sure I didn't relive past mistakes," he says and kisses my forehead.

"What happened?" I ask.

"When I started dating my last girlfriend, she told me she was single. Things were going great and then she started to…*change.* She became more distant and I found out she'd been seeing someone the entire time we were together, it wasn't long that we dated, but it still crushed me. When I found out about David, that's all I could think about."

"You know I feel horrible about that. I'm sorry I wasn't honest and up front with you from the beginning. I promise no matter what, I'll always be honest with you."

"I know. I trust you, Bridge."

He wraps me in his arms and I get comfy, thinking of his words. *I know. I trust you.* I never knew something so simple could impact me so heavily, but hearing him say the words did just that. I trust him too, utterly and completely.

Chapter 15

Perfect

I don't think we could have picked a better time to leave town. After finding the note David left for me at the condo, I've been on edge. Needless to say, I'm looking forward to some time alone with Troy and to just…unwind.

"How much longer 'til we're there?" I ask Troy.

"Not long, babe, maybe another thirty minutes. We might just make it in time to see the sun set," he says pulling onto a dirt road.

The Jeep bounces about as we ascend the steep hill. Looking over the edge, it's a steep incline, covered with thousands of trees. Normally, I would be nervous, but seeing as I'm with Troy, and he's so confident behind the wheel, I'm not one bit scared.

"Do you come up here often?"

"Not anymore. Growing up, we spent a lot of time here as a family. There were many holidays and celebrations, but as the years passed, that has fizzled. I love it here and I think you will too."

"Are you kidding me? I'm going to spend the weekend alone with you, of course I'm going to love it."

"That's the plan. You and me, baby. No distractions. We'll go four-wheeling tomorrow and I have a little surprise for you, if you're a good girl."

"Troy, I hate surprises."

"Well, I love them, so tough shit, Bridge."

I begin to pout until I see a beautiful log home come into view. It's on the top of the hill and all alone. "Is that it?" I ask.

"Yup, that's her."

"Wow, it's gorgeous."

"It is, huh?"

I can't keep my eyes off of the beautiful home as we approach. It's amazing – the windows are huge and it has an expansive deck wrapping around the entire front of the house. As we pull around the side, there is an attached two-car garage on the bottom of the house, and stairs leading to the deck. "Ready to head in?"

I nod my head and once the Jeep is in park I hop out and stretch my legs. It was a long drive and I feel stiff. "Are you ever gonna learn?" Troy asks, shaking his head and opening the back to take out our bags.

"I'm sore."

"Oh, you'll be sore after I'm done with you," he retorts. I swat his ass, but miss when he moves out of the way and he catches my wrist, pinning it behind me. "God, you're feisty today." He nibbles on my ear and intertwines our fingers. "Come on, bad girl, let's go watch the sunset.

As we approach the door, Troy slides the key in to unlock it and sets our bags down. "Hop on and I'll give you the grand tour." I climb onto his back clinging to him as he carries me inside. As soon as we enter our weekend retreat, I'm in love. I never want to leave this place. The interior matches the exterior and the outdoor surroundings flawlessly, not to mention how huge it is. Surprisingly, it's modern and looks to have been recently renovated.

"Here you have the kitchen, with cool marble counter tops, which I plan to fuck you on later. This is the great room/dining room and we'll do plenty of fucking in here too, especially in front of the fireplace. Upstairs is just a bunch of bedrooms, which we'll get to know them all very well, but that sun looks enticing."

My insides are on fire from his words. I'm probably hotter than the fireplace and the sun combined. As we exit the house and walk out onto the huge deck, the view from up here is even more spectacular than I imagined. The sun is gorgeous as it cascades down to the horizon, getting ready to set. Troy doesn't set me down, and that, I like. Leaning into him, I breathe him in. His scent drives me absolutely mad. I think it's one of the things that exudes confidence from him – that and many others. Troy is without a doubt one hundred percent real, confident, and sexy as fuck. Oh, and all mine.

Pressing my lips against his neck, I relish his scent as

the sun quickly diminishes. Neither of us speaks and I enjoy that. It's one of the things I enjoy most, when we're just…together. No words or worries. I don't have to stress about what he's thinking or where the next moment will take us.

"Damn, it sets fast," he says.

"It does, but it always comes back."

"That's one of the best things about the sun; it always comes back."

"That's true, it does. I promise I'll always be your sun."

"And I'll be yours."

With those words, for the first time in years, I feel secure. I truly believe Troy will never leave me. That's been my biggest fear all along. My father left when I was two, and there have been countless people since then that I have had to say goodbye to – but not with Troy. Finally, he sets me down and I don't waste another second threading my fingers into the wild strands of his hair.

He holds my face like he always does, kissing me so gently, while looking into my eyes. We hold one another's expressions, but his is a bit unsure. It's as if he's reading into me, "Do you trust me?" he asks pulling away.

"With my life."

"You'll always be my sun?"

"Of course. Why would you ask that?"

He looks down at the ground and for the first time since I've met Troy, I see self-doubt. "Just trust me, okay?"

"You know I do."

"I'll never hurt you."

"I know that. Troy, I have to be honest with you, you're starting to scare me."

"No, no. Please don't be scared. This is a good thing, or at least I hope it will be."

Looking up at him, I fully absorb his words. I trust him. Infinitely, I trust him and will continue to do so until he gives me a reason to feel otherwise.

Waking up the next morning it feels like I am in a dream. Honestly, I'm having a hard time telling the difference between what's reality and what's not. I love being in Troy's arms; my back is to his front and we are tucked nicely under the plush, warm covers.

My eyes are closed, which I prefer, since I cannot see his face. Moving his large hand, Troy rubs my body, paying attention to all of the right places. "So perfect," he whispers.

I smile, agreeing with his words more than he knows. This is perfect – *he* is perfect. Troy rocks his hips into me and his hard erection is ready. Moving his hand under the covers, he tweaks a nipple and then glides it the rest of the way down my body. When he reaches my thigh, he cups the inside of it, like he always does. Instinctively, I lift my leg and push my butt into him. Taking two fingers, he separates my wet slit and caresses me.

I moan with need as Troy starts to suck on my neck and a soft finger plunges into my aching pussy. His lips are so tender, yet urgent. He moves his mouth and hand in sync and it's driving me absolutely mad. Although this feels amazing, I want more. Reaching back I clutch his velvety soft organ and begin pumping it. A low growl escapes his throat and he pulls his finger out of me. I take his cue and guide his rock-hard dick towards my opening. Troy holds my leg up and nudges himself inside of me. My body burns as he enters me. Moving slowly, he pulls himself in and out until he's soaked and nestled deep in my wet core.

Then he lets go of my leg and I lower it. Tightly, he holds my body against his and I reach behind me, gripping his ass as he moves. Troy doesn't speak and neither do I. This is by far the quietest either of us has been while having sex. The morning sun is crowning the sky and shining in all of the windows, casting bright and beautiful heat throughout the room. The window is cracked and I can faintly hear a few birds chirping. Inside the room, the only noise is our erratic breathing, quiet moans of contentment, and the sound of our skin slapping together as our bodies work as one.

Sliding my hand up Troy's body, I knot my fingers into his hair and pull him to me, kissing him as my body builds close to climax. Troy grunts as we move and the moment his tongue enters my mouth, I lose it, letting go and allowing the ecstasy to take over. God, I enjoy this pleasure. He grabs a handful of one of my breasts, which only intensifies the feeling.

He pulls away from kissing me and grips me tighter than ever as he comes. I turn to watch him and realize this is probably the first time I've ever really focused on him when he's come. He's gorgeous, so handsome and sexy all at the same time. His eyes are tightly shut and his lip is tucked into his teeth. I love it when he does that. Each pull and push of his cock is flawless.

"So perfect," he finally whispers.

Chapter 16

Rough Ride

-Troy-

Staring at Bridgette's ass is such a fucking turn on. I can see her clearly through the window, as she's bent over in the kitchen. We're about to go four-wheeling, but seeing her like that has me so fucking tempted to say fuck it, and tie her up. *Focus, Troy.* I shake my head to clear my thoughts and remind myself of what I have planned for this evening. It took everything I had to not do it when we got here last night, but we were tired after the drive. Plus, when I show her that side of me, I want it to be just right.

Walking inside I say, "Hey, baby," and kiss her chastely, seizing her tiny, little body. "Are you ready to get going?"

"Yup, I think I have everything packed. Let me grab my sunglasses."

She walks off and I snatch a blanket off the couch and

carry our lunch outside. It's a beautiful day, so I decided to take the top off the Jeep. As I pack everything in the back, I hear the door to the house close and see Bridge emerge. *God, she's hot.* Today she's wearing a little pair of jean shorts, with a black tank and some Nikes. She sees me staring at her and gives me a cocky half smile. She knows damn well what she's doing.

"Wanna drive?" I ask her.

"Oh, hell no."

"Come on, babe, I've been dreaming about you handling my Jeep climbing up the mountain all week."

She scrunches her eyebrows and looks at me. "Really?"

"Yeah, really. Won't you make my fantasy come true?"

"Let me watch you take it up and maybe I'll drive it down."

"Fine. You can drive a clutch, right?"

"Come on, Troy, what do you think?"

"Okay, okay. Point taken. You can definitely handle a stick."

"Yes, I can and very well," she says stepping to me and grabbing a handful of my junk. Her touch makes me fully hard. That's the affect she has on my body; Jesus, it's crazy. Just being around her has me at half-mast most of the time. Then you add the slightest touch and my dick acts like a starving animal that's craving it's next meal.

"Are you gonna open my door?"

I smirk at her and like that she's finally listening.

Swiftly I plant a kiss on her lips and walk to her side of the Jeep to let her in.

I back out of the driveway and start to head down to the main road. I reach across the Jeep to grip Bridgette's thigh. I know once we are wheeling I won't be able to, and I just can't keep my hands off of her, especially her legs.

She's got her head rested back, and I can see through her shades that her eyes are closed. I wish I could get into her head, even if only for a few minutes. Lately, I've been worried about her. I know David is lurking in the back of her mind and I'll do everything in my power to protect her. Still, it pisses me the fuck off. The guy is fucking crazy and needs to let her go. I hope that he's not what's on her mind right now. Since she didn't respond to his letter, his calls have pretty much ceased, or at least to my knowledge they have. But I'm not about to ask her either. I don't want to be the one to bring him up.

"God, it's beautiful up here." Her soft voice interrupts my mindfuck, reminding me of what's important.

"It really is. We can come up here anytime, baby."

"I would love that. It feels so different than the city. I guess it's being away from all of the hustle and bustle. Plus, there's virtually no one around; we're all alone."

"It's a great feeling. I love being up here. Any time you want to come you just tell me, okay?"

She nods her head and a gust of wind whips through her hair. I love watching her mane of dark strands become a complete and total mess. I don't know if I like it even more that she doesn't care – she's so free.

We reach the bottom of the dirt road and begin to make our way over to Devil's Canyon; it's my favorite spot to wheel. I know soon I'll have to remove my hand from her thigh, but being the greedy bastard that I am, I slip my fingers into her shorts and push her panties to the side.

She looks at me for a moment and the second I find her clit she begins to whimper. She's putty under my fingers and I love it. Unfortunately, it's not long before we arrive at the base of the canyon and I have to stop.

I pull my fingers out and indulge by sucking her sweet taste off of them, devouring her wetness. My girl's always ready for me.

I look at her and I swear she's panting, staring at my erection through my pants. I know she wants it; she always does. Staring at her lips, they remind me of the first time she sucked me off. It seems so long ago, but I know it's not. There has never been another woman in this world that can push my limits like she can.

The road starts to wind and becomes rocky. I take both of my hands and hold the wheel tightly. "Are you ready?"

"Yup, I'm so excited."

"Well, I hope I don't let you down."

"You won't. You never have."

I smile at her comment. "And I never will," I say as we begin to climb small piles of rocks.

She looks up ahead scouring our surroundings. "Is this

how it is the entire way up?"

"Nope, you better get ready for a rough ride."

"I love a rough ride," she jibes with an ear-to-ear smile.

Oh, she's gonna pay for that later.

"We'll see how rough you can handle it." I have to pause in talking as my Jeep crashes over a huge boulder. We both bounce in our seats and I know I now have to focus. "Stop distracting me, woman."

She laughs and I bring the Jeep to a stop, carefully picking my line before I start the climb. I need to concentrate to get us safely up this mountain. I figure I can teach her better, once she's driving. As we begin to move, I lean my head out the window and watch my front wheel. The traction seems to be good.

We continue up the trail, and I love having Bridge next to me. She's got a huge smile on her face and she's just enjoying herself. I feel like whatever stress she was holding on to, she's let go. I've never taken any of my girlfriends four-wheeling before. She's my first. Well, she's my first of many things.

"Are you scared of heights, baby?"

"Not really. Not when I'm with you."

"Good, because we're heading to the top of that ridge." I point high in the sky.

"No way! We're gonna drive up there?"

"Yup, if you look closely you can see tracks from where others have driven. The farther up we get on the mountain, it's just covered in dry grass and some low-lying rocks. It's about a fifty-degree angle at some points, so it's a bit trippy, but the summit is so worth it, babe. I can't wait to show you."

"I bet it's amazing. How much longer?"

"Maybe thirty minutes. Are you sure you don't wanna drive any of the way up?"

"No way, Troy. I'm great right here, watching you. Keep doing your thing," she says.

I wink at her, turning my baseball cap backwards, just like she likes. Her body melts into the seat and I swear she presses her thighs together. Now she knows how I feel walking around with a fucking hard-on all the time. I've never jerked myself off more than I have since I met her and it's barely slaked the lust I feel just thinking of her sweet body.

After another thirty minutes of driving and eye fucking, we make it to the top. I park so we are looking out over the incredible view. Goddamn, the Rocky Mountains are something else. She hops out and runs to the ledge. I'm not far behind her and tightly hug her, breathing in her delicious scent. As I kiss the top of her head, we both take a deep breath.

"God, Troy, this is stunning. It's absolutely breathtaking."

"It's my favorite spot in the whole world."

She reaches her arms back and holds my body. Her touch has become a drug to me. I swear I'll never get enough of it.

"Let's eat and enjoy the view." I kiss her again and go to the back of the Jeep, grabbing our food and blanket. I decide to lay it on the hood of the Jeep. It'll be more comfortable than the ground. As I spread it out, she turns to me. "Oh, you brought a blankey," she teases.

"Yes, I did. So you better stop teasing me if you wanna sit on it." She glares at me. "Oh, I'm sorry. Would my little cock tease of a girlfriend prefer to sit on the hood and get her thighs burnt?"

"Cock tease," she repeats.

"Yes. Cock. Tease. Did I stutter? Nope, didn't think so. I watched you clench your thighs the whole drive up here. That's not to mention how you eye fucked me. I almost drove off the mountain a few times."

"I'm sorry! But you were the one gripping the steering wheel 'til your knuckles turned white. Then you had to keep biting your lip, and don't even get me started with that damn hat."

She's standing with her hands on her hips and fire in her eyes. I've pissed her off. *Note to self: don't call her a cock tease.* Dropping our lunch to the ground I stalk her. The moment my hands are on her, I unbutton her shorts and tug them down a little. Then I lift her up and carry her to the hood of my Jeep setting her on the soft blanket. Thank God my man brain brought this. Swiftly I remove her shorts and panties all the way.

I look up at her as she is resting on her elbows watching me. Her feet are on the front bumper and I know I'll never look at her tight cunt the same way again. It's staring at me and I don't waste another second. I close the distance and take what's mine.

"Hmm, you taste delicious," I say, pulling away. I lift her shirt above her head and toss it aside. She reaches for me, touching my hard skin though my clothes. I slide my hands under her bra teasing those sweet nipples. "Does this make you wet?" I ask against her skin.

"Uh-huh."

"Tell me what you liked most about today?"

"When you came in my mouth."

"Is that right?"

She nods her head traveling her hands down my body and into my shorts. My cock is hot and wet awaiting her touch. As she begins to stroke me, I unclip her bra. Before I know it, she's naked, out here in the middle of the Rocky Mountains on the hood of my Jeep. "Take your shorts off," she demands, watching my every move.

Once I'm fully unclothed, I begin to stroke myself. *Oh fuck*. It feels good, but not nearly as good as what she can do to me. "Is this what you want?" I ask stepping inches away from her.

"Yes, please."

"Oh, I like your manners. Don't bother playing nice with me though, I know how dirty you really are." My words remind me of our first time, and the endless hours of sex we had. She surprised me that night. I told her I couldn't stop, but neither could she. It was mind blowing and I will forever keep it etched in my memory. Stepping to her, I nudge the head of my dick against those wet folds, moving in the slickness. Gripping her sides as I watch myself slowly move in and out of her tight cunt.

"Fuck me, please," she begs.

"My pleasure, baby," I say sinking deep into her, filling her completely to the hilt, with all of me. "Wrap your legs around me." She listens to my direction as pleasure surges through me. "Oh fuck, Bridge," I rasp, now moving with urgency. Her back is pressed against the hard metal of the hood, with only the thin blanket providing comfort.

My brows are creased and I've got a firm hold on her hips. Taking my thumb, I begin to massage her clit and it causes her to moan loudly. "Oh yeah, baby, let me hear you," I say, pulling her harder against me. She starts to slide off the hood and I pull out of her. "Bend over the Jeep and let me see your perfect ass."

She listens right away and I take both of my hands, massaging each of her ass cheeks. *Mmm, her body feels so good.* I squeeze down hard spreading her wide and slide back into her pussy, circling my hips. "Hmm. You look so good from this angle," I say and spank her. Electricity charges through my hand from the spot I just hit. God, she's driving me crazy. Her noises become urgent and she tilts her head back meeting me thrust for thrust letting me fill her as deep as I can.

I smack her ass again and can't help, but moan. "You

like that?" I ask grabbing a handful of her hair and pull her up to me. Reaching back she touches me and relishes in the pleasure.

"Are you ready to come, baby?" I ask in a harsh tone, completely out of breath.

"Oh. God. Yes."

"Let go, Bridge. Come around my cock."

I'm barely able to focus on reality as we transport from this world we live in. I keep my eyes closed and go with her. We work together so well, you would think we'd been doing this for years.

Quivers take over my body and I begin to shudder. I lose focus, and faintly remember her screaming my name and God only knows what else. I love it when she comes.

Once I'm back down to earth, I don't stop my smooth movements or end our connection. I just slow and say, "I don't want this to end."

"Keep going," she says gripping my cock with her pussy muscles.

"Goddamn, woman, you and your tight cunt will surely be the death of me."

"Not if you kill me first."

I smile to myself, holding her body closely against mine. Her words *keep going* strike something within me and I do exactly that, enjoying being in the middle of nowhere, with her. The air is fresh and sun is bright. Everything is surreal, except holding Bridgette. Being with her is as real as is gets.

Chapter 17

Trust

"Oh my God, I still can't get over your face today," I say laughing.

"Troy, you're such an asshole. I had no idea it was going to be so hard to actually drive that thing down the mountain."

I can't stop laughing and I actually have to bend over, it hurts so badly. "Well…I'm sorry. I'm sorry, just give me a minute."

"Troy!" she snaps and whacks me with a kitchen towel.

"Come on, baby, it was funny. Did you really think you were supposed to hit the gas on the way down?"

She glares at me and checks our dinner, which is in the oven. I continue slicing vegetables for the salad and try to stop laughing.

"Are you done making fun of me?" she asks.

I nod my head and somehow hold back the smile.

"Good," she says, setting the table. Then the timer

goes off on the oven and she removes the huge pan of lasagna that we made together.

"Salad's ready, let's eat, babe."

"Jesus, are you that hungry tonight?"

"Nope, it's what's after the meal I'm excited for."

She smirks at me and serves our plates. "Should I be excited or scared?"

"Both," I say, taking two beers out of the fridge and carrying them to the table with our salad. She approaches and I hold her chair out for her, helping her get situated. My mom taught me from a young age to be a gentleman and it's always stuck with me. I'm glad Bridge respects it; some of my previous girlfriends wanted nothing to do with it and it was weird to have to change who I am.

"Is that why you said you would never hurt me yesterday?"

"Yeah, that and I can tell you're still stressing over David. You're constantly checking your phone; I know you're dreading him calling. I want you to know, I'm not him. I haven't brought this up, because I don't want to bring up the past. I'm not going to let anything happen to you. I'm going to protect you. Don't let him cloud what we have."

A thin layer of tears fills her eyes. "No, Bridge, don't cry."

My strong girl blinks them away and nods her head. "You promise you'll always be my sun?" she whispers in a hushed tone. It's so quiet I can barely hear it, but I know exactly what she's saying.

"I promise. You can trust me. Always, okay? I'll never let you down."

I take her hand in mine and squeeze it tightly. Then she picks up her fork and I crack our beers. We both proceed with our meal and I hope I haven't ruined the night. I decide to change the subject in order to bring a smile to her face.

"Can we talk about your face today, just one more time?"

She glares at me. "If you want me to stab you with this fork, then have at it."

"Tempting…but I'm not in the mood to deal with your feistiness."

"You always say I'm feisty. Why don't you do something about it?"

"Maybe I will. Why don't you tell me what you want tonight?"

"Whatever you want," she says.

"You know, you're not giving me much to work with."

"I'm sorry."

"And you should be," I tease, lifting her in my arms. She's got the biggest smile on her beautiful face and I know now is the time. Without speaking another word, I walk us both upstairs. Her legs grip me tightly and I know I'll never get over how my hands feel on her body.

When we reach the bedroom, she begins to kiss my

neck and threads her hands into the back of my hair. Gently I lower her onto the plush bed, taking her mouth with mine. I love how her hands feel on my body as she begins touching me. Her body's restrained below mine, unable to move.

"Trust me," I say in between kisses.

"Always," is her response and my heart speeds up in anticipation.

Taking my time, I continue kissing her, controlling not only her mouth, but also her body. My erection strains my shorts and is dying to be free, so I remove them to regain some comfort and throw my shirt off in the process. Her pupils immediately contract, before moving a trail down my body. When she reaches my cock, they dance in excitement and she licks her lips. I grab the base of my shaft and begin pleasuring myself. She whimpers, wanting me. I know what this does to her. Scooting over on my knees, I sit atop her chest. "Suck it," I demand. Right away, she listens and takes me into her mouth. This is such an awkward angle for her, but for me it's such a fucking turn on to see her struggle to get a good mouthful. I love making her work for it.

Her plump lips are so wet as they tightly grip me from the tip to my base and over again. *Damn, she can take it so deep.* I know that's why I'm able to come from her naughty mouth. She pushes me so close, so fast. I begin to panic, not wanting to let go. It's too soon. She stops me before I pull all the way out and grips my hips, keeping my cock in her mouth.

She bobs her head like a fucking machine and my hand weaves into her glorious brown hair. I begin to pump my hips as I feel my balls tighten, ready to let out a violent blow. Bridgette digs her nails into my skin holding me. That reinforcement from her sets me off. I groan like a fucking animal, gripping her hair as my cum coats the back of her throat. She never falters, keeping pace with my every move. That's my girl. She's just as insatiable as I am. Her ravenous need for my cock just reminds me she'll never get enough of me, as I'll never get enough of her.

Looking down at her still holding me in her mouth, is so fucking sexy. *Now it's my turn to please her.* Pulling away, she sucks with all her might, not wanting to let go. When my dick finally pops out, I say, "You're a greedy little thing, aren't you?"

She nods her head and I slide the strap of her tank off of her shoulder. With as much force as she used on me, I begin to suck her sensitive skin, dousing her with kisses. Then I pull the other strap down and move to that side. Taking my time, I work my way across her collarbone and then to those perky boobs. My cock twitches and drips a little cum, wanting them. She reaches for my shaft when the cum hits her leg, and I back away.

"Not yet. Trust me."

She looks at me through heavy lids. I can tell she's horny and ready for me, but she trusts me to take care of her. I remove her tank all the way and slide it down with her panties and shorts. As I toss her clothes aside, I walk to the other side of the room and get into my bag. When I turn back and look at her, she's watching me and the items in my hands curiously. I like that there's *no* fear in her face when she sees what I have – only passion and excitement.

"Greedy," I say and slide the blindfold over her eyes. When I cover those beautiful greens she just smiles at me. Jesus, it feels so good to be with someone who trusts me. I'm not a dominant or anything like that and I don't have rules. I just want to pleasure my lover. And I do so with rope. There's something about the art of the knots and the trust the two people have to have to find desire in those situations. I've been with women that are gone, once I've shown them this side of me. Some have even freaked out by my stamina. I can't help that I can fuck for hours; this is how I was born.

Staring down at the beautiful diamond beneath me, I'm grateful. "If I hurt you, just tell me, okay?" She nods her head and I flip that gorgeous body over. Her ass is ridiculous and my eyes travel up her back to where all of her tattoos are. I love them. "Get on your knees." She listens, but is on all fours. I only want her ass in the air. "Head down, baby."

She complies and I land a smack to her plump ass. God, I love to spank. I want to know how hard she can take it. She freezes and I reward her with a soothing touch, then I invade her wet slit with my fingers. A long moan escapes her sweet throat as I begin to please her. I pull away and she tenses. "Trust me, Bridge. Find pleasure in this."

"Does it turn you on?" she asks.

"Like nothing else."

"Do it," she commands and I land another hand, this one a little firmer. As I pull away to touch that sweet clit, her skin starts to turn pink. She catches on quickly to my game and knows if she takes the hit, I'll reward her with pleasure.

Her pussy is swollen and wet, but I'm not quite ready for it. Gently, I take her hands and bring them behind her back. As I grab the soft nylon rope and begin to bind her, I ask. "What are you thinking about?"

"You. Your cock."

"What about?"

"I want you inside of me."

"You're not worried that I'm tying you up?"

"No, I trust you. To be honest with you, I've dreamt of doing this with you."

No shit. "Really?" I question, completely thrown off. I never imaged she would have that type of fantasy and it pleases me to no end. I'm never letting her go, no matter what. She's fucking perfect. Once her hands are tightly bound, I lift her up and pull her back against my chest. "Are you ready for my big cock? Do you want me to make you come hard, baby?"

Whispering my dirty thoughts into her ear causes her breathing to pick up and I push her forward. She keeps her head down and I begin to finger that delectable pussy, spreading it wide and stretching it. Doing things like this is such a turn on; nothing in the world compares. She starts to whimper and moan, and I know I'm driving her crazy. As I slide a third finger into her tight cunt, she gasps and grips my hand squeezing it hard.

"That's it, baby, squeeze it for me," I tell her.

She does so and her noises get louder. I grab the lube and squirt a little on my fingers. As I adjust and move around, I find her G-spot and begin to work it. I stimulate the sensitive area and she arches her back. At this angle I barely have to pull my fingers out. The attention to that special spot causes her arousal to push her close to orgasm. "Fuck me, Troy," she murmurs.

"Come for me, then I will." With my free hand I rub her red skin and land a firm hit. She whimpers and says, "Again. Please spank me again, baby." I definitely don't have a problem with that and I take my time, pleasing her just right as I land each calculated smack on fresh untouched skin.

Her moans turn to screams and she comes hard from my persistent torture to her pussy combined with her newfound pleasure in being spanked. As the trembles in her body stop, I remove my fingers and nestle my throbbing cock deep inside of her soaking wet core. I fill her balls deep and she begins to move, meeting my movements. Her back is glistening with sweat, arched and so sexy. My eyes follow the line of her spine to those beautifully bound wrists, and concentrating on them is almost my undoing. We work so well together. My hard cock filling her so full while her pussy keeps a tight hold around me. Fuck, I'm already close. This is not normal, this is not what I'm used too. *Goddamn this woman.* I slow my movements and pull her up to me. She clenches my dick adjusting to the new position and I know I can't handle more. "Don't do that," I instruct her.

"Untie me, please."

Immediately I do so, without asking why. I told her to tell me if I hurt her and the truth is, I want her hands on me. I need them on me. As much as it's a turn on to see her wrists bound, I can't be without her touch for long and I've quickly learned that. I can't seem to unknot the rope quickly enough. Finally her small hands are free and she reaches for me, pulling our bodies tightly together. I hug her closely to me and breathe her in. She smells delicious, like sex and Bridgette. Her scent is indescribable; it's a sultry mix of lilies and eucalyptus. That's why I brought her those flowers – they reminded me of her. For the first time in my life I have what I want, a beautiful partner who accepts me. There are no lies or secrets between us. She knows my biggest enigma and is sexy as hell partaking in my desires.

"Was that okay?" I ask, directing her to lie down. For some reason, I need the reassurance from her.

"Yes," she pants and rakes her nails over my back. I push my cock back into her, moving slowly and ask, "So you liked it?"

"Yes! A lot." She starts to squeeze me again and I have to stop.

"Good. Now stop squeezing my dick with that vise of a cunt, and let me fuck you. I'll make you come again, I promise."

She releases the death grip she has on my shaft and I feel like I can breathe again. As I begin to move, I hold her face the way I like, kissing her passionately, showing her that she's mine. Tiny whimpers move through her with each plunge of my cock. Without her gripping me so powerfully, I can move and fuck like I normally do. I want to make her come good, so I take her thighs and lift them up, holding her knees down on the bed next to her ribs. She's so limber and gorgeous. Once I have her spread open for me and held down, I rhythmically move my cock in and out. Each push and pull is calculated to hit her U-spot. I bet no one's ever made her come from it. I can't wait to see her go wild from pleasure when I stir it awake.

Her noises become extreme and I know I've found it. Keeping steady, I hold my angle and hers. She makes my body writhe, wanting more of her. Sweat covers our skin and the moment she turns her head to the side reaching above her – I lose it. Her tits shake and bounce as I pound her, they're spread wide as she reaches for anything to grab onto. I grunt violently, pumping my cum inside of her. My release is so intense and my movements are insanely urgent as I let go. "Ahhhhhh," she screams thrashing back and forth. I push her legs down even harder and slam my cock so hard and deep, she convulses. Her eyes are tightly shut as she fists the comforter.

"Yes, baby, that's it," I shout as I move with speed. "Come hard for me," I rasp.

Her body finally settles and I let go of her legs, touching her clit. *Fuck, that was hot.* She pushes my hand away and I smirk at her as I nudge myself in as far as I can and lay down on top of her. I intertwine our fingers and kiss her cheek. When she turns to me, I kiss her lips and then settle sprawled on top of her, nestled to the hilt. *If only heaven was this good, I would die today…*

Chapter 18

Grease

I have to get the Jeep fixed before we can leave today. But being in her arms is so much better. She's resting peacefully and I know she needs it after the weekend we've had. She's good at keeping up with me, but I'm a machine and have to be careful how I push her. We're on the couch and I hate to get up, especially because I don't want to wake her.

Checking the clock, I know it's now or never. As gently as I can, I slide my arm from underneath her. She rolls over and tucks herself into a tiny ball. Covering her up, I kiss her forehead and slip outside. The sun is in full effect and hot as hell, so I pull my shirt off and throw it on the railing before I head down the stairs. I approach my Jeep and look at the tire. Fuck. I am so pissed that it's flat. I just bought this set and it cost me a fortune. I could understand if we hit something wheeling, but to wake up today and see it like this just blows my mind. I get everything out to put the spare on. It's mundane work, but has to be done.

While I go through the familiar process, my mind takes me back to last night. Binding her, blindfolding her, and spanking her. Those are my three favorite things and she gave them all to me. I would love to spread her body wide and tie her to my bed. Then blindfold her, making her hypersensitive. I would drag my tongue across every bit of her skin.

My cell phone rings, interrupting my daydream, and I wipe the grease off of my hands before answering it. "Hello," I say leaning up against my Jeep.

"Hey, Troy. It's Alexa."

"Oh, hey. What's up?"

"Nothing much. Can you step away real quick?"

"I'm alone. Bridgette's sleeping."

"Really?"

"Uh-huh. Why?"

"Well, she just never naps. I mean she has *never* napped, even when we were kids."

"Huh. Maybe it's the altitude," *or the mind-blowing sex,* I lie and hope she doesn't question me any further.

"Maybe. So did you get a chance to talk to her about her birthday?"

"Not yet, but I will."

"All right, will you text me as you soon as you have any ideas?"

"Yeah, for sure."

"In the meantime, I'll talk to Cara and Vince and see

what we can come up with."

"Sounds good."

We hang up and I get back to work, removing the spare and dropping it to the ground. Then I get down and remove the flat, sad one. It's just ridiculous, that this happened. I make quick work of swapping out the tires and once I have everything tightened up, I give the flat a good look over. There are no puncture marks and nothing is piercing the rubber. I'm going into that tire shop on Monday to give those pricks an earful.

Just as I finish cleaning everything up, Bridgette emerges from the house with a book in her hand and a smile on her face. "Hey, gorgeous. Did you have a nice nap?"

She walks down the stairs and says, "I did, thank you. I can't remember the last time I was actually able to sleep in the middle of the day."

"Good, baby." I go to grab her face but she pulls away.

"You're dirty."

I look down at my hands and they're not that bad. I reach for her but she runs off. "You wouldn't," she says and heads up to the top deck.

"I would."

"Well, here's a little advice for you – don't."

"Or what?"

"You don't want to find out. Just let me read before we hit the road. I wanna enjoy the serenity up here one last time. It kills me that we have to leave today."

"Fine," I grumble walking away. "What are you reading?"

"It's a new book by L. Sidon."

"Huh. I didn't know you liked to read."

"Yeah, I always have."

"Is it good?"

"Yeah. It's pretty fucked up, but it's a great story and there's some hot sex in it."

"Oh, sounds interesting. Do you have one of those reading thingies?" She laughs at me as I put the last of the tools in the Jeep and close it up. "What?"

"Troy, you can't be serious." She closes her book and I stalk towards her.

"You better stop laughing at me, if you know what's good for you."

She heaves over in her chair amused, clearly not taking me seriously. Once I reach her, I take the grease-covered rag that I just cleaned my hands with and grab her tit, squeezing it hard through her white tank top. She freezes and looks from my hand to my eyes. I smile and remove it, dragging the rag across her chest, leaving a trail of grease.

"Troy, I'm gonna kill you!" she yells, bolting out of her seat and running after me. I sprint into the house and she follows me. *Damn, she's fast.* I throw the towel at her and fly up the stairs, heading straight for the bedroom. I know there's a lock on that door. Just as I go to close it, she squeaks in. I put my hands up signaling defeat and slowly walk backwards. She marches towards me with irritation in her eyes.

I can't help but smirk at her. "Do you see what you did to me?" she asks trying her hardest to maintain her composure.

"You were laughing at me," I contend.

"Well, now you're going to have to pay for it."

She walks me all the way into the bathroom. I reach for her, but she skims out of my grasp and breezes past me, starting the shower. Taking her time, she slides out of her clothes and stands before me naked. My cock throbs, wanting her. I adjust my shorts and lean against the sink adoring the perfection that is her body.

"Don't do this," I plead.

"Don't try and guilt me now, Troy. You did this."

She steps into the shower and lets water cascade down her sweet body. Her nipples harden from the temperature change and she pinches them, pulling out and squeezing hard. *Goddamn it.* I lunge towards her and she puts her hand up, stopping me. I take a deep breath, pushing aside my frustration, and pull my shorts down, gripping my cock. If she's going to make me watch this, I need relief. My dick is about to explode, so I move my hand up and down my length. She smirks at me and fills her hand with soap, drenching her body in it and washing away the grease.

She rinses clean and cups her sex. Her small hand finds her delectable cunt and the moment her fingers sink between those smooth folds – I lose it. I attack her, pinning her against the cold tile wall. She spreads her legs for me and I sink inside of her. She's so ready; my cock slides in effortlessly. "Do you like to tease me?"

I begin to move and clasp her hands behind her back. She moans and moves her ass pushing against me. "Tell me. Do you find pleasure in teasing me?" Her words are inaudible. "I didn't like that. I'm the only one who pleasures you, understand?"

"Mmmm."

Letting go of her hands, I move mine around and touch her clit, rubbing it aggressively as I fuck her. Jesus, she's something else. Her noises are so sexy and hot that they set me on fire. It's still hard to comprehend how fast she pushes me to climax. No woman has ever done that before. She tightens around my shaft, pulling my orgasm to fruition. Releasing her hands, I bind my arms around her body holding her tightly. Then I close my eyes and explode, coming far inside of her. My noises tell her to let go and on cue she does, coming with me. I can't help, but nip and suck her shoulder as we stand together. I just want this feeling – this moment – with her to last forever.

Looking over at Bridge, she's fast asleep and it has to be one of the sweetest sights ever. I could watch her for an eternity. Unfortunately, I can't. Work calls and it absolutely rakes my heart to leave her. Damn, I'm falling fast. Taking my hand, I sweep the hair out of her face and tuck it behind her ear. This might be fast, but she's totally worth it.

Pressing my lips to hers, I breathe her in. It's about six in the morning. We had a late night so I won't wake her. I leave a few kisses on her neck and shoulder, then cover her up and slide out the front door. I feel safe leaving her at my place. Although, I shouldn't be worried – Vincent said the grounds security at Bridgette's condo are keeping an extra eye on things. Plus, she was smart enough to not give David the gate code when he came over. I hate even thinking his name; it sickens me. Maybe I'll get lucky enough to run into him alone and give him a taste of his own medicine. I would force my fist on him and see how he fucking likes it.

My knuckles are white on the steering wheel and I loosen my grip. She's safe and in my bed. I pull into the parking lot of the station and all is quiet. Well, it's early as hell. I park and walk up the stairs to the firehouse. A few of the guys are in the kitchen making breakfast, while the others are packing up to leave.

"Morning."

"Hey, Troy," they say and I walk to my bed, leaving my bag, and run smack dab into Abel.

"Hey, what's up, man?" he says.

"Not much. How are you?"

"I'm good. How was your time off?"

"It was great, thanks for letting me have the extra day."

"Oh, no problem, man. Nothing exciting happened here."

"Good. How's Cara?"

"She's great. Did you hear we have a date to move into the new place?"

"Nah, man, I didn't. When is it?"

"This weekend. You down to help?"

"Of course. If you can get me out of work."

"Consider it done."

"Are you getting excited?"

"Extremely, I never knew I would feel like this."

"I know what you mean. Fucking Bridgette, dude, she's something else."

"Yeah?" he questions.

"Yeah, I think I'm falling for her."

"That's good, bro. She's a good girl. Let it happen; don't fight it."

"Don't you think it's a little too soon?"

He punches my shoulder and says, "Not when you find the one, it's not."

He walks off and leaves me standing alone contemplating his words. Is she the one? No way. That is absolute crazy talk. We just met, but she does accept me and I know I don't want anyone else. Thinking of not being with her makes me sick. I shake off the feeling as Abel calls us over for our morning meeting and let go of the whirlwind swirling through my mind.

"Morning, guys. I take it that everyone had a nice weekend?" We all agree and he continues. "Good, good. Well, it's business as usual around here. Tom is going to be stopping by in the next few days, so make sure the trucks and the bays are in tip top shape. Also, Troy needs this weekend off; are there any volunteers to work his shifts?"

A few of the guys grumble. "He just had yesterday off," Sam says under his breath.

"Yes, he did, Sam," Abel says. "Thank you for pointing that out. He needs this weekend off to help me move. So unless any of you would rather help *both* Cara and I move, I suggest someone volunteers for him."

"I'll do it," Matt says.

"Thanks, Matt," I say.

"Yes, thank you," Abel says. "You all know your duties, so unless anyone has anything else to add, this meeting is over.

As I walk down the stairs, the August sun is hot on my back. I pull my shirt off and walk into the bay. I notice myself paying extra attention to the bench where Bridgette sat not too long ago while I fixed her finger. Things were so innocent and cute then; now I would love to have my way with her on that bench. In fact, I would tie her to it.

"Earth to Troy? You gonna answer your phone, dude?" Matt asks.

I realize then that it's ringing and pull it out of my

pocket. There's my girl on the screen, splayed across the bed this weekend with her mane of hair sprawled around her. "Hey, baby."

"Hi," she responds in a raspy voice.

"How are you?"

"Tired," she yawns. "And wondering why I'm alone in your bed."

I growl a little thinking of her, naked under the covers and alone. "Trust me, I didn't want to leave you. There's something about watching you sleep."

"Mmmm," she sighs heavily and asks, "Do you still wanna have lunch today?"

With a cocky ass grin on my face I say, "Of course."

"Good, I'll see you later then?"

"Yes, baby, you will."

Neither of us wants to hang up. This is shit I did in high school. What am I doing it for now? I'm a grown ass man. Finally, we get off the phone and I walk over to help the guys clean the rig. It's a shame it's not lunchtime now. My filthy mind is missing my girl and her lips.

I pull my head out of the gutter and think about her birthday. Alexa is going to be calling soon and I need to have some good ideas. I can't tell her that I want to tie Bridgette to my bed and stay inside her all day.

We finish washing the truck and I hop in the shower, before I go meet Bridge. I wanna be clean for her. I know she'll want my cock; she always does.

I park in front of her work and check my phone as I

walk up to the building. When I look up, I notice her and Alexa outside. They are seated on one of the benches and deep in conversation. I don't want to interrupt them, but I glance at the time and it's 11:58; I'm only a few minutes early. I think about waiting, until I see Bridgette brush tears off her cheek with the back of her hand. No way will I wait when I know my girl is upset. As I approach, they embrace one another. Bridge has her face towards me and I can see how deeply upset whatever they are talking about has made her.

"Hey," I say. She looks up at me and Alexa releases her. I sit next to them and she turns, clinging to me. "What's wrong?" I ask almost laughing with how tightly she grips on to me.

The moment I hear the sobs leave her throat, I know something is terribly wrong. The noise breaks my heart. "It's all right, baby. I'm here." Those are the only words that I speak, but I don't even know if they are what she needs. For me, I need to fix this. I say them almost more for myself.

"Do you want me to tell him, sweetie, or would you rather?" Alexa asks.

Bridgette pulls away from the comfort of my arms and in that moment, I don't give a fuck what's wrong, I want her back in my hold. Seeing her tear-stained face is heart wrenching. It absolutely kills me. Her eyes are puffy and swollen, their normal clarity lacking. What were once bright green are now covered with a gloss of pain.

Finally, she speaks, "Lex, you tell him. You got the call and know more."

I kiss the top of her head and she locks her arms around my body as her sister begins to speak. "I got a call this morning from our estranged father, Robert. Let's just say I was shocked and wanted to slam the phone down. He begged me to hear him out; he said Bridgette and I are his only shot at surviving cancer."

Bridgette clutches me more tightly when her sister says, "his only shot." I grab her face and pull her lips to mine wanting to calm her hurt – her suffering – and take away her anxiety about the situation. I'll do anything to make it go away. As I press her lips to mine she lets out a deep sigh and Alexa continues. "The cancer has spread through his entire system. In order for him to have a fighting chance, his whole immune system needs to be wiped out. Typically they would just take his healthy stem cells, but they are infected. He needs a transplant and asked if Bridgette and I would consider being tested to see if either of us is a match."

"Jesus Christ, you guys. I'm so sorry. After all this time, this is how he comes back into your lives? What about your brother?"

"He has a different father. Our mother cheated on him."

"When does he need an answer by?"

"A week, maybe two at the latest."

"What did Vincent say?"

"He doesn't know yet. He's in court."

"Well, we have some time to decide what to do, right?"

They both agree and Alexa says, "Why don't you guys go enjoy your lunch. Bridge, don't let this ruin your day."

She nods her head and says, "I'm gonna run in and use the restroom real quick."

I kiss her softly and watch her walk off. She's so cute in her short, black skirt with a white top and matching heels.

"Troy, don't let her beat herself up about this, okay?"

"What am I supposed to do?"

"Keep her mind focused on the painlessness of the test, then we decide. She's so upset about this because she took him leaving really hard. Even though she was so young, she used to cry for him and wait for him to come home from work every day – and of course he never did. I know she remembers it. I think that's why she was so attached to our mother."

"Then why get tested?" I ask. "If he did that to your family, why help him?"

"Because he's a human being and it's what's right. I watched cancer kill our grandfather and I'll be damned if it hurts another person, especially if I have a chance at stopping it. Troy, I'm tired of living with regrets. I did that with our mom and now it's too late. Don't let Bridge make that same mistake. I know you want to protect her and you will. Make sure she keeps her head up and be the man she needs right now."

I nod my head looking at Alexa. God, she's a strong woman. I never really realized until now what these girls have gone through. Bridgette emerges from the building and I notice her the moment she hits the sun. She's bright and beautiful, just like it is. She takes tiny steps to keep her balance in her ridiculous heels.

"I won't let you down," I say to Alexa as we get up to meet Bridgette.

The girls hug and Alexa heads back inside. I look down at my fragile Bridge. She's so scared and unsure. It kills me to see her like this. Taking both of my hands, I place them on her face and look deep into her eyes. I'm searching as far in as I can. Looking into her soul to let her know how serious I am right now. "*We* are going to get through this, okay?"

Her lips quiver and I crush them against mine. Keeping my eyes shut tight, I want to kiss away her fears. She's hesitant at first and then I growl a little, letting out a low noise to let her know what I want and she gives in to me. She melts in my arms and I have to remove my hands from her face to brace her body against mine.

Being the greedy man that I am, I slide my tongue into her mouth and caress hers. I don't know what makes me think I can kiss away her fears, but I'm going to try. I will not let something like this bring her down. Not right before her birthday and when we are starting something so new.

She moans a little and I know I have her. I pull away and say, "You hear me, baby? We're going to get through this. I'm going to be right by your side. As long as we have each other, we can get through anything." I scoop her up into my arms, and walk away from her office. She smiles, wrapping her arms around my neck. My strides are long and purposeful, and as I set her in my Jeep, I have déjà vu, remembering not so long ago how it felt to dream of being in this place with her.

I lean over her clicking her seatbelt into place, and she kisses my cheek. Swiftly I kiss her lips back, then walk around and hop in the driver's seat, starting the vehicle. "Where do you want to eat?" I ask.

"I'm not that hungry."

"Bullshit," I quip and drive off to her favorite place. As I pull into the lot of Drain Café and park, it's busy, but it's the lunch hour so that's to be expected. Most people get their food here to-go and leave, like we normally do. Not today. As much as I want her mouth around my cock, I want to talk about this clusterfuck of a situation and calm her mind.

Like a good girl, Bridge waits for me to walk around the vehicle and open her door. We walk in the eatery hand in hand. "I'm really not hungry, Troy," she says.

"Bridge, please. Just order something. For me. Anything."

Giving me a small smile, she nods her head and we get in line looking at the large menu that hangs over the back of the food line. As she stands in front of me, I wrap my arms around her, resting my chin on top of her soft hair. "What are you going to get?" I ask.

"Probably the summer salad. What about you?"

"Come on, do you even have to ask?"

"Right, I forgot how you feel about the chipotle chicken here."

"God, it's so good," I say and lean down to whisper into her ear. "It's almost as good as your tight pussy."

The smile that follows from those words is instantaneous. I leave my lips by her ear and continue to say filthy nonsense to her. My words change her mood and that's what I want. As we wait, I can feel someone staring at us. I look over to the check-out line and see a guy watching our every move. I feel like I know him, but I just can't pinpoint it. As Bridgette pulls away from me to order her lunch, she grabs my hand. The moment our fingers intertwine, he tenses.

My minds flashes a million miles a minute, then the pieces of the puzzle come crashing together. They all click into place when she turns and kisses me. "I ordered for you."

"Thank you," I say kissing her back. Then I plunge my tongue down her throat and grab her snug ass. While I kiss her, I look over at him. The cashier keeps repeating himself, trying to get the guy's attention. Then Bridgette pulls away from me breathlessly.

I'm speechless holding her as I watch David flip me

off and walk out of the restaurant. The cashier looks stunned and I can't help but feel good that he saw us. *Yeah, fucker, see that? She's mine.* "Are you all right?" she asks as I am still possessively holding her body.

"Yeah, baby. I'm great. Sometimes I can't help myself. Talking dirty to you like that sets me off. I want your cunt."

She shakes her head, as we are next up to pay. Thankfully we get a different cashier than the tool bag had. I hand the girl my card and we decide to eat outside. "Are you sure you don't want to eat in the car?" she asks.

"I'm sure. I think that's a bad idea right now. You don't have much longer before you have to be back. Plus, we need to talk about this situation with your dad."

"Don't call him that," she snaps. "His name is Robert."

"Okay, then we need to discuss the Robert situation."

"I don't know what to say about it, Troy."

"Just hear me out. I get that he's a shitty…Robert and what not." I stop myself from calling him her dad. "Trust me, I know all about that. I have one of those at home, remember?"

"I know, but my situation is way different. You know your dad."

"I know, baby, and I'm sorry you don't know yours. I'm not asking you to do anything more than, a) not stress, and b) take the test. We'll go from there."

"But—"

I cut her off. "But what? You're just going to overanalyze the situation. Nothing has changed, babe. Okay? You have to remember that. Focus on what's important; work, us, your birthday. Don't forget we're flying to Vegas to get married."

She busts out laughing and starts to eat her salad. I was teasing her the other night about flying to Vegas and getting married, when we were discussing her birthday. I hope my comical distraction can keep her content for a while. Especially while I figure out what in the world to do about seeing David. Should I tell her? We promised each other to always be honest. Right now, I just can't. If she got this upset and worried about a tiny test regarding Robert, I could only imagine how she would take knowing David saw us together. Not to mention he saw me maul her in public.

Chapter 19

Sneaking Out

Dropping Bridgette off after lunch today was hard. Not being able to be at home with her tonight is becoming absolutely unbearable. As I stare at the screen of my laptop, I'm awake and it's so late. I'm in the kitchen of the station and can't sleep. She texted me about an hour ago and said she was going to bed. Since then, I have been searching the internet for places to visit for her birthday.

I was texting Alexa and she agrees it might not be a bad idea if we skip out of town. I see an advertisement on the side of my screen for Vegas as I search hotels and I click on it. I wonder what she would do if I took her there.

I click through the site and the probability of going seems so real. We would have a crazy time for her special day. Abel walks in the kitchen half asleep and startles me. "What's up, man?" he says with a yawn.

"Not much. I can't sleep."

"That shit with Bridge got you wound up?"

"Yeah, and lately I hate being away from her. I'm so

worried that she's stressing out."

"Go see her."

"What? No way. What if we get a call?"

"Then I'll handle it. We're training Scott so we're technically a man up."

"Really?"

"Yeah, really. Take my key," he says removing it from his ring on the counter. "I've been where you are myself. I know how you feel."

"Thanks, I owe you one. I'll be back early, I promise."

With the key to Bridgette's place in hand, I can't seem to get to her quick enough. There's no traffic and I definitely push the speed limit. In record time, I'm entering the code to her community and driving through the gate. As I park in her driveway, I hop out, jog to the door, very quietly slide the key into the lock, and enter the dark house.

I lock the door behind me and make my way into her room. The bathroom light is on, splaying a small amount of light across her bed. There she is, fast asleep. Her hair is fanned out around her and I can't keep myself from kneeling next to the bed. I'm a sucker for watching her sleep. I do it often, but normally there are no lights on. With the small amount of light shining in I can finally see her – really see her – at peace.

Miniscule breaths move through her and I don't last long. I stand and remove my clothes, stripping down to nothing. In this moment, I need to be as close to her as possible. I slide in facing her and she doesn't wake until my hands pull our bodies as close together as they can get.

She blinks a few times like she doesn't believe I'm real. "Baby?" she questions.

"I'm here."

"Is everything okay?"

"It is now. I needed you, Bridge."

She holds me as close as she can and exhales. I know she needs me just as much. She begins to leave tiny kisses on my bare chest. Her touch sparks something inside of me. It awakens my body, like it's been asleep for a century. Roaming my hands all over her, she surprises me by clenching my shaft. I look down at her and her eyes are closed. She strokes me for a few moments and then disappears underneath the covers.

She huddles between my legs and takes my hard organ into her mouth. Sucking from top to bottom and back over again. The feeling of her mouth clenched so tightly around my sensitive skin, followed by her hand moving along my length, is almost too much to handle. She's persistent and continues to bob up and down. I don't want to let go, not yet anyways. I want to come inside of her, filling her with all of me.

The moment she lets up, I guide her back to me. She straddles me and I direct the tip of my dick towards her opening. When our skin touches, it's exhilarating. I gasp out in pleasure keeping her near me as she moves that skilled body, working me just how I like. Finally she pulls away from me and sits up, looking down at me. My hands are around her hips and she pulls the soft cotton t-shirt she is wearing above her head. I'm grateful she didn't have underwear or pants on, because had I been forced to remove anything, I would have shredded all of it like a savage animal. Her tits are so fucking plump as she sits atop of me and wiggles her hips. She has my cock engulfed so deep inside of her, I'm afraid her movements will make me come.

"Stop," I rasp.

She looks down at me smiling. I'm not sure what pushed me so close, so fast. Was it those simple movements coupled with the fact that she has her hands above her head and intertwined in her hair? Or maybe it's just her. Fuck if I know, I'm just glad she's not moving. I need a minute to compose myself. My dick craves her in a different way. I want her like nothing else; then once I finally have her, I can't last. She can unman me like no one else ever has.

Leaning forward, she rests her hands on my chest and starts to move again. Each movement causes her to whimper. Her head is tucked down and I move her hair so I can see her face. I want to watch her and see her expressions change – she looks so beautiful while fucking me.

She looks at me as I have a fistful of her hair and bites her bottom lip, moving with determination. I can tell by her breathing that she's close, that and the urgency in her hips. Aggressively, I grip my hand onto her hip and buck upwards, thrusting myself inside of her.

She begins to orgasm and when she clamps down, tightening her pussy around me, I let go, coming along with her. She keeps her eyes closed; however, I cannot close mine. They are fixated on her as she trembles above me. I release her hair and she collapses, falling against my chest.

I pull the covers up, keeping us both warm and wrap her in my arms. I know I can't sneak out every night I have to work; we are going to have to spend some nights apart. But for now and tonight, I'm here and that's what I'm focusing on. I close my eyes and the world quickly turns heavy and dark as sleep takes over.

Thank God for Abel – I really don't know what I would do without him. My shift for the week is over and he let me off early to get everything booked for Bridgette's birthday next weekend.

I'm on my way over to Alexa's to work out the details. Now, convincing her sister of what I want is a totally different thing.

I hop out of my Jeep and make my way up to the front door. When I ring the doorbell, I place my hands in my pockets and wait anxiously. She answers after a few moments, with a huge smile on her face. "Hey, you got here fast."

"Traffic was light," I tell her, when really I bolted early. The sooner I'm done here, the sooner I'm with Bridgette. It's been since Monday that I've spent the night with her and that's made it a tough week to say the least. I've missed her. I've also been beating myself up for not telling her that David saw us. I know I need to, but I can't do that to her. I know it set him off and I don't want to worry her.

Alexa has her laptop set up in the living room. "So I've done a ton of research and I think I found the perfect place."

Please say Vegas, please say Vegas, please say Vegas.

"Napa," she blurts out.

Sonofabitch.

Although it's not the worst option, I'm kinda set on Vegas, and no, it's not to get married. I know how much her tattoos mean to her and there is a world-renowned artist there that has an awesome shop.

"Well, what do you think?"

"Hmmm, Napa sounds nice. But what do you think about Vegas?"

"Oh, hell no. She said she didn't want to party this year."

"What if we stayed at a really nice hotel and just relaxed? We could sit by the pool, eat out, shop, and see some shows."

"I'm not saying it's a bad idea, Troy. Please don't get me wrong, but I know Bridge said she didn't want to get hammered like she did last year. She just wanted to relax. I know we could try planning that in Vegas…but it's Vegas!"

"Fine," I grumble. "Show me what Napa's all about."

She claps and bounces in her seat. "So I found this amazing hotel that is right by a vineyard, and the spa they have…oh my God, she would die."

"Does she like spas?"

"Yes!" she basically screams. "Troy, don't let those tattoos fool you. I never even knew about them for years. She's a girly girl."

If Alexa thinks she will like it, then I agree. I'll take her to Vegas myself another time. "Napa it is. Let's book it."

We go through the process of picking the flights and then the rooms and when it's all said and done, I feel like I just got punked. She paid for it all. This was supposed to be my present to Bridgette. She wouldn't take no for an answer and I wasn't about to wrestle her away from her laptop. That would have been a little awkward.

I guess that gives me that much more money to use buying her a gift. Speaking of which, what in the world am I going to buy her? I've never really bought a girl anything minus flowers and I can't show up with only flowers in hand for her special day.

I have a little less than two weeks to figure that all out. Tonight is my focus right now. Bridgette and I are meeting at my place and I can't wait to take her to my bed. I need to have her for hours, to tie her up, and do God only knows what else. My phone rings and I'm blessed with that sexy picture of her. "Hey, baby," I say, answering with a shit-eating grin on my face.

"I'm so sorry, I'm running a few minutes late."

"Don't be sorry. It'll give me time to get things ready for you."

"No!" She's breathless and I hear the elevator ding. "Don't go inside your house until I'm there."

I laugh at her demand. "Why?"

"Just trust me, okay? I'm on my way. I promise."

She hangs up before I can get out another word. Great, what the fuck am I supposed to do now? I'm not about to sit on my own front porch and look like a transient. So I shoot her a text. ***How long 'til you're there?***

Maybe thirty minutes. Trust me, babe.

You're going to pay for this later.

What in the world is she up to? I'm tempted to go into my house and see what she's hiding. I mean, I'm the one who lives there after all, but her words ring in my head. *Just trust me.* I've said the same thing to her and she's done that. I decide to stop and fill my Jeep up with gas and then I run it through the carwash.

Checking the clock on my way out, I should arrive at the same time she does. Good grief, she's lucky I'm fucking smitten with her, or I would have said *oh, hell no, you don't tell me when I can and can't go into my own house.* That's one of the best things about Bridge, everything is different – everything.

Arriving at my house, all of the lights are on and she's made it before me. Her car is in the driveway and I pull up blocking her in. She's not leaving without me, so it doesn't matter. When I walk up to the front of the house, I'm a little irked that she has the door cracked. Then I remember that this is my place and David doesn't know where I live. I need to calm down about that asshole; he *has* left her alone and will continue to if I have anything to do with it.

She only left the door cracked, as a sign for me to come in. I push it open and blink a few times taking in the sight in front of me. She turns from lighting a candle and runs to me. "Baby, you weren't supposed to come in yet."

"The door was open. What's all of this?"

"You said your place was a little bland, so I took it upon myself these last few days to spruce it up."

My house looks incredible; she's really outdone herself. There's a new rug, accessories galore, pillows, candles, and pictures. My eye catches a picture of us she's had blown up and hanging on the wall next to the couch.

"Did you do all of this yourself?" She nods her head. "Bridge, it's amazing. I love it, especially the picture."

"I'm glad you like it. It feels more like home, doesn't it?"

I nod my head and lean down, filling her mouth with my tongue. As we indulge in each other, she slinks her arms around me and stands on her tippy toes. Her sweet mouth tastes like a dream and her body so close to mine feels like heaven. I begin to walk us upstairs, but she pulls away.

"Not yet. I have something in mind."

"What's more important than me cherishing your body for hours and repaying you for this amazing decorating job?"

"Trust me?" she asks.

"Always."

"I want you to take me to your favorite sex shop. I've never been before and after our weekend at the cabin, I'm curious. Show me what turns you on."

Before she can say another word, I'm dragging her out of my house. She doesn't need to ask me twice; this is one of my biggest fantasies. She giggles when I open the passenger door and toss her inside. Then I jog around and start the engine. "Buckle up, baby."

"What's the rush?"

"Are you kidding me? This is a dream come true. That's the rush. Come on, buckle up."

She reaches for the belt and I lean over taking it from her and click it in. My mind is going a million miles a minute with all the different scenarios. God, they are endless. I can taste the possibilities as they absolutely drench my mouth. I can't help, but speed down the road; all the while her eyes are on me.

"Are you all right?"

"What, do I not look all right?" I gesture towards my pants and she blushes.

"Oh."

"Yeah, oh. You've unleashed the monster inside of me. I can't believe we're about to do this together."

"So… I mean… Sorry. You've never done this with anyone else?"

"What? No, baby. I…" I trail off thinking of how to say this without sounding like a bitch. "I've never had a girlfriend that's been into what I do, like you are. I've had girls let me tie them up, but after a time or two of it, they're gone." She looks deep in thought. "Let's just say not all girls are like you, baby. Most are prudes and afraid to think outside of the box. I've had a hard time finding someone to share my desires with. That is, until you."

"That's the last thing I expected you to say."

"Really?" I ask a bit puzzled.

"Yeah. I don't know why anyone wouldn't be into it. How you are in bed has to be the biggest turn on. Like I told you, I dreamed about you doing that stuff to me long before we even started dating and I've never experimented with any of it 'til you. I love that side of you. I also love the sweet, soft side of you when we have gentle, slow sex."

"I'm a man of many personalities, baby. I mold to the moment and the time. I can tell you, tonight, I won't be soft or gentle."

"That's good. I need it rough, I want it rough," she says leaning over, caressing my erection. "I've been deprived for a few days."

As traffic comes to a standstill, I know it's going to be a bit longer until we're there – and I'm about to explode. "Suck me off," I order.

She unbuckles her seatbelt and I second-guess my decision. Safety is always a priority to me, but that all washes away when her soft hands remove my hard member from the rough fabric of my jeans. She doesn't waste a moment going down on me, taking my full cock deep in her throat.

Christ, her mouth is going to kill me one day. However, I would gladly die if this feeling were the cause of my death. She's aggressive and knows what I like. Reaching into her shirt, I search for her nipple. Like the horny little thing that she is, it's hard and ready for me. I roll the end between my fingers and she pushes it into my hold.

Moving my hand over, I search for the next one and find it just as ready. Traffic is still slow and I lean back, enjoying this moment, thankful that my Jeep has such tinted windows. They are darker than the other cars around us, so I know no one can see. I weave my fingers into her hair and hold onto her head as she lets me fuck her mouth. My orgasm catches me off guard. Dammit, I don't wanna let go. With her, I never want to.

God, she's a little spitfire. As she quickens her pace, I pull her hair, giving in. My entire body hardens as I come; it feels like I haven't had a release like this in weeks. Each force of her hand moving in sync with her lips causes me to shudder and I remember that I have to keep an eye on the road. My body finally settles and Bridgette stays close to me, kissing my shaft. She whispers something I can't make out, but I'm too dazed to ask.

"Damn, that was—"

"Satisfying?"

She finishes my sentence for me and I smirk at her as I tuck myself back into my pants.

"What are you smiling at?" she asks me.

"I don't smile, I smirk. See this?" I point to the smirk that's plastered on my face. "This is a smirk of prime satisfaction."

"God, you're cocky."

"Excuse me? I'm cocky?" I ask, grabbing her thigh as we finally pull off of the freeway. "You're the cocky one, with that mouth of yours. Sucking me off in my car like that."

"Well, I'm glad you approve. Maybe later you can repay the favor?"

"I would love nothing more."

I smirk at her again and park the Jeep. "So this is it?" she asks.

"Yup."

"It doesn't look like what I pictured it to be."

"Really? What did you think, some seedy place with bars on the windows?"

She whacks my arm and I grab her hand. "Hey, let's save the hitting for the bedroom, okay?"

We walk inside hand in hand. I can't help, but keep my eyes on Bridge as I try to read her body language. At the entrance are all the outfits, which I'm not opposed to… but they also aren't my thing. We take our time walking through and I don't say much, or point anything out, I want her to soak this all in. She observes all of the sex toys and even stops and tests out a few of the displays.

A saleswoman approaches us and I put my hand up, signaling that we are okay. She smiles and goes back to shrink-wrapping pornographies at the checkout counter.

"Have you ever used one?" I ask her, observing the large dildo she's holding.

She shakes her head.

"Let's get one. The orgasm can be quite intense. I can get you there too, but this will be different."

"I don't know, this feels so hard. Don't they have softer ones?"

That's my girl, always wanting the best in pleasure. I take her over to the display of silicone ones and she smiles right away. "I like these."

"Good, pick your size."

She blushes a shade of crimson and asks, "How do I know which one?"

I kiss her cheek and since I'm standing behind her I reach my arms around her and carefully go through the different options. She picks the waterproof one, and that's a-okay with me.

Once we finally make it to my section I feel my cock

start to throb. Watching her stand here in front of all of the things I like most is such a turn on. She looks at the wall of restraints, whips, rope, crops, and more. I look along with her, trying to judge her thoughts and pick out which one I'm going to use. For me I'm really all about the control of tying up my partner. Then you add in knowing how to inflict the right amount of pain, and it surges pleasure for me.

"Tell me what you're thinking," I say.

"I don't know if I can give you what you need."

What? No, this is not how this was supposed to go. "Bridge, you already have. Honest to God, I'm not some sex freak. Yeah, I like a little kink and spanking, but that's it. I don't need any of this. I have rope at home and my hand is my favorite prop."

She looks into my eyes, like I'm lying. "You promise?"

"I swear. Does it turn me on to play with this stuff? Yeah, hell yeah, it does. But I would also be fine if we left."

"No. I wanted to do this and I believe you. I know you'll always be honest with me. Tell me what you like?"

Dammit, I haven't been honest. I need to tell her about David seeing us. She wraps her arm around my side and asks again. "Tell me what you like?" Fuck that mother-fucker. He's not going to ruin this moment for me. Another time. I'll tell her another time.

"I want you to pick out a crop, anything will do. I'll be gentle and bring you pleasure, I promise." She picks out a red weighted vinyl heart.

"Interesting choice. Let's get one of these too." I grab a large foam wedge pillow that I can use to position her body any way I see fit.

"Troy, that costs over a hundred dollars."

"I don't care. How much did you spend on my house?"

She sulks back and shakes her head. "Exactly. We're buying this stuff."

"I got a sign-on bonus at work, so it's different."

"Don't start with me, woman, or I'm buying handcuffs."

She doesn't speak another word about price as we finish up our time inside the store. I love how curious she is about everything. She scrunches her eyebrows as she scrutinizes the displays of items. The best was the anal section. I had to fuck with her for a minute about wanting to buy a huge strand of anal beads. She swallowed hard and before she almost fainted, I busted out laughing.

Driving home, she's rubbing her forefinger over her lips and staring out the window. I wish I had a glimpse into her head, even for a brief moment. She's so intense and I'm almost positive dirty thoughts are clouding her mind.

Chapter 20

Spending

"Dude, I can't do this without you. You've got to help me." Abel basically begs.

"Come on, man, you've got Vincent."

"Yeah. That's exactly why I need you. That fucker is made of money. I don't need his superficial opinion getting in the way of a logical one."

"He's your brother. I can't believe that's how you talk about him."

"Whatever, it's nothing I wouldn't say to his face."

"Fine, but I have to get Bridgette a birthday gift and a good one while we're out."

"I'll help you, if you help me?"

"Deal. Want me to pick you up at noon?"

"Yeah, that works for me. Thank you, and remember, don't mention this to Bridgette. I don't want Cara to have any idea what I'm up to," Abel says.

"I won't, man. Stop worrying."

We hang up and I go in search of Bridge. She's out in

my backyard, enjoying the August heat, reading. "Still on that book, huh?"

"Oh my God, Troy, you were right about what happened with his wife, he just found out."

"See, I told you. I'm glad you're enjoying it. Listen, I'm gonna run a few errands. Are you still going to that wedding thing with Alexa today?"

"It's called a Bridal Expo and yes, we're going at one o'clock."

"Okay, well, have fun and I'll meet you back here for dinner?"

"Sounds perfect." She opens her book and sticks her nose back in it. I smile and know what I need to get her for her birthday. I kiss the top of her head and walk back inside, grabbing my car keys before I head out. It's hot and muggy today. We've had a bit of rain lately, giving it an east coast feel of humidity.

The drive to Abel's is quick. I park in front of his building and text him. He comes right down and hops in. "What up? Thanks for picking me up."

"Of course. Where's Vincent meeting us?"

"The mall."

I head in that direction and notice Abel is particularly anxious. He keeps bouncing his knee and is picking at the skin around his nails.

"You all right?"

"Yeah…no…dude, I don't fucking know. This is such a huge step."

I chuckle at him and think how I can calm his nerves. "What's got you so worked up?"

"I don't know, maybe that this is…forever?"

"Do you see yourself spending forever with someone else?"

"Fuck no."

"Then it's settled. She's the mother of your child and you love her. Stop questioning this."

"I know, dude. I shouldn't be nervous, but I am."

"Then don't do it."

"What? But I want to," he says evenly.

"Then do it and stop being a bitch about it. I swear it would be easier for you to get her name tattooed than it's going to be to buy a fucking ring."

He's watching me and I glance over at him. "How can I not be nervous?"

"It's not that hard. Just live your life, knowing what you want and going after it. I know how determined you are. Don't let that confidence slip away. Is Cara your forever?"

"Yeah."

"Then?" I ask.

"I'll do it."

"Atta-boy," I joke with him.

He rubs his face with his hands and I go in search of a parking spot at this nightmare of a shopping mall. Finally I find one and pull my Jeep into the small spot. We hop out and both walk up to the entrance. I see Vincent as we approach, getting a valet ticket.

"What's up, guys?" he says.

"Not much, just calming your brother down," I say.

Vincent laughs, "I can't blame him. I was nervous as fuck when I went through this."

"I'm not nervous. It's just forever, you guys."

We both laugh at him and head through the mall. "Nothing's forever, Abel. This is only for the rest of your human life," I say.

"Same difference."

"Where do you guys wanna go first?" I ask.

"Jewelry store," they both say at the same time.

We make our way through the mall and I scan all of the stores, looking for the perfect gift for Bridge. Although I have one in mind, I wouldn't mind getting her another.

"So when are you going to ask Cara?"

"I think in Napa. She loves the ocean and I want to do it before the baby gets here. Do you think Bridgette would mind?"

"Nah…she'll be happy for you. Bridgette's not like that – at all."

"Then that's the plan. Unless I get the balls to do it before then."

"When the time's right, it'll happen," Vincent says.

He bobs his head and we walk into the top of the line jewelry store. I'm a little thrown off by the security guard standing by the door, but then again I've never actually been inside one of these places. An overzealous saleswoman immediately greets Vincent and Abel. I keep my distance for now and browse the cases. There is nothing right off the bat that catches my eye. However, I'm not sure if Bridge would wear any of this.

I walk over and check on the guys. They are in full engagement ring mode. The woman pulls out option after option, 'til I hear Abel say, "That's the one."

Vincent snatches the ring out of his hand and nods his head. I glance over at it and it looks nice – really nice. "What do you think, Troy?" Abel asks.

As I hold the heavy metal in my hand and inspect the diamonds, I'm shocked. How could I argue? "Dude, it looks pretty fucking amazing to me." The woman scowls at me and I give her my sincerest smile.

"I looked at rings with her when she helped me pick out Alexa's and this one reminds me of what she liked," Vincent says.

"Yeah, this is definitely it."

"I think it's a great choice," the woman adds. "Now if you would like to pick out a center stone, let's head over here."

"Do you guys mind if I peace out real quick and grab Bridgette a few things?"

"Go right ahead. We'll catch up with you," Abel says. I love how calm he looks. I know he's making the right decision and I can tell he now knows that too.

As I leave the store, I head straight for Apple. She needs something to read her books on. The place is slammed and I kick myself for not making an appointment. But to my surprise, as soon as I tell the guy I'm here to buy an iPad he has a sales associate right over to help me.

As I weigh my different options, the harder question isn't which size. The color is what's throwing me off. Who knew choosing between black and white could be so hard? I settle on black, because I know that's what she'll like, and then I pick out a case before heading out to find the guys. On my way to meet them, I see a line of people, and as I reach the front of it, I notice an author signing books.

I look through the line once more and notice everyone is holding that book Bridgette's been into. I would love to get her an autographed copy. Then I realize I can get her iPad case signed. I hop in line and text the guys. Fuck, the lines so long.

Surprisingly, the line moves quickly and before I know it, I'm almost up. I fish the case out of the bag and package to get it ready for her. Then it's my turn and she asks, "Hey, just that signed today?"

"Uh, yeah. Unless you have any paperbacks."

"I'm all sold out, I'm sorry. Do you want me to make it out to anyone?"

"Bridgette, please."

She spells the name back to me never looking up and signs away.

"Thanks," I say as she hands it back to me. I place the case back in the bag. With this gift, I might've won boyfriend of the year. I try to think of anything else that I could buy her, but I think this is perfect. Maybe the guys will have some better ideas. I see them emerge and Vincent pats Abel on the back.

"All done?" I ask.

"Yup, it'll be ready before we leave."

"What about you, did you find her a gift?"

"Yeah, I'm all good."

"What did you get her?"

"An iPad with an autographed case from her favorite author."

"No shit," Abel says.

"Should we eat since we're done so early?" Vincent asks.

"Hell yes. I'm starving."

We both laugh at Abel's comment. He's always starving, so of course he would want to eat. My phone chimes with a text and I check the message, it's from Bridgette. *Can we just go to Vegas and get married? I'm so not down with the whole wedding thing.*

I shake my head at her comment; it's the last thing I expected her to say. I guess my joking about taking her there for her birthday has paid off. It puts a shit-eating grin on my face. ***Let me know when I should book our flights.***

Chapter 21

Your World

It's my last shift of the week and I'm stoked. Although I do have to help Cara and Abel move, I'll be with Bridge and that makes any situation better. I'm showing Shawn how to check the inventory on our medical items when we get a call. The sirens go off in the station and that familiar feeling of adrenaline courses through my veins.

We both drop what we were doing and run over to our gear. Quickly, I step into the pants and grab my coat. Abel flies down the pole and gets dressed next to me. "Wanna drive?" he asks.

"I wish," I respond.

In order to even dream about being behind the wheel of the rig, you have to be certified. I've been working my ass off to pass the test. Hopefully, soon I'll be able to say, "Fuck yeah."

Abel hops in the driver's seat and I get in behind him, sitting in the passenger seat of our beautiful rig. He starts the engine and she purrs to life. As the guys start to pile in, we do a head count and then pull out of the stall. The ambulance leaves before us like they always do.

Putting my headphones on, the dispatcher gives crisp, clear details of the situation and the directions to get there. Abel turns the sirens on and I love how all the cars part to the sides of the road as we pull out. We're headed to a house fire. It's been weeks since we've been to a fire. Lately, we've had a lot of car accidents and medical incidents, but this is what we do and the adrenaline of knowing we are about to fight what each of us has trained for, is exhilarating.

It sounds like the house is vacant, so no one was inside. I smile knowing Bridgette will be happy that we don't have to go in. It's complete chaos as we approach the scene and Abel starts to give us all orders. The fire is huge and completely out of control. The neighbors are all out ogling, standing far too close in my opinion, and the cops are doing their best to keep them at bay.

We park and I hit the switch to drop the hydraulics. I can tell right away that we are going to need to send someone up in the bucket to fight this one from above. Smoke's billowing out of the windows and as we start to disburse, a loud explosion goes off.

"That's likely propane," Abel says over the radio. Let's tackle this bitch. I run over to Shawn as he's struggling a bit with the fire hydrant to get the line attached.

"Calm down, man. Don't be nervous. It's no different than in training."

He nods his head and attaches the hose. I give him a slap on the back and turn the water on. Then I report to Abel over the radio, that we have water. Immediately the guys start to spray the house. Shawn and I run over and remove another hose to tackle the right side.

The pressure is so strong; I love the fight the hose puts up. Water gushes out of the end and we drench the house. Abel gives clear instructions like he always does. We're really lucky to have him as our Chief.

The flames begin to dissipate and I'm grateful. The last thing we want is for this fire to spread to any of the surrounding homes. I glance up at Matt in the bucket. That kid always has a grin on his face. I chuckle at his expression; it's as if he's taking on the world.

We work well together as a team, smothering the last of the flames. Within an hour of arriving on the scene, we are done and packing up. I can't wait to get back and take a shower. That's one of the worst parts about this job – the smell. I might think it's worse than some of the other guys, but I'm a freak about being clean.

Abel drives us back and I sit in the back of the truck, bullshitting with some of the other guys. These are my brothers and funny as can be. Shawn's beginning to fit right in. I think he'll be a good addition to the team. Abel pulls in front of the station and I hop out to guide him into the bay. I've parked our rig before and she's a bitch to maneuver.

While I'm guiding him in, I hear my phone ring. It's

on one of the benches and I grab it and answer it without looking at the screen; I regret it right away. My dad's voice is stern and cold.

"What's that noise?" he barks.

"I'm helping Abel back the truck into the bay. What's up?" Irritation flows through me. I try to stay nice; he is my father after all.

"I can see you're still not taking your job seriously. Just call me when you're not putting other people's lives at risk."

"Fine," I say and hang up.

It's easier than arguing with him. What I wanted to say was a lot worse than fine, but I bit my tongue. I'll text my mom later. Who knows what in the world that man wants. I know if I wait and call him any later, he'll be drunk. Since retiring, that's what he has become. A drunk.

I put my hand up signaling Abel to stop and the guys all pile out. I check my phone on my way up to shower and notice a missed call from Bridge and a few text messages.

The test has been scheduled.

I'm kinda freaking out. If I'm a match, I did some research and I'm not liking it. Call me.

I dial her number and go sit on the bottom of the stairs to the house. She answers, and I can tell right away, she is down. "How are you holding up?"

"I don't know."

"Listen, babe, I know this is hard. The unknown

always is, but remember what we've talked about. It's just a test. You don't have to do anything more."

She huffs into the phone. "I know, but what if I'm a match? I don't think I can go through with the procedure."

"Come on, baby, stop getting ahead of yourself. You know Googling shit is always worse than the facts. Please, don't let this ruin your night."

"I know, It's just—"

I cut her off. "No, baby, stop worrying yourself. For me?"

"Okay. Are you almost off?"

"Yeah, we just got back from a call. I'm gonna shower and leave. Do you still want me to grab dinner on the way?"

"Please, that would be great."

"I won't be long. I should be home by the time you get there."

"I'm gonna leave in a little bit, so I'll see you soon."

We hang up and I fly inside past the kitchen full of animals, eating like they have been starved for weeks. I shower and dress, then pack my bag. I don't see Abel anywhere inside so after I say bye to everyone. I head down to the garage and find him.

"Thanks for helping Shawn today. Are you outta here?"

"Yup. I'll see you for the move."

"Sounds like a plan. Cara and I appreciate it more than you know."

I give him our signature goofy high-five and walk to my Jeep. I toss my bag into the back thinking of what I can grab us for dinner. I want something fast so I can get things set up for tonight. I know I can't go wrong with Drain Café, plus, they're quick. As I drive, my mom calls and I'm happy to answer knowing it's her.

"Hey, Ma."

"How's my baby boy?" she asks.

"I'm good, just leaving work."

"Oh, that's nice. Well, I wanted to see if you and that special girl of yours want to have dinner soon. I would love to meet her."

"Yeah, of course. We're going out of town for her birthday, but after that should work. I'll talk to her and text ya, okay?"

"Oh, honey, that's great. I can't wait to meet her."

"Thanks, Ma. Hey, Dad called me earlier. Do you know what he wanted?"

"No, sweetie, I don't. I can ask him."

"Nah, don't bother. I'm sure he's only calling to bitch. Is he taking care of you and Brittany?"

"He's doing his best, dear. You know I'll call if I need anything."

"I love you, Ma."

"Love you too, honey."

As I walk into Drain, I'm happy that it's quiet. There aren't many people inside and I put our order in. As I wait, I check my phone and look at the weather for the move this weekend. It's going to be hot as hell. Great.

Within a minute or two I've paid and am on my way outside. As I walk across the parking lot, a black SUV cuts in front of me and slams on its brakes. I throw my arms up and yell at the driver as I walk around it. Then the window rolls down. *You have got to be kidding me.*

"What's up, douchebag?" David says.

"What, do you hang out here now hoping you'll be able to see Bridgette again?"

"Piss off. Where is she?"

"Don't fucking worry about it," I snarl back.

"What, did she already leave your sorry ass?"

"Fuck you. No, in fact she's at my house – naked – in my bed – waiting for me."

His face turns to disgust and he spits at me. It lands on the inside of his door. "Nice. I can see why she left you. You got some fucking class, bro."

I turn my back to him. I'm not going to give him any more of my time. "We're not finished. She'll come to her senses," he yells and speeds off. I shake my head and watch his SUV as it peels away. Every detail about it, I'm engraving into my memory.

Jesus, what are the chances that I would run into him – again? I hop in my Jeep and look around, he's nowhere to be seen. On the drive home, I pay attention to the cars around me. I want to make sure he doesn't follow me. The last thing I need is that strung out fuck knowing where I live.

My anxiety spikes thinking about him. He looked like he hadn't showered in a week, and he was so skinny. His face was all fucked up. There were a ton of scabs that looked like he'd been scratching them. He's definitely on something. God, I really need to tell Bridgette about seeing him. Especially now that it's been twice. She'll understand and know the only reason I'd kept it from her was to protect her.

I push that all aside. No, fuck it; I'll handle him later. Right now I need to figure out how to calm Bridge. I know she's going to be upset about the test when she gets off of work. I park in the driveway and take our food inside. I head straight for the kitchen and grab two beers from the fridge. That's what she's going to need first. I know a little alcohol always calms her nerves. Then I shoot her a text. *I'm here waiting for you. I can't wait to see your beautiful face.*

She doesn't respond promptly like she normally does. I take our food upstairs. I think she'll enjoy relaxing in bed and eating there. Then I can take care of her, wash away her worries, and relax her fears.

As I sit on the edge on the bed, I contemplate what she'll want tonight…I'm not sure if she's going to want me to be gentle with her or take her out of this world and into mine. Quite frankly, I hope it's the second option because I need it. I follow my gut and grab the blindfold, rope, and the heart-shaped crop she picked out.

If she doesn't want this, I'll give her anything, whatever she thinks she needs. I know her well enough to judge that this is the perfect dose of medicine to cure her rapid thoughts. I know her mind – it races a million miles a minute. However, once I slide the blindfold over her eyes, that all washes away. She has to focus on *me* – *my* voice, *my* commands, and trust where *I'm* taking her.

I hear the front door close and bolt downstairs. She smiles at the sight of me. I engulf her in my arms and breathe in her delicious scent. When we pull away she looks up at me with a bit of an uncertain expression. "How are you, baby?" I ask.

"I'm better now. A lot better."

"Good, come upstairs with me and we can talk."

She tilts her head to the side, questioning my motives. "I promise, dinner is up there." I reach for her hand and she takes mine. I lock our fingers together and begin to move. Her heels click on the stairs and once we enter my room, she takes them off.

We both sit on the bed and I hand her a beer. She gives me a sideways smile and says, "Thank you," before she takes a small sip. I sit behind her, placing both of my legs around her body and lean us backwards. She exhales deeply.

"Talk to me, baby. What's going through your mind?"

She shrugs her shoulders and says, "I don't know. I keep reminding myself that it's only a test, but it's more than that. It's seeing Robert twenty years after he abandoned us. I mean, how am I supposed to handle that?"

"Babe, you stay true to who you are. He's lucky you both have agreed to get tested."

"But what if he wants to act like everything is normal? What do I do?"

"If it were me, I would let him know how great you're doing. You have a fabulous job and are starting a new, *healthy* relationship. Plus, I'll be right there with you. I won't let him make you feel uncomfortable."

"You will?" she questions, turning in my hold.

"Of course I will. Did you think I would let you go through this alone?"

She rests her head on my chest. I squeeze her a little harder and look down at her small frame, resting so securely between my legs. "You have a way of making everything seem so easy."

"It is. This is all minor stuff. Is he going to be there for the test anyways? Isn't it just a blood test?"

"You're right, I don't think he will. I don't know why I get myself so worked up."

She looks up into my eyes and I move my lips to hers, brushing them gently across her sweet skin. She exhales a long breath. It sounds like she's been holding it for a while. "Your lips…" she trails off.

"Mmm, your lips," I repeat and plunge my tongue against hers. I set her beer down and don't wait for her to tell me anything else. I just go with what I'm feeling. In this moment, I need her, all of her. I roll us over and pin her beneath me. Taking my hands, I hold her face. Her mouth feels like satin as our tongues work together, and she makes the sexiest noises. Anything she does in bed turns me on, especially the sounds. She has me so hot.

Pulling away for a brief moment I look into her eyes, they are so green. I can see myself in the reflection. They are clear and certain looking up at me. "Tell me what you want?" I ask. I need to hear the words from her. I want to know that she's ready for me to push her limits.

"Take me to your world."

"Are you sure?"

"Yes," she responds breathlessly and slides her hands under the thin fabric of my gray t-shirt. I help her out and sit up removing it all the way. I toss it aside and look down at her, slowly unbuttoning each of the delicate buttons of her top. Once I'm all the way done, it hangs open, exposing her body. Forcefully, I pull down each cup of her bra, revealing her.

Taking my hand, I pinch a hardened nipple and wrap my mouth around the other. This special attention causes her body to buck underneath me. Pulling away, I blow on the wet nipple and say, "Calm down, baby. We're barely getting started."

Blinking a few times, she looks up at me, and I kneel between her legs unbuttoning her pants. The moment I'm done, I rip them off of her, underwear and all. She closes her legs and shyly turns from me. "Oh, no, you don't. Open your legs, or I'll tie them apart."

Slowly, she complies. With a smug smile on my face, I

step off the bed and remove my pants. As I stand before her, naked, she licks her lips and rolls on her side. "Your shirt and bra off, please."

She immediately listens. And when she's done, she crawls to me, stark naked with that long brown hair framing her face. When she reaches the edge of the bed, she sweeps it to one shoulder and says, "Touch yourself."

Without hesitation, I grab my cock moving my hand from the base to tip over and over again. She watches what I'm doing and pinches her nipple. The touch causes her to squeeze her thighs together. She signals that I come to her and I can't wait. I want my cock in her sweet mouth.

As I step to the bed, she opens wide and takes all of me in. I close my eyes and pull out almost all the way before I push back in, following each movement with my hand. She reaches her hand up my body and rests it below my chest. Finally, I let go of my dick and place my hands on my hips, balancing myself on my tiptoes as I fuck her sweet mouth. Each movement is amazing.

Jesus, my girl sucks a good cock. As I move and thrust, I think of how good it's going to feel to tie her up. She spreads her legs a little and I can see her cunt. The sight stops me dead in my tracks. I push her backwards onto the bed and grab the rope off of my nightstand. "Flip over, baby, and grab your ankles.

I slide the blindfold over her eyes and admire this view and how obedient she is. Hovering above her, I kiss between her shoulder blades. Her skin is damp from perspiring in anticipation. I love how her body responds to me, that I have such a powerful effect on her body. I know we are just beginning this journey, but the trust she has shown me tells me there is nothing she wouldn't give me.

Taking a piece of rope, I wrap it around her delicate wrist and ankle, binding the two together. In this position, she has her ass raised and I have a perfect view of every intimate part of her.

I'm methodical with my knots. I've done it a lot and researched the shit out of what's right and what's wrong. The last thing I want to do is hurt her. I've gotten quite good at this; what I do never leaves deep marks. At least it hasn't for years. When I first began and was young, I fucked up once and it's taken years for me to forgive myself. The marks on her wrists were detrimental to my confidence in this world I love. I'll never fuck up again, especially not with Bridge.

With both of her legs bound, I lean in and taste her, diving right into her cunt. I flick my tongue constantly, making her squirm against my face. "Fuck, you're wet," I say when I pull away. "Are you wet for me?"

"Only you."

"Better be," I say and land a firm hand to her plump ass.

"You remember the little crop you picked out, don't ya?" I run it down her back and over her ass.

"Uh-huh."

"Tell me why you picked it, Bridge."

"'Cause I want to know what it feels like."

"Do you think it'll feel better than my hand?" I ask and land another smack to her prize ass.

"No," she shrieks. "Nothing's better than your hand."

"We shall see, baby." And with those words I begin to work her. Building the anticipation by running the crop over her skin, watching it tighten everywhere it touches. She stays still as the heart moves, tickling her entire body. Then she tenses and I wait on using it. I want her calm and relaxed. "Trust me, baby," I rasp out, so hot and turned on by the sight of her and the control I have right now, it's unreal. My cock is dripping pre-cum. I swear all it would take from her in this moment is the slightest touch and I would lose it.

She moans and arches up, moving towards the crop, and I take my hand caressing her ass and then smack it. "Yes," she retorts.

I can tell she's loosening up and trusting me. Finally, I make my move, landing a soft smack of the crop to her ass and she moans. I do it again and she moans louder. I know she likes this. I push her and enjoy watching her ass turn pink with little hearts. Then, I cannot take it any longer, watching her hands and ankles bound together. They are how I want them. And I invade her pussy, sinking my cock deep inside. She's drenched in slickness for me and I slide right in. I drop the crop and grip her ass cheeks, squeezing them hard.

I'm in a trance as I look down and watch myself move

in and out of her. We fit together like God made us for one another. I can't move fast, I need to cherish this – her. That is until she says, "Fuck me hard, Troy."

I grab her ass and do as she asks, picking up speed and piling into her. She makes the hottest sounds. I love that the room is silent minus her moans and the noise from our bodies hitting one another. "Spank me," she orders. And in that moment, I know she's perfect for me. I've never had a girl ask for it – ever. I do as she wants, loving the response I get out of her when my hand makes contact with her supple ass. "More. Harder," she demands.

"You like it, don't you?" I ask, needing confirmation for some reason, although she's telling me exactly what I want to hear.

"God, yes."

"Come for me."

"Yessssss."

I grip her hips and really work her pussy, needing to push her there. I move my angle to where I'm now almost standing over her. My cock runs so deep inside of her and I love it. I take advantage of her tits, squeezing the nipples as I work us close to release. Each movement has me so near, but I want to wait for her. I want us to come together. And come together we do as she tightens her pussy around my cock – I explode – grunting violently. She screams my name and shivers with pleasure underneath me.

Chapter 22

The G

"So tell me when the test is," I ask Bridgette as I dry off from the shower. We spent the day helping Cara and Abel move and it was exhausting. I can tell from the look on her face that she's as tired as I am. Thankfully, there wasn't much heavy stuff to move since they ordered a lot of new furniture, but man did they have a lot of boxes and other odd and ends. Plus, it was hot as hell, like brutally, excruciatingly hot.

"It's the Monday after my birthday."

"Okay, I'll talk to Abel about taking the day off."

She applies some of my lotion to her legs and says, "You don't need to take the whole day off."

"I want to. Who knows how things are going to go? So I would rather have the time off."

"Well, thanks, babe. I appreciate it."

"It's what I do. Are you still up for the movies tonight? We can just stay in if you would rather."

"No, I want to go."

"Cool. Do you wanna eat there?"

"God, yes." She's too cute. "Can I get a pizza, a hot dog, nachos, and popcorn?"

I tease her. "What, no candy?"

She wraps her arms around my neck, touching our naked bodies together. "Oh, I want candy too. I only told you what I wanted for dinner."

"I'll get you whatever you want, baby."

She smacks my ass and walks off. I'm a bit shocked at what she just did. No one has ever spanked me before. I run my hands over my face. I guess I shouldn't be surprised. There's a lot that she does that shocks me.

When I walk back into the bedroom, she's dressed in a black pair of yoga pants. I head over to my dresser, and when I walk behind her, I unclasp her bra and it falls right off. I can't help but laugh at her. "Troy," she snaps at me.

"Yes, baby?" I innocently ask, sliding on my underwear.

She laughs shaking her head and picks her bra up off the floor, putting it back on. I smirk at her as I pull on a pair of shorts. We've been keeping the mood light all day, which has been nice. Since the moment we both woke up with smiles on our faces, it's been fun. I know last night calmed her and took away a lot of her fears. She knows I'm going to be with her no matter what, through anything that life throws at her.

"Have you decided what movie you want to see?"

"I told you I don't care."

"Are you sure?"

"Yup."

We load up in her car and head to the theater. She told me earlier that I'm the one who always drives. It's not that I don't want her to drive, it's just me following what I think is right. Damn my mother for instilling such manners in me. Speaking of my mother, I should ask Bridgette about dinner with them. I really don't want to subject her to my father, but it has to happen eventually.

"What do you think about having dinner at my parents'?"

She glances at me for a moment trying to read my expression. "Are you asking me what I think, or if I want to go?"

"Both."

"Troy, I think the better question is what do you think?"

I laugh nervously. "I want you to meet them. I really do. Well, let me rephrase that. I want you to meet my mom and Brittany. My dad, I couldn't care less."

"Is he really that bad?"

"Yes!" I blurt out. "He's an asshole. He hates me. I'm like the devil's spawn that has never been good enough for him. Then, add the fact that since he's retired he's become a master alcoholic, and being around him is horrible."

"Then why don't you invite just your mom and Brittany over? We'll cook for them and that way you'll be more comfortable."

I think about what she's proposing and although it sounds like a great idea, I know it'll only cause my mom that much more stress to lie to him. "Babe, I think it's sweet of you to worry about me being comfortable and all. But…I don't want to ask my mom to lie. If you're down to go with me and get through this, I'd love to take you."

"You know I want to meet all of them, including your dad. I'm sure he'll like me."

"I know he'll like you. Hell, he'll probably try to convince you that you could do so much better than me."

Her mouth drops open as she parks the car in front of the theater. "Would he do that?"

"I don't know. Let's not talk about him, okay? I'll talk to my mom about a date and we'll discuss more then."

We get out of the car and I grab her hand, holding it tight. She leans her head on my shoulder and we walk in, getting right in line. I look over the board of options trying to decide which movie to see. I decide on one that's been out for a few weeks, figuring the theater will be quieter. To be honest, I'm not really here to see a movie.

"Is that okay with you?" I ask Bridge.

"Yup, I told you, babe, whatever you want to see is fine with me."

I whisper in her ear as I pay the cashier, "I wanna see you come."

She looks at me shocked and I give her a devilish smile. "No," she protests. "Not here."

"Okay, babe. Whatever you say."

We make our way through the line and find out which theater we're in. Then we proceed to order all of our food. And by *all*, I mean Bridgette goes overboard. I love how excited she is with her arms full of food as we find our theater. When we walk in, I lead the way. It's quiet inside and quickly we find an empty row. We sit close to the back, with our food occupying the seats on either side of us.

"Are you really going to eat all of that?" I ask, watching my little woman take the first bite of what I assume will be many.

"Uh-huh. You didn't think I bought it all and planned on letting it go to waste, did you?"

"I bet you a hundred dollars you can't eat it all."

"Deal," she says taking a bite of her hot dog.

"Shake on it, woman."

"I don't want to set my hotdog down," she whines.

"Then no deal."

She sighs in frustration setting her hotdog down and takes my outstretched hand. "What movie are we seeing anyways?" she asks.

I shrug my shoulders. "I don't know, whatever they are showing in theater four. It must not be that popular considering how many people are *not* in here.

"Stop fucking with me," she snaps.

"Shhhh, be quiet. We're in a theater, babe."

She finishes her hotdog and pulls her feet underneath her as she turns towards me in her seat. "Will you hand me the nachos, please?"

"These are my nachos."

"No, they aren't," she says.

I look at her confused; she knows damn well that they are. "I ordered them."

She whispers in my ear. "I'm on to your game. Do you plan on touching my pussy while we are in here?" I nod my head at her. "Then hand them over, mister. I don't welcome jalapeño fingers on my lady parts."

Sonofabitch.

She knows that I absolutely cannot eat nachos without jalapeños on them. I sulk back in my chair handing over my favorite item. I settle on the popcorn, hoping it will taste half as good, but it doesn't.

As Bridgette eats bite after bite she moans and lets me know vocally just how good it tastes. "That good, huh?" I ask.

"God, yes."

"You're lucky I don't make you get on your knees and suck me off."

She smirks at me and I have to do a double take. *Did she really just smirk?* As I stare at her beautiful face, the lights turn down and the previews begin. I'll give her time to finish eating, then that's it. She's mine.

As we watch the previews, they all look good. Like really, really good. I might have to bring her back here to actually see a movie. When ours starts and it's taking place in 100B.C. she rolls her eyes at me. I smile taking a sip of soda and act like I'm really into this shitty ass film.

I can tell she's anxious, wanting me to touch her. I look to our left as a couple starts to walk up the stairs. I'm nervous they are going to come down our row. I watch them like a hawk but they settle a few rows in front of us. I'm thankful and lean forward. I can sense her fidgeting next to me. *She's such a greedy, little thing.* No matter what, she always wants more, more, more.

"Good movie, huh?" I whisper. She glares at me and I reach over her grabbing the popcorn off of the empty seat. I make sure my arm brushes against her chest. Dammit, touching was a bad move on my part. *Now I want more.* My game is over and it's of my own accord that it ended. She crosses her arms over her chest and I set the popcorn next to me. I uncross her arms and she lets out a deep sigh. Placing them next to her, I tweak her nipples looking around to make sure there is still no one behind us. I lean into her neck with my mouth, kissing her soft skin and then take a bite between my teeth. She throws her head back and grabs onto my arm. I kiss the skin and sit back in my seat. Getting comfortable and propping my feet on the chair in front of me. No one is sitting in the next row, thank God.

Placing my index finger over her soft lips, I insinuate that she stays quiet. She nods her head and sits back in her seat. Softly I rub my hand over her breasts and then down her stomach and between her legs. She pushes herself against my hand and I know how bad she wants this. I'm sure it's just as much as I want to give it to her. Taking my time, I slide my hand under the waistband of her pants and work my way beneath her panties 'til I reach her sex. She's wet for me, but I'm not surprised. She always is.

Gradually, I separate her pussy taking extra time before I pay any attention to her clit. This little amount of torture is pushing her to frustration quickly. I can tell she does *not* like it. That's not what I want, although I do enjoy teasing her. So I give in, sinking a finger inside of her wet core while keeping my thumb out to touch and tease her clit.

I watch her body change as everything within her begins to relax. She's enjoying this. Letting my palm rest on her clit, I quickly find her G-spot. I know it's risky to play with the G in public, but that makes the whole experience that much more fun. *Bingo.* I've found it and can tell right away. She reaches for me. Needing to hold on to something. I welcome her touch and wish we were alone, and naked, and didn't have to be quiet.

However this is about Bridge, not me. She starts to whimper and I cover her mouth, stopping my movements. She looks at me and closes her eyes when I start to move again. Each movement is pushing her there. I remove my hand and take her mouth with mine. I know how loud she is when she comes and she's close. I kiss her like I love, controlling and invading. Matching my hand and tongue. She keeps her sounds quiet and I know it's not an easy thing to do.

Taking her hand, she reaches over for me. Her touch causes me to stop. I bite down on her lip and look into her eyes. Although it's dark, we can see each other perfectly. She moves her hand insistently over my erection and I want more. Taking my free hand, I unbutton my pants. She helps me unzip them and then snakes her hand inside, clenching my hard member.

Her touch is so invigorating, it makes me stop kissing her. With my hand still inside of her pussy she takes over the pleasure and leans in sucking on my neck. God, this feels so good, almost too good. I don't want to come in my pants so I rest my hand on hers and whisper in her ear, "This is for you, baby."

As I begin my movements, she loosens her grip but cups my balls. Gently she massages them and I like this. I work hard pleasing her and it's not long until I'm quickly rewarded by her orgasm. She wraps her hand around my thigh, holding on tight. Trembles move through her, nothing like normal, tiny shakes and when she lets go I think of how good it will feel to fuck her later. To fill her tight cunt with my cock, balls deep, and make her take me rough and hard.

Her next movements catch me off guard. She pulls my hand out of her pants and leans down, removing my shaft and wrapping her tight lips around me. A hiss escapes me when she glides her teeth down. She swirls her tongue and moves with urgency. I know she wants this, just like I wanted to give it to her.

My body begins to spasm and I know this is gonna feel so good. Taking my hand, I weave my fingers into her hair and meet her mouth by gently thrusting my hips. I look around to make sure no one is watching and then let go. Fuck, it feels amazing to come in her mouth. She keeps a firm grip on the base of my cock and milks out every last drop of cum.

Finally, she stops and sits up. I lean into her and she whispers, "Thank you," into my ear. I smirk at her. I should be the one thanking her.

Chapter 23

Shock

"Are you really not going to tell me where we are going for my birthday?"

I shake my head, lying on Bridgette's bed as she packs for our impending trip. She squats in front of me, taking my attention away from my phone. I'm trying to research what we are going to do while in Napa. Pulling her shirt down she begins to tweak her own nipple. I grab her wrist stopping her as I feel my blood boil. I think most guys are into that, but *not* me, definitely not me. "That's my job," I snarl.

"Then do it," she says.

"No, not now. I'm busy and you pissed me off. Don't even think that's going to get me to tell you where we're going."

She stands and I smack her ass hard, a popping noise echoes through the room and I love the sting in my hand.

"Carry on," I say.

"You so need to be tied up."

"Never gonna happen, babe."

She storms into her closet and starts throwing out clothes. "Hey, what are you doing?" I ask.

"Packing," she yells.

I guess I did push her buttons. I lay there and let the clothes cover me. She'll get 'em off of me. "So what do you want to do on our trip?"

"Well, if I knew where we were going then I could tell ya, couldn't I?"

I decide to mess with her again. It's been fun fucking with her lately. "I told you we're going to Vegas, babe, so don't forget to pack your wedding dress."

"Troy!" she yells in the way only she can.

"Yeah, babe?"

"God, you're driving me nuts."

"Touché."

Her phone rings and she comes out of the closet grabbing it off the bed. I see it's Alexa calling, right on cue. We decided to really surprise her. She's calling to say goodbye and see if she needs anything before we leave. Little does Bridgette know, Alexa is joining us with Vincent, as well as Cara and Abel.

A text chimes in on my phone from Vincent. *I'm sending a car to pick you both up in the morning. Are you going to be at Bridgette's?*

Jesus, he really doesn't need to do that. ***Yeah, we're here, but you really don't need to do that.***

It's already done. See you at the airport.

Bridgette walks back into the room with tears in her eyes. "What's wrong, baby?" I ask.

"Oh, it's just my sappy ass sister. I'm going to miss her. I always see her on my birthday; this will be the first I won't."

"I'm sorry, Bridge. I promise the trip will be worth it."

She gives me a small smile and starts to fold her clothes. "Hey, we agreed. No stressing on this trip and getting upset. That includes crying."

"But the trip hasn't started."

"Well, our vacation has. I'll be right back."

I sit up and remove the clothes she threw about. I can't wait any longer to give her, her birthday present. I've had it for what feels like months, even though it's barely been a week. I run out to my car and grab the bag from my back seat.

I might as well bring my suitcase in since Vince is sending us a car and all. When I walk back in she's in the kitchen filling up her water bottle. She turns to me and I hold the gift out to her. "What's this for?" she asks.

"Your birthday."

"My birthday isn't for two days."

"I know, but I can't wait any longer. Open it, I promise you'll love it."

She takes the bag from me, setting her water down and removes the card first. I didn't really know what to write in it, so it's only a few lines, but I wanted her to know how much she means to me. She reads it and wraps her arms around my neck hugging me and then kissing me hard on the lips. I hold her tiny hips and look into those green eyes.

"Open your present; I don't want to wait another minute."

She lets go of me, looking into the bag and removing the tissue paper. I keep my arms around her and look over her shoulder. Pulling out the sleek Apple box, she turns to me. "No way, Troy."

"Yes way, babe."

She shakes her head clutching the iPad to her chest. "But why?"

"'Cause you needed one of those reading thingies." I can barely keep a straight face as I say the words.

"Okay, that has to be a joke. I can buy books. This costs too much, and the trip too."

"You can buy books on here too. Don't worry about the money, just enjoy it. Plus, there's another gift in there that I promise you're going to love even more."

She sets down the iPad and reaches into the bag, pulling out the matte black case with the popping silver autograph on it. She looks at it and smiles. "Thanks, baby."

"Of course. Flip it over."

Immediately she does and her breathing skips a beat. She stares at it stunned. "Is…? Wait… How…? No way!"

"Yup, it's L. Sidon's signature."

"You're fucking with me."

"No, I'm not, babe. I promise, I waited in a long ass line for her to sign it."

"Motherfucker, Troy! What did she say? Was she nice? Did you ask her when her next book is coming out?"

I can't help but laugh at her. "Errr, no. I just asked her to sign this for my girlfriend, Bridgette. She did and I said 'Thanks.'"

"Uhhh, Troy," she whines whacking me with the case. "How could you let an opportunity like that go to waste?"

"I'm sorry, babe. I was just excited to get the case signed."

"Haven't you heard it's been rumored that she's done writing? I can't lose her, she's my favorite author. Without her stories I'm going to be so bored. She also has an unfinished series I'm itching to get my hands on. The next book in it is supposed to be BDSM."

No way is that normal looking chic into BDSM. "Well, fuck, why didn't you tell me all of this sooner?"

"I don't know."

"Hey, don't be down. At least now you can stalk her via social media any time of day. This bad boy has built in 4G so you can go online wherever you are."

"God, Troy, this is truly the best gift ever. Thank you so much."

"Of course. Now let's finish packing, we have an early morning flight."

Our bags are loaded in the trunk and the feeling of leaving town with Bridgette is amazing. She's sleepily wrapped in my arms on the drive to the airport and I'm grateful that Vincent sent this car. The further away we get, the more I feel her relax. Her breathing is calm and even; she's almost a different version of herself. Lighter. Freer.

"Are you getting excited?" She nods her head. "Are you tired?"

"Yeah, I haven't been sleeping well."

"I'm sorry, I promise you can rest as much as you want on this trip. It's just me and you, so whatever you want to do is fine with me."

I know the minute she sees the girls she'll perk right up. She's gonna be so shocked. "When are you gonna tell me where we're going?"

"When we check in at the gate."

"Can I guess?"

"Sure," I say resting my cheek on top of her hair.

"Vegas?"

I falter for a second and figure I better stop messing with her. "No."

She turns in my hold and looks at me "Really? We're not getting married?"

I smile at how cute she is, so small and sleepy in my arms. "No, not yet, babe."

Leaning up, she kisses me and then leans back against my chest.

"New York?"

"Nope."

"Mexico?"

"Nuh-uh. But that's a great idea." The limo comes to a stop and the driver gets out. "No more guessing, we're here." She sits up and reaches for the door. "Will you wait a minute and let the man do his job?"

"I'm excited and he's slow."

I know what's taking so long. I love watching Bridge fidget and pick at her nails. Then the door flies open and Cara and Alexa yell, "Surprise!" I get a good look at her face and the expression is priceless. Vincent did a flawless job coordinating all of the cars' arrivals together for this moment to be perfect. Bridgette slaps her hand over her mouth and looks at me. The girls pull her out of the car and I exit right behind her.

As the three of them are squealing like children in an amusement park, I head to the guys. "What up?" Abel says.

"Hey, douche," I respond and we both laugh.

"Vincent, this is great, man. Thank you."

"Of course. I'll do anything for those girls. Look at how happy they are."

Our driver sets our luggage down, then we head inside to check in. "Baby, did you do all of this by yourself?" Bridgette asks.

"Nope, I had a lot of help. You've got some really great people who care a lot about you. We all pulled together to get it done."

"I can't even believe it."

"Well, believe it, babe." This is how *our* life's gonna be. This is our life, and every day is what we make of it. I know each day is a gift and you better believe I'm going to make the most of every moment I get with Bridge.

Chapter 24

Embarrassed

We land in California fifteen minutes ahead of schedule. The flight was smooth and filled with lots of laughter. Surprisingly none of us have ever been to Napa, even Vincent. I hear Bridgette say to the girls that she's always wanted to go. I'll have to thank Alexa later for pushing the idea. I know I was set on Vegas, and maybe more for selfish reasons. Deep down, I have to be honest with myself. No, fuck, I can't. Things are great the way they are, we couldn't possibly get married right now. I have a habit of rushing things. I'll be damned if I do that again.

"I'm so excited to be here, babe."

"Me too," I say and kiss her on the lips.

As we start to get off the plane, Vincent says, "I only booked us one limo so you girls better not have packed too much crap."

Alexa glares at him. "Baby," she snaps.

"What?" he asks shrugging his shoulders.

"Don't be rude."

"I was joking. What, did you think I would make you leave one of your precious suitcases at the airport?"

I can't help but laugh at them. Then you have Cara and Abel – he won't let her carry anything. And by anything, I mean he even has her purse in his hands. I know we're far from normal, but these people have become my family. Bridgette slides her arm around me as we follow the crowd off the plane to find the luggage carousel.

"So what are we doing first?" she asks.

"Uh, Alexa is our tour guide. What's on the agenda for today?" I ask her.

"Today we shall squish grapes and tour the vineyard."

"Yuck," Cara gripes.

"Whatever, Cara. What about tomorrow?" Bridgette asks.

"It's your birthday, so that's up to you. I have lots of options though. I was thinking the spa in the morning and we go from there."

She smiles and I notice how quiet Abel has been. "You all right, bro?"

"Yeah, man, I'm good," he responds.

"It'll be fine," I say as Cara walks ahead with Alexa.

He shakes his head and says, "I know."

I feel bad for him; I know he's been stressed all day. I hate to see him like this. He's planning on asking Cara to marry him on our last day. That way it doesn't take away from Bridgette's birthday, but at this point, he needs to get down on one knee right now.

"So, do I have to partake in the grape squishing?" Cara asks.

"Yup. We're even going to make some non-alcoholic wine for you and the baby," Alexa says.

Cara grumbles under her breath and I can't wait to see how painful this is actually going to be for her. Bridgette seems to be excited for it and that's all that matters. Finally, we find the luggage carousel and one by one, pick off everyone's bags. Thankfully, everything fits into the limo and since we are traveling with Vincent, check-in at the hotel is a breeze. Of course, Alexa upgraded our rooms to suites, after I told her *not* to.

As I close the door and am finally alone with Bridge, I can't stand another minute of not touching her. I slide the chain in place to ensure privacy and walk over to her as she's checking her phone. She doesn't look up at me and I throw her body over my shoulder. She squeals, dropping her phone God only knows where.

"What, does your phone excite you more than I do?" I ask slapping her ass.

She laughs and reaches behind herself to cover from another smack. All that does is make it easier for me to hold her wrists together with one hand. "Troy! No! Don't!" she protests as I begin to tickle her with my other hand. I toss us both onto the bed and she tries to scramble away.

She's too small and quite frankly, not fast enough; it

doesn't take me but a second to regain control and drive her mad. Popping her boobs out, I suck hard on the skin around her nipples and she settles. She's no longer fighting me because she's enjoying it.

I glance up at her as she moves her hair out of her face and watches me take my time with these precious girls. *Christ, I love her tits.* I love everything about her. Her confidence, poise, beauty, and most of all her heart; she's so caring and compassionate.

She's eager and lifts those little hips, shimmying down her pants. I go back to sucking my prized possessions. Then she reaches into my shorts, catching me off guard.

She strokes my cock so perfectly like she knows how and asks, "Slide him in?"

"I will in a minute."

"I don't care if we lay just like this, I need you inside of me."

Because of her words, I slip out of my shorts and brace my weight above her. As I look down at her, I hold her face like I always do and slip inside of her tight, wet core.

She moans as I take my time filling her. Once I am in as far as I can go. She pulls me to her and kisses me, invading my mouth, like the little vixen that she is. As our tongues work together, she pulls me against her. I kiss her back, moving slowly inside of her body.

Having sex with her always pushes my boundaries. It's a test of how far I can go and now ultimately how long I can last. The man I used to be, the machine I once was, is no longer. She took that from me. I guess you could say it's because of the connection we have. Each interaction we have, every movement, pull, push, noise, they all drive me mad.

I realize then how close I am to coming. She has her legs wrapped around me like a vise. Her hands are woven into my hair and we haven't broken our kiss since the beginning.

I hear a knock on the door. *Fuck, not now.* I can't stop. It would take a wrecking ball to move me from her. "Come with me," I whisper, taking her mouth again as I pummel myself inside of her. She moans as I rub her spot; I know what she needs. I hear the knock again and control my tone as I let go, pouring myself deep inside of her.

She whimpers, raking her fingernails down my back. I open my eyes and watch her body change as her release takes over. I love her face when she comes, she's so hot shuddering underneath me. "Bridge, are you in there?" I hear Cara call through the door.

I kiss her hard on the lips and fly off of her and into the bathroom to shower. "Troy!" she yells out after me. I throw her a towel and close the door.

"I'll be right there," she says.

I know I'll totally pay for this later, but it's worth it. Not stopping and having to force out our orgasms was something else.

I take my time letting the water rush over my skin. I

know my clothes are on the other side of the door, so I want to wait 'til they leave. After probably twenty minutes of wasting time in the shower and scrubbing 'til my skin hurts, I rinse and finally turn the water off. I can hear the girls laughing so I know this is gonna be fun. Wrapping my towel around my waist, I open the bathroom door, and feel all three sets of eyes as I walk over to my suitcase.

"Hey, girls," I say, hurrying as fast as I can.

One of them whistles and Bridgette says, "Right? Isn't he fucking delicious?"

"Hey, I'm right here," I say.

"Oh, we can see that," Alexa says.

I shake my head and grab my clothes, heading back into the bathroom.

"Damn, girl, what did you do to his back?" Cara asks.

I lock the door, feeling a bit scared of the vultures on the other side. Setting my clothes down on the counter, I turn and look in the mirror at my back. Running down each shoulder blade are red lines that must be from Bridgette's fingernails.

God, I should've stayed in the shower a little bit longer. I decide I need to have an evacuation plan upon leaving this room again. Dressing quickly, I grab my phone and text Abel. ***Where are you? I can't hang out with these chicks.***

We're down at the bar in the lobby. Come meet us.

I take a deep breath before walking back into the pack of hyenas. I open the door, looking only at Bridge and she smiles at me. "I'm gonna meet the guys, babe. Text me when you girls are done doing…whatever it is you're doing."

I kiss her and bolt. I hear them say bye as the door closes behind me. As soon as I'm in the elevator, I shake my head. I've never had three chicks make me so uncomfortable. I know they are only joking, but Jesus.

When I emerge into the lobby, I spot Abel and Vincent right away. They are laughing at the bar and I can't wait to have a beer with them and just relax. "What up, douchebags," I announce as I sit down next to Abel.

"There he is," Vincent says.

"What took ya so long?" Abel questions.

"Sorry, I had some business to handle."

"Right, right," Abel says. "I take it you got the job done?"

"Fuck yeah, I did. I would have been longer had your two ladies not interrupted."

"I told Lex to give you guys some time."

The bartender walks up and asks me what I'm drinking. "I'll take a Corona, bro." He cracks it open and slides it to me. "Let's toast," I announce.

Both Abel and Vincent raise their drinks, as I think of something funny to say. "To Abel's manhood. It will forever be missed."

"You're such a prick," he gripes.

"I'll toast to that," Vincent says, clinking bottles with me and we both knock back a drink. I forgot how much I love the taste of Corona. It's been so long since I've indulged and gotten drunk. Tonight, I think I'll do just that.

"Why do you both hate me?" Abel asks.

Vincent pats his back. "We love you. That's why we're giving you a hard time. Don't stress, bro. Remember what you told me when I went through this?"

"I know I just hate waiting to ask her."

"Then don't wait," I say. "Ask her tonight."

He takes a sip of his beer and looks at me. "But what about Bridgette?"

"Trust me, she won't mind. Do you want me to ask her?"

"Yeah. 'Cause I would hate it if she felt like I was taking away from her trip."

"Dude, she's not like that – at all."

I look to Vincent as he's on his phone. "What are you doing?" I ask.

"Texting Alexa."

I glance at Abel and his face turns a pale white. Poor guy, he really is nervous. When I think about my future, I see Bridge. I know one day I too will ask her to marry me and I don't get the slightest bit nervous thinking about it. I'm excited. I guess for some God unknown reason, I got lucky.

Chapter 25

One More Present

"Good morning, my sweet birthday girl," I say nuzzling as close as I can to Bridge. Thankfully, I feel good. Maybe I'm a little groggy, but considering how much I drank last night, this is good. She stirs awake as I kiss her back, slowly moving next to me, immediately making me hard.

I kiss her shoulder, grinding my erection into her ass. "Hi," she whispers in a hoarse voice.

"How are you feeling?" I ask.

"I think I'm okay. How 'bout you?"

"I'm good. It's my baby's birthday, I couldn't be happier."

"You're sweet. But you drank a lot last night, are you sure you're all right?"

"I'm good, babe." She looks over at me and I kiss her cheek. "I promise."

"What should we do today?" she asks.

"Whatever you want. But first I have one more gift for you."

She looks at me confused and I pull her on top of me. Staring into her clear and beautiful green eyes, I hold her face in my hands. "Bridge, my beautiful girl, I've been thinking about this a lot and how to tell you. But the truth is, there is no right way to do it, so I just need to say it. There is no denying how much you mean to me. You have become my best friend and my reason for happiness. I know this might seem fast, but *I love you.* I can't let another day go by without speaking the words to you. You have such a special place inside of my heart and it consumes all of me. You are what I have searched for my entire life. You let me be myself and the freedom of no longer living a lie is invigorating. I'm not scared any more of the what-ifs, because I know no matter what, we'll get through them and we'll do it together. I love you, Bridgette Schaefer, and there isn't anything you need to do or say, I just had to let you know."

She looks at me, blinking a few times then linking her tiny fingers behind my head, she clings to me. To say I'm not a little disappointed to not hear her say the words would be a lie. It hurts, but I know what we have. It's real and something that will last forever. I kinda sprung this on her, and deep down I knew it was a risk. That's why I told her she didn't have to say anything back.

Her cell phone rings and she lifts her head looking for it. I grab it off the nightstand and hand it to her. "It's my brother," she says.

"Answer it, babe."

She does so and gets to talking to him. I sneak off and shower before we head down to meet everyone for breakfast. As I emerge from the bathroom, Bridge is dressed in a short, black, strapless dress.

"Is that new?" I ask.

"Yeah, I got it for the trip. You like it?"

"Hell yeah, I love it. Do you have a bra on?" She nods her head. "Will you take it off for me?"

"Troy! For real?"

"Yes, babe, please. I want to be able to see your nipples all day."

She turns her back to me, lifting her hair and I reach into her dress unclasping her black strapless bra. As I pull it out of her dress, I ask, "Is this new too?"

"Uh-huh."

"Fuck," I mutter and lift her dress. I'm greeted by a pair of black, lace underwear, which barely cover her ass. *I'm doomed.* We have to leave the room and head downstairs, but goddammit I want her. Kneeling down, I slide off her panties. There's something about knowing she's completely naked under the dress that makes me horny as fuck. Standing back up, I look into her eyes, trying to read her expression.

Her breathing is heavy and I know what she wants. Taking my hands, I pick her up by the hips and set her on the bed. As she leans back and looks at me, I flip her dress up and open her pussy wide with two of my fingers. I growl a little, staring at her and want like nothing else to make her come and come good. Taking a deep breath, I breathe her in before I wrap my mouth around her clit. She falls back onto the bed and moans. Not hurrying, I kiss and love her body, like she deserves.

Pulling away for a brief moment, I slide two fingers inside of her and get back to work. Right away, her noises increase and I keep my rhythm slow and steady. Pleasing her and pushing her body to orgasm is by far the biggest turn on. I glance up and watch her body. Her back is arched and knees are slacked to the side. She has both of her hands threaded into my hair.

"Ahhh…. Fuck, Troy. It feels—"

She can't get out the rest of her words because her body lets go. Twitching and pushing against me, with her fingers knotted tightly into my hair. I smile watching her release and as I finally slow, I kiss her sweet cunt. We stare at one another for a minute and she says, "Thank you."

"Happy birthday," I respond and help her up. She smiles at me and we gather our stuff before leaving the room. "Are we okay?" I ask.

"Of course. Listen, I'm sorry I didn't say anything earlier—"

I cut her off. "You don't have to explain anything. It's all good, baby, as long as you heard me and know where my feelings lie. I know it's fast, but I had to get it off my chest."

"I heard you. Thank you for the best birthday gift ever."

"It's my pleasure."

She smiles and hugs me tight. "Are you ready to meet everyone and see how Cara and Abel's night went?"

"Yup, I can't wait to hear all of the details." As we emerge into the hallway, Alexa and Vincent greet us.

"Oh my God, happy birthday, sis!" Alexa says giving Bridge a huge hug.

"Thanks."

Vincent hugs her as well and wishes her a happy b-day, then we pile into the elevator. "Have you guys seen Cara and Abel?" I ask.

"Nope and he's not answering his phone," Vincent says.

Hmm, that's not like him at all. I hope everything is cool. I glance at my phone, briefly checking the messages, but there are no new ones. "I'm sure they're good; I bet they're still sleeping."

"Well, if they are then we're eating without them," Bridgette jokes.

"Whatever you want to do is fine with us. It's your day, honey." Alexa says. "I forgot to tell you, I did book a little session at the spa this morning."

"God, that sounds amazing."

When we get to the restaurant, the hostess takes us to a table that is tucked in the back. As we approach, there are Cara and Abel. They are intimately talking and I'm not sure if we should interrupt them or not. That is until Cara sees us and waves us over. "She looks happy," Bridge says.

"Happy birthday, sweetie," Cara says directing us to sit at their table.

"Yes, happy birthday, you little knucklehead," Abel tells her.

"Sooooo?" Bridgette asks looking at Cara's hand that's resting in her lap.

Cara smiles from ear to ear pulling her hand out showing off the beautiful diamond ring. "We're getting married." Everyone whoops and hollers in congratulations. Looking over at my best friend, I've never seen him happier. He takes her hand in his and kisses the ring.

"Do you guys have a date in mind?" Vincent asks. I know this has been weighing on Abel, as he wants to marry Cara before the baby's here.

"So kitten, what do you think?" he asks her.

"Let's do it."

"What do you guys think about a weekend in Vegas?"

I look to Bridge and bust out laughing. She slaps my leg and I try to contain my excitement. "What's so funny?" Abel asks.

"Troy's been fucking with me this whole time about going to Vegas for my birthday."

"You might have thought he was joking, but he tried to talk me into booking it for your birthday," Alexa says.

"Well, it sounds like we're all down for Vegas," Vincent interjects. "To Cara and Abel."

We all clink our water glasses and I lean down whispering into Bridgette's ear. "I can't wait to get your ass to

Vegas."

"Did you have a fun day, babe?" I ask Bridgette as we enter our room.

"It was the best. Thank you for my necklace. I love it." She found a long silver chain with multiple beads strung along it in black, silver, and purple. As soon as she put it on, I had to buy it for her. I really wanted to see her naked in it. I love the way it drapes into her cleavage.

As she turns out of my arms, there is a gigantic vase of lilies on the table and a bottle of champagne. "Oh Troy, this is all too much."

Hardly, I think to myself. I want to give her so much more. "It's your birthday, babe. Let's toast to the best year of your life."

She nods her head and says, "It will be, because of you." I pop the bottle and pour us each a glass. Then before we toast, I make a decision.

"Wait here," I say as I direct her to sit down.

She nods her head and as I walk off she says, "Troy?" I can hear the underlying question in her tone. I don't respond. I know how much this will mean to her. I've asked so much of her, this is the least I can do to repay for what she's given to me, and it is her birthday after all.

I stare into my bag for a few moments…then take a

deep breath and remove my much loved nylon rope. As I turn back to her with it in my hands, she smiles ear to ear and sets her glass down. I smile back sitting down inches away from her. She takes her wrists and places them together, presenting them to me. I smirk like the cocky bastard I am. I've trained her so well.

I shake my head and open one of her hands, placing the rope in her palm. "You're in control tonight."

She looks at me, wildly searching my eyes. I know she's looking to see if I'm telling the truth or not. She begins to shake her head and passes the rope back to me saying, "No, baby."

"Yes," I reaffirm. "You've been saying you want to tie me up, so do it."

"I don't know how."

"And neither did I at one time. Use common sense and I'll walk you through the rest. You don't want to go too tight. Always think about marks – you *never* want to leave marks."

"But what if I do?"

"You won't." I say leaning back and showing her my erection. Talking with her about this has me so horny. There's an underlying bit of anticipation to all of this. Deep down, I think I want her to tie me up.

"Are you sure?" she asks. I nod my head and she contemplates her next move. "Are there any rules?"

"No spanking."

"Wait here," she murmurs. I'll happily do anything she

wants right now. Her ass is so beautiful in that dress as she leaves the room and goes into the bathroom. As I sit there waiting, I'm tempted to get undressed. She takes forever and I figure, fuck it, standing up and tearing my clothes off, heaving them across the room. Sitting back down, I'm in direct view of the door and begin slowly pleasing myself.

I don't want to come, not without her. However, I do know how much she likes it when I touch myself. The door clicks open and my movements falter. Where is my girlfriend and who is this impeccable, picture-perfect woman before me?

"Hmmm, I like it when you touch yourself," she says walking towards me.

"Goddamn, you look hot." She's only wearing the necklace and a pair of black, suede heels. Her hair's big and wavy, and she's done her make up. Her eyes are so green, and her lips are plump and sparkly. With the rope in her hand, each step causes my body to twitch with impatience. I stop touching myself and place my hands on either side of me. She straddles my lap with her naked body; her pussy is so close to my cock that I want to be inside of her *now.*

Reaching down, I rub her wet, little nub. She pushes me away and shakes her head. "Who's in charge?"

I lean my head back regretting not having control in this moment. Reaching down she guides me inside of her. I look at her nervously. *What is she doing? No oral sex? Fuck!*

She sets the rope next to us and holds my face in her hands. I hold on to her hips and guide her because I know soon enough I won't have my hands.

Ah, I love her body. Watching how she moves on top of me is such a turn on. She's so beautiful, there's something so special about her. They way our bodies work and react to one another is something else. She's constantly contracting and releasing her muscles around my cock. It makes me want to come and I have to stop her with my hands, holding her in place by the waist.

"No, no, no. Don't stop," she cries as she falls into orgasm. I fall with her, slamming her down hard onto my shaft, pumping myself inside of her as we come together, moaning and sweating, twitching and cursing. *Fuck, this is so good.*

Her body settles, but her movements don't abate. They only slow as she keeps moving above me. That doesn't last forever though. They finally cease and she asks me, "Are you sure you want to do this?"

"Yes."

"Have you ever done this with anyone else?" she asks as she gets off of me.

I shake my head and reach for her outstretched hand. She takes it and snatches the rope, walking me over to the bed. "Lay down with your head on the pillows." I do so, but give her one last smack on the ass.

"Give me your wrists and walk me through how you do this," she says hovering above me.

Sitting up, I place my hands together presenting them to her. She takes a piece of the rope and binds it around both of my hands. "Weave the rope around my wrists in a figure eight." She follows my order. "Tie a single knot in the middle but leave some slack to wrap the lose end around."

"Like this?"

"Yup. Perfect." She wraps the long end around and around and around.

"Now tie those two lose ends together. Do you know how to do a square knot?"

"Nuh-uh."

"Tie a knot like you normally would, then tie the next one in the opposite direction."

"So when you tie me up, there's not much tying to it, it's more wrapping?"

"Right. It's more about control. You don't want the person to get free, but you want to be able to free them quickly if needed."

"So what's next?" she asks.

"You tell me, babe."

"Lie back and put your arms above your head."

Happily I comply, watching her take more rope and looping it through the wooden headboard. She threads it through my bound wrists, tying me securely in place. "Are you okay?" she asks.

I nod my head, biting my lip, watching her every move. Leaning down, she presses her lips to my chest. Her hair fans out around her, covering my body. Patiently she kisses her way down my body and around my cock. The anticipation of her mouth is too much, causing me to close my eyes. Instinctively, I pull my arms against the rope to touch her. I want to feel her, but I can't.

Sonofabitch.

She hops off of me and I watch her sexy round ass walk over to my bag. She takes out the blindfold and slings it around her index finger as she walks back over to me with confidence written all over her face. She crawls next to me and slides the silk over my line of vision. Her lips are the last thing I see and the first thing I feel as they mold around my cock.

Chapter 26

Stalking My Girl

"So are you really getting married in Vegas?" Matt asks Abel.

"Hell yeah, I am. You should come."

"Right. I know Troy's not gonna stay and keep an eye on the station so it's going to be my job."

"Are you sure?" he asks. "I think that nurse Cara works with is going to be there."

"Damn. In that case, let me think about it."

"Have you guys started to book things?" I ask.

"We're looking."

My phone buzzes on the kitchen counter and I get up from the table to check it. The message is from Bridge. *I can't make lunch today. I'm so sorry.*

Damn, I was really looking forward to seeing her. We just got back from Napa and I got really used to being around her, like all of the time. ***It's all good, babe. Do you need me to bring you anything?***

A few minutes pass and then she responds. *No, thanks.*

I'll grab something.

Okay, I can't wait to see you. I love you.

I know she hasn't said the words back to me yet, but I can't mask my feelings. It feels wrong to not say them. I wait for her to text me back, but she doesn't. I start to get a little bored and head outside with a few of the guys to play a game of basketball.

We haven't had a call all day and that always makes the time drag. Playing a good old game of ball with the guys always passes the time. None of us is ever serious when it comes to basketball, well, none of us minus Abel, and he's inside looking at drive–thru wedding chapels. "How's your girl, man?" Shawn asks me.

"She's fucking hot," Matt says. "Have you seen her Facebook picture?"

"Dude, what, are you stalking her?" I ask.

"She friend-requested me," he says.

I can't help but laugh out loud. Bridgette told me when Matt friend-requested her. "Right."

"She did and she's gorgeous."

"Well, she's mine. Enough about my girlfriend's looks, okay?"

"So you really like her?" Shawn asks, shooting the ball.

"Yeah, I love her."

"Whoa. Let me see the picture, Matt," he says.

I snatch the ball away from him and shoot as they pull up Bridgette's Facebook page. "Damn, bro. She is fucking hot." Shawn says.

"Don't you two have someone else's girlfriend you can stalk?"

My phone rings and I answer it without looking. "Oh, hey, Ma."

"Hey, Troy, I was making sure you and Bridge…that's what you call her, right?"

"You can call her Bridgette."

"Oh Okay, I was making sure that you and Bridgette were going to make it for dinner this weekend."

"Ma, it's Monday."

"I know, sweetie, but I have to get to the store this week and buy groceries."

"Yeah, we'll be there. What did Dad say?"

"Not much, dear. But Brittany is really excited."

"I know. She texted me about it."

"Well, I'm so excited. Should we plan on six o'clock?"

"Sure, Ma. See you this weekend."

We hang up and I check my phone, Bridgette still hasn't texted me back so I send her another message. We've been sexting a lot lately; maybe this will get her to respond. I'm sure she got busy with work. ***My cock misses you.***

I head inside to check on Abel and we get a call. *Hell yeah.* I fly down the pole getting into my gear and then into the truck. Abel's not far behind me, getting in the truck, and strapping up in the driver's seat. Once we have a head count, we pull out of the garage.

I listen to the dispatcher over the radio. She explains

it's a fire alarm in a downtown Denver building. Dammit! Immediately, I regret the call. We'll have to check all of the floors to ensure that everyone's safe and each floor is clear of fire. Nine times out of ten with these calls, there's no fire.

It takes us a few minutes to arrive on site and there are tons of people that evacuated the building, plus it's tall as fuck. Our team heads in and the sirens are blaring as we head for the stairs. It's quieter in here and Abel gives us orders to clear the floors.

I'm with Shawn like I have been a lot lately, but I like him. He's a good guy and has been taking his training seriously. We sweep through our floors with precision, with too many flights to count. When we've cleared our assigned areas, we head back down to meet Abel. He's talking to the building manager.

"All clear, Chief."

"Thanks, can you reset everything?" he asks me. The sirens are off, but I go into the utility room and reset the alarms and the flashing lights. The building turns back to normal and I head outside with the other guys. It's a cool afternoon and I can't wait to be off with Bridge. She's been getting so frisky and letting me do things I never dreamed of.

The guys and I load up in the truck and wait for Abel. "Dude, are we ever going to get a massive fire that takes us all day and night to contain?" Matt asks.

I laugh at him, "Why don't you see if there are any

wildfire details that need help out of state?"

"It's too late in the season. Plus, you two assholes are going to Vegas. I might as well drive this baby," he jokes getting into the driver's seat.

It's a horrible time to do so, as Abel emerges from the building to see him screwing around behind the wheel. He flings the door open and shouts, "Out."

We all bust out laughing as Matt tucks his tail between his legs getting out of the driver's seat. His face is red and I whisper over to him, "You know the rules. Never get behind the wheel unless you have permission."

He nods his head, beating himself up while Abel drives us back to the station. After he backs in, I find my phone. There are no new calls or text messages from Bridge. I'm sure something came up at the office and that's why she cancelled our lunch.

I hop in the shower and bolt. "Have a good night," I say on the way out. It's nice having Shawn around. It allows us to come and go early if needed. Since I haven't heard from Bridge all day, I'm going to surprise her at her office as she's getting off of work.

Chapter 27

Fear

I pull up to Bridgette's work and check my phone one last time. She hasn't texted me all afternoon. It's 4:59 and I know she should be off any minute. Hopping out of my Jeep, I notice how hot it is again today, almost unbearable. Walking into her building, I look a little odd to be taking an elevator up considering everyone else is leaving, but I'm on a mission.

Upon exiting on the 29th floor, that whore of a woman, Spring or Summer or whatever her name is, is packing up. She gives me the biggest smile. "Well, what brings you here this evening?" she asks like I'm here for her.

"Uh, my girlfriend. I'll just go back," I say without even giving her the time of day.

As I round the corner, Alexa is on her phone. She doesn't notice me, so I continue on to Bridgette's desk. When I arrive, it's empty. She's not here, she's not packing up…my stomach drops when I see a vase full of red roses on the corner. Who sent these to her? Anger flares inside of me as I snatch the note that reads *Meet me at Drain at noon – I have a surprise for you. Troy.* Reaching my hand down around the top of the vase like it's his neck, I pick them up, squeezing so hard I wish the glass would shatter. It doesn't, so I chuck them against the wall. The glass breaks and water gushes everywhere, leaving the roses lying there lifelessly. It doesn't help my rage. I wish it would, but it doesn't.

Alexa comes running over and I can see the pure shock on her face.

"Troy, what are you doing here? And what's wrong?" she asks.

I don't answer her. Instead, I call Bridgette. I have to get through. Maybe this is all a misunderstanding. When there is no answer, real panic starts to set in – something isn't right. I look at Alexa and now Vincent is staring at me too.

I swallow hard before speaking. "Did I just miss Bridgette?" I ask trying to stay calm. Praying to God that what I think is happening isn't.

They look at me confused and Alexa says, "No. Why would you ask that? She's been with you all day."

"No," I snap. "She hasn't, I haven't heard from her all day."

"Uh, wait? What…? But…"

"Goddammit," I snap. "What time did she leave?"

"I don't know, around noon. She said she was meeting you and then she texted me later asking if she could take the rest of the day off."

"What did you tell her?"

"Yes, of course I told her yes. She said she was with you."

"Fuck, Alexa." There's fear in my tone as I think of my girl out there with some sick freak. The thought almost brings me to my knees. "The flowers…the flowers on her desk were signed by me, but I didn't send them. The card says meet me at Drain at noon, I have a surprise, and it said from Troy. Drain is the place where I have run into her ex, twice." Vincent looks at me and I get in his face. "She's gone, man. Bridgette's fuckin' missing."

"Okay," he says calmly. "Let's not jump ahead of ourselves. We'll figure it out, man. Lex, baby, will you check the delivery log?" he asks. She nods her head and leaves us. "Who do you think did this?" he asks.

"David, 100% without a doubt it's David."

"The flowers came at 11:30 this morning," Alexa says, jogging around the corner.

"What time did she cancel lunch with you?" Vincent asks me.

Quickly I scroll through my log of text messages and find the one. "It was 12:23. We normally meet at 1:00 so it seemed normal."

"I'll call Cara and see if she's home," Alexa interrupts. "She could be there."

"What about the other messages after that? Do they seem like they were from her?"

I read the few I have, and I guess they do. Then it hits me. I only have a few, which is unlike her. "She didn't respond to the last one that I sent her; I know something is wrong. She always has to have the last word."

"Liam!" Vincent yells. Immediately a tall, light-haired male exits a corner office. He's in a suit like Vincent is and comes right over to us. "Everything all right?" he asks, looking at me questioningly.

"Not exactly. This is Bridgette's boyfriend, Troy. Troy, Liam." I shake his hand as Vincent proceeds. "It seems she's gone missing."

"No, she's been taken by her ex," I correct him.

"Sorry," Vincent says.

I glance at Alexa on the phone with Cara, a sheen of white covering her face. The news from Cara must not have been what she was hoping for. She must have been holding things together in hopes that this wasn't possible. Now the realization is sinking in for her like it has for me. Vincent pulls her to him and wraps an arm around her as she continues to talk with tears running down her cheeks. "No, Cara, she's missing." The words are choked up and almost inaudible.

"Can we call the cops?" I ask.

"Without proof, Colorado law prohibits us from filing a missing persons case for twenty-four hours." Liam says.

"Fuck, what can we do?"

"Follow me," Liam says. "I'll hack into her credit cards and bank accounts to see if there have been any charges."

We head into Liam's office, leaving Alexa on the phone with Cara. She's talking a million miles a minute and is so upset at the same time. Liam sits behind a large desk that has four huge, flat panel monitors.

He begins to furiously type away and Vincent asks me, "When was the last text she sent you?"

"Earlier today after she'd cancelled lunch."

"Why don't you try and send a message? Let's keep in contact with this asshole, but don't let him think you know anything."

I stay calm thinking about his idea, although my blood is boiling. I would love for one second, just one second, to have my hands on him. Vincent's idea is a good one; I need to remember her safety first. We can play into this and possibly get the upper hand. "What should I say?"

Liam interjects. "What do you do for a living?"

"I'm a firefighter."

"Tell her that you are working an extra shift for one of the guys. Use a name, but the wrong one, not someone you work with. In these types of cases, the perpetrator wants to hurt the victim in anyway possible so he'll likely read the message to her to accomplish that. He'll want her to know that you are cancelling on her, that he's more reliable than you. The name switch will let her know that you're onto things. She's gonna need to keep up the will to fight until we get there. Be casual, and don't get too sappy. You don't want to piss this bastard off."

I won't be able to make it over tonight. Jacob asked me to work his shift.

I reread my words out loud before I press send. Everyone agrees with the message and now we wait. The room is silent except for Liam's fingers as they busily work the keys of his keyboard. I stare at the screen of my phone, concentrating on Bridgette's picture. I pray to God that I'll receive a message back. She has to be okay.

"What are you checking first?" Vincent asks Liam.

"I pulled her credit report and am hacking into her credit cards. I want to see if there are any hits there. That's normally what they go for first since they tend to have higher limits. If I don't get anything there, I'll check her bank account."

"What's going on?" Alexa asks as she comes into the office.

"Liam is checking Bridgette's credit cards for any new charges," I say.

"Are you all right?" Vincent asks.

She nods her head, hugging him, and then asks, "Can you track her cell phone?"

"It'll take longer and with how cell phone towers bounce signals, it could lead us astray."

I watch Liam. He works like he could do this in his sleep. His eyes bounce from monitor to monitor and his hands move with Mach speed over the keyboard. "How do you know how to do this?" I ask.

He laughs, shaking his head. "You don't want to

know. I've been doing this since I was a kid."

Just then my phone chimes and I squeeze it hard. I swear to God I can't look at it. "Check it," Vincent orders.

Pressing the unlock button, I read the message that's from Bridgette's number. Right away from the words, I know it's not her. *That's all right, love.*

"Love" is what David used to call her.

"What does it say?" Liam asks.

I can't bring myself to speak the words, so I pass my phone to them. *He better not have laid one goddamn finger on her or I swear to God, I'll kill him.* Alexa tears up reading the words. Vincent holds her, handing me back my phone.

"Motherfucker, nothing on the credit cards," Liam exclaims. "I'm going to try her bank account next. Cross your fingers."

We are all silent as everything hangs on the man in front of us. I have no clue how Liam is doing any of this, but that's not for me to worry about. I just need a hit. I need for something to connect so that I have a clue how to find Bridgette. I close my eyes and picture the pure innocence of her face. I can't imagine David doing this to her and how scared she must be. I do my best to stay calm.

"I found something," Liam declares.

"No shit." I run around his desk and stare at the monitors.

"There was a charge at The Up-Country Motel."

"Up-Country? I've never heard of it," I say.

"I believe there's only one in Denver."

"Where is it?" I demand.

"In Denver off of Colfax. I'll drive," Liam says.

We bolt out of his office jogging towards the elevators. Vincent is talking to Alexa and I don't want to be cold-hearted because I know how hard this is on her, but we have to go. Now. Liam and I press the call button and wait. Then Vincent runs after us and Alexa is right behind him, but he stops her. "I'll make sure Abel is here in a few minutes, okay? He'll take you to Cara's. Just please wait, baby, we don't have time to argue."

She sobs, "Please, Vince, she's my sister."

"Alexa, you are not coming with us – end of story. Especially not being pregnant. Go to Cara's with my brother," he snaps, kissing her, and then the three of us get into the elevator. She stands frozen for a moment and then nods her head a few times, blinking through the tears.

Jesus, I had no idea she was pregnant. This stress is the last thing she needs. "I'm sorry, Alexa," I say.

"Don't be. Please just get my baby sister back safely."

I nod my head before the doors close. As the elevator descends, I watch the numbers count down and it has to be the slowest thing I've ever seen. I pray that it doesn't stop. But sure enough, it does on the eleventh floor. *Fuck, please don't let this be a glimpse of what we're in for. No more.* A woman enters and I press the close door button repeatedly, none of us speaking as we head to the ground floor. We all evacuate the elevator in a rush, leaving the lady feeling a little speechless I'm sure. As we race across the parking lot, Liam unlocks the doors to his white Yukon Denali. I get in the passenger seat and Vincent slips behind me.

"Vincent, get me alternate directions in case there's traffic," Liam says backing out of the parking spot. As we are about to exit the lot, he honks at a car taking their time turning, then he guns it and pulls onto the freeway. "I got the directions. I have to call my brother real quick." He's not on the phone but for two minutes and I know Abel is worried because as soon as they hang up, he texts me. *Hang in there. I can't imagine what you're going through.* There are no words I can respond with so I don't text him back. Instead I focus on what's ahead.

"So what's the plan?" I ask.

"We're going to need to find out which room they are in first. If he's dumb enough to use her card, then I'm hoping he'll make this easy on us. I swear I handled a murder case at this hotel, God, over ten years ago. It's pretty run-down, so if we can find the room, we should be able to kick the door in."

"Fuck! Don't say shit like that." His words make my world spin. My breathing escalates and I can't imagine losing her. "Fuckkkk!" I scream.

"Just breathe, man. She's all right or he wouldn't have texted you back."

I swear to fucking God, I'll lose it! It takes everything I have to calm myself. She's my everything, my life, and my future. She is my happiness and I need her. Glancing at the clock, it's 5:54. He's had her for almost six hours. What a fucking nightmare. I'm sure she's scared – so, so, scared. I can't even picture what she's had to endure. I don't want to. I won't let myself go there – not now.

Vincent rests his hand on my shoulder and I know now is not the time to break down. I have to be strong for her. Liam slams on the brakes and yells, "Vincent, I need another route.

He pauses for a brief moment scrolling through his phone and then begins to give out new directions. My phone chimes and instantly everything within the car silences. "It's him," I say looking at the screen.

"What does it say?" Liam asks.

What time are you off?

"Don't respond. We'll be there soon enough."

Sitting in silence I do my best not to text him back. I want to stay in touch, that way he'll be preoccupied and won't hurt her. Maybe this is my entire fault. I should've told her I saw him at Drain – not once, but twice. Had she known, maybe she would've been more cautious than to go to the place where I'd run into him. The guilt I'm experiencing for lying to her is too much. It's so much to handle. Then there is the disappointment she's going to feel when I tell her. However, none of that matters now. As long as she's okay, I don't even care if she hates me for the rest of my life. Did I fuck up? Yes! I never should've lied. I mean, I broke my *own* number one rule.

"Okay, we're here," Liam says, putting the car in park.

I go to get out and he stops me. "NO! Not yet. What does he drive?"

I grip the door handle squeezing so hard my hand hurts and survey the parking lot of cars around us. "There, that black 4-Runner."

Both of the guys follow the direction of my hand and we all stare. Sitting here isn't going to help me, so I ignore his command to stay put and get out and walk towards his car. What if she's inside of it? I have to know. If she's not, then I don't give a shit what room he's in. I'll make sure he hears me and comes out!

"Troy!" Vincent yells, running after me and grabbing my arm. "Would you wait a minute? We don't know what room they're in."

Anger boils my insides; every nerve ending is ready to snap. As I turn to him with my fists balled at my sides, I ask, "What would you do if this was Lex?" He shakes his head and lets go of my arm. I cup my hands around my eyes and look into the dark tint of the windows. It's empty; she's not in there. I begin to search the ground hunting for anything big enough I can use to throw at his car. I need to get this motherfucker out of his room.

Liam slams his door as I find a rock the size of a watermelon. I lift it with all of my strength. I can see Vincent and Liam staring at me. I know they agree with me or they would be stopping me. This is the fastest way to find out which room she's in. Taking every ounce of force, I toss the boulder through his front windshield. It pops likes a firework on the Fourth of July and then caves in, a million little pieces around it, crumbling.

His alarm starts to go off and the three of us stand, staring at the motel. I'm looking for any signs of movement in the windows. There's commotion in quite a few. Curious onlookers stare out to see what all the ruckus is – then I spot him. His black eyes lock with mine as he peeks through the fabric of the curtain. I'll never forget the depth of despair in those eyes. He's so fucking pathetic.

I race for the stairs, running as fast as I can, and the guys follow me up. Immediately I begin to bang on the door. "Bridge," I scream.

"Move," Liam orders and he begins to kick the door with all of his might. Each blow he makes causes the door to budge. He's making progress – it's slow, but progress. Then the manager comes running up the stairs yelling at us. I can't focus on her right now, all I see is red. We need to get this door open before she stops us. Thankfully Vincent intercepts her, stopping her dead in her tracks. Then by the grace of God, it flies open.

"Troy!" is the next thing I hear. It's the best noise I've ever heard and from the sweetest set of lungs. There's a ring of panic to it, but that's okay – I'm here and she's alive. I don't look for David or anyone else. My instincts move me right towards her; there is nothing in this moment that could stop me. Once our eyes connect, the sight of her hits me hard. She's huddled on the top corner of the bed, tied to the headboard. Dried blood runs down her mouth, and her cheeks are tear-stained with mascara. Through it all, I can see the reassurance in her eyes.

"Where is he?" Liam asks.

She tips her head towards the bathroom door. Reaching into my pocket, I grab my keys and knife to begin cutting her free. I can hear Vincent fighting outside with the manager, and then he finally runs in.

"Where is he?" he asks.

I point in the direction of the bathroom and keep working on the ropes. Jesus, he used enough to tie down a grizzly bear. Finally I get the last piece off of her wrists.

"Does he have any weapons, baby?"

"A Taser."

Then Liam opens the door. Both Bridge and I watch him; he looks like a machine as his chest puffs out breathing heavily. I prepare for God only knows what. Then he stands back and says, "It's empty."

Both he and Vincent run out of the room. As much as I want to catch David too, I can't leave her, not now that I finally have her back. I breathe her scent in, enjoying being right next to her. Then I make the mistake of looking down at her wrists. Bile rises to the back of my throat at the sight of her poor, mangled arms. I place my hands gently over them. They have been rubbed almost raw and are completely black and blue. "Fuck, baby. He hurt you." I say, embracing her in my arms, pulling her to me as tightly as I can.

She shakes her head and I hold her close. She clings to

me, sobbing into my neck without answering. "Dammit, baby, what did he do?"

"Just get me out of here, please."

Faintly, I hear the sirens in the distance and it's such a reassuring feeling to know that help is on the way. Pulling away from Bridgette, I look into her eyes and hold her face in my hands. "Are you okay?" I ask, needing some form of reassurance from her. She nods her head, I help her up, and we head out to meet the ambulance together.

Chapter 28

Get Away

For the first time all day I feel calm. My breathing has come back to me; I'm no longer grasping at it like it's lost in the dark. What was once stark terror is nothing but a distant memory. I know we will forever be haunted by today's events, but it's nothing we can't fight through together.

I put my Jeep in park in front of the cabin and look at my sleeping girl. I hate to wake her; I know this is the only time she will feel at peace. But I want to get her inside. The moment we were done with the cops and all the crazy shit of the day, I knew this was where we needed to be. Quickly, I walk around the car and lift her out, cradling her in my arms against my chest. She looks so comfortable in her soft sweats. I'm happy she talked me into stopping by and packing a bag for us. On the way inside, the stairs below my feet creak, but she doesn't move. Gently, I lay her on the couch and cover her up with a soft blanket from the back. I bring in our bags and the cooler of food I emptied from her fridge. As I set everything down, I lock the door and run downstairs to make sure the other doors are still locked. Call me paranoid, but I will not risk her safety *ever* again.

Once I have her in my line of sight again, I cannot help but stare at her. It takes everything inside of me to not lie on top of her and crush our bodies together. I yearn for her, like nothing I've ever known. Pulling my eyes away I decide to start a fire to keep busy; I know how much she loves the sound of crackle. I figure it will also help her stay asleep.

Quietly I place a fire starter log on the bottom and then stack a few pieces of dry wood on top of it. I strike the match, lighting the paper of the log and watch the amber colors slowly come to life. It doesn't take long until all of the wood is engulfed. Sitting down in front of it, I watch the flames so wild and precious all at the same time.

I can't even begin to imagine what she went through. However, when she's ready to tell me, I'll listen and be there for her. I'm sure it'll hurt worse than any experience in my life, but for her, I'll endure it. Then I'm going to need to learn how to put all of this shit behind me – it's done. *But it's not.* David's still out there somewhere and who knows what he is thinking and plotting. It's not really over with until he's behind bars.

Resting my head on my knees, I close my eyes and images of the police officer snapping photos of her wrists flash before my eyes. They jerk open and I blink a few times, checking my reality. She's still asleep and peaceful. I don't know why he had to hurt her arms. Had it been any other part of her body, I probably could have handled it better. But fuck, her sweet and delicate wrists. I know I'll never be able to tie her up or hold her down. Not again.

My body is so tense, I decide to sprawl out on the plush bearskin rug and watch her sleep. It's brown and soft; I've loved it ever since I was a kid. Resting my head in the crook of my arm, I stare at Bridge. I don't dare close my eyes. It's too daunting, and the images of what I might see…frighten me. She stirs a little and makes a small noise. I can't help but smile at how adorable she is. My phone buzzes in my pocket and I pull it out checking the few missed text messages. They are from everyone wanting to know how Bridgette is. Thankfully, Alexa and Cara met us at Bridgette's place so the girls got to see her and know for themselves that she is all right. Well, as good as can be expected. All in all, everyone agreed this was the best plan and the best place for Bridgette.

I take my time responding and then a flash of movement catches the corner of my eye. I look to see Bridgette awake. She walks over to me, wrapped in her throw and is as comfortable as ever. "Hi," she whispers.

"Come here, baby," I say opening my arms to her. She snuggles under me as I'm on my side and looks at me with a lost expression.

"Please tell me this was all a dream."

I shake my head and blink back the pain as water wells

up in my eyes. For the first time in many years, I feel like I could cry. Tightly, she closes hers and tears slip over the sides. In that moment, I'm at a loss for words. I search for the right thing to say, but there's nothing. Without knowing what else to do, I kiss her, pressing my lips to hers. The guilt I feel is almost unbearable. This is all my fault so I try and give her some of my strength as a measure of consolation.

"What's wrong?" she asks.

I shake my head, holding her face. "I'm sorry. I'm so, so sorry."

"Troy, this is not your fault. Please don't think for one second that it is."

I know now is when I have to be honest. I hope to God that she can find it within her heart to forgive me. My stomach is nauseous with fear. I don't know what will follow, with her knowing the truth, because I can't bear losing her. How am I supposed to protect her if she doesn't want me?

"It *is* my fault." I pause and wait for a reaction while she looks at me confused. She doesn't speak so I continue. "I saw David twice at Drain, once was with you and I acted like an asshole kissing you and manhandling you in front of him." I pause again. "The next was when I grabbed some to-go food. He asked if you had already left me. I…I told him you were naked and in my bed waiting for me."

"Why didn't you tell me about this?"

"I wanted to, trust me. The first time you'd just gotten the news about Robert and then it was your birthday. The time never seemed right. I knew I should be honest with you. I regret that now more than anything. I'm so sorry, baby, you have to know that. I love you more than anything and I *never* meant for any of this to happen."

She's looking into my eyes and it scares me. I mean, she's really looking into me. The world moves in slow motion in the next few moments, as she opens her mouth and begins to speak, I cannot believe her words. I must have heard her wrong because she should be running away from me and slamming doors. I lied to her and broke *our* number one rule, *my* number one rule, but she isn't. Instead with more clarity than I've ever heard before, she says, "I love you, Troy. Goddammit, I fucking love—"

Before she can finish her sentence, I invade her mouth, crashing my tongue against hers. She wholeheartedly accepts me and loves me. Fuck, I need her. I have to have her and that is all there is to it. I know he didn't do anything to her sexually, that's the one thing I had to ask. It was eating me up. Thankfully, what happened was physical and mental. I can fix the mental part. That's what I'm good at.

Her body fits beneath mine perfectly. Taking one of my hands I slide it across her stomach and work my way up 'til I have a handful of one of her breasts. "Say it again."

"I love you," she speaks breathlessly as I leave a trail

of kisses down her neck. I unzip her hoody, exposing her dark swollen nipples as they strain the fabric of her white tank top.

"Again."

"I love you, Troy." Her words drive me out of this fucked up world and into my zone. Where I can be *me*. Where I don't have a care in the world. Uncontrollably, I tear the fabric of her tank, splitting it right down the middle. I'm rewarded with a moan and she says, "Take me with you."

Following her wishes, I continue to tease her nipples. My touch causes her to wiggle underneath me and I grind my erection into her.

The moment she rakes her fingernails down my back, my body becomes pure sensation. Jesus, her touch does crazy things to me. Pulling away from her mouth, I kneel between her legs, sliding my hands under the waistband of her pants. As I remove them, she watches my every move.

"Will you take your top off? I need you naked."

Sitting up, she removes her hoody and shredded tank top, then lies back down and I can't stop myself from spreading her wide and loving her clit – my clit. She's so special; I never knew I could feel this way and have it be with someone who accepted me, knowing who I truly am.

Taking her hands, she locks them into my hair and I'm rewarded with her sweet moans. I know what this does to her. She's so close to coming and so quickly, and I want to take her there. Insistently, I move the way she likes, giving her clit the right amount of pressure. She begins to spiral and mumbles some nonsense; she's dirty like me. But the last part, I hear clear as day. *Fuck, those words*. Once she settles, I pull away and remove my shirt and pants. I barely kick them off before descending into her, filling her with all of me.

Once I am nestled to the hilt, she wraps her arms and legs around me. I slide my arms underneath her fragile body holding her tight and nuzzle my face into the crook of her neck. As we stay connected like this, a wave of emotions takes over and the events of today crash into me. Fear – anger – panic – they all come barreling down. Everything I experienced earlier all wrapped up into one hard blow and it knocks me sideways.

Finally, I give in and begin to cry, letting out all of the pent up emotions. She doesn't speak or try to calm me and tell me that everything's going to be okay. Instead, she holds me, giving me time and her strength. We are a good team like this, the way we feed off of each other and support one another. With Bridge, things have been like this since the beginning. That's how I knew deep down she would accept me.

She forces me to look into her eyes, holding my face tightly in the palms of her hands. I'm almost ashamed to be crying in front of her. I've never let anyone see me like this, and I never would have – until her. Tightening the walls of her pussy around my cock, she reminds me of what's important… Us. This. Our future. Her safety. Not the past. Yes, it's part of us and now molds who we are. But hell, today I almost lost her and I'll be damned if I forget how that feeling of fear affected me.

Pressing my lips to hers, I begin to move. Taking my sweet time with each pull and push. Being with her is amazing; it's honestly hard to tell if this is real or if I'm dreaming. Her movements become intense as each slow, deliberate filling causes her to want more. I can't help the intensity of wanting to please her. My instincts tell me to grab her wrists, but I don't. I know I'd never forgive myself. Finally, I pull away needing to see her, I need to know that she is real. She has her eyes closed as I hover above her and her arms are stretched above her head. My eyes become fixated on her breasts as they bounce with each thrust.

"Fuck," she whines. I know I've got her spot and I stay right where I am. Watching her like this, so close, pushes me over the edge. I keep a steady rhythm as I pump myself inside of her. God, I love coming in her. It's such a turn on. I can't help my noises, but dammit I never can. She knows me far too well and lets go simultaneously, gripping the rug above her, as amber shadows blaze over our skin.

She cries out, letting go, coming into my world where I will forever keep her. The pain cannot hurt her here. This is our safe haven and a place I wish we could forever live.

Chapter 29

The Story

"Do you want to eat something?" I ask.

"You," she jokes.

"I'm serious."

"Fine, what can you make us?"

"Let me check." I pull out of her and hate the feeling – so desolate. She goes to sit up. "Stay there, please. You are so gorgeous after being fucked." There's not much to do up here but have sex and…have sex. We've only been here for two days, but that's all we've been doing besides sleeping.

"I don't know how gorgeous I look right now, but thank you."

"I'll still spank you for talking like that."

She smirks at me, rolling over and propping her ass up in the air. Immediately, I jog over to her, squeezing one of her round cheeks while I swat the other. Her breathing halts and she lays back down.

"Didn't think I would do that, did ya?"

"Definitely not."

"You liked it and you know it."

"Damn you for being so fucked up and turning me on by it. You know it's one of the things I love about you."

"I'm glad to know it. I love you too." I open the fridge and there's not much inside. I take out a loaf of bread and some jelly. I open a cabinet looking for the peanut butter I left from the last time we visited. "How does a PB&J sound?"

"That's good with me."

I make our sandwiches as fast as I can and grab a bottle of water. As I return to the couch and sit back down next to her naked body, she rolls on her side looking a little glum. "What's wrong?"

"I…I just…I need to get what happened off of my chest. You haven't asked but a few questions."

"I don't want to upset you, baby. I figure when you are ready you will tell me."

"I'm ready."

"Then I'm ready too, as long as you'll eat a little."

She takes a nibble off of half a sandwich and then sets it back down. Swallowing hard, she begins to speak and I kiss the top of her hair, knowing I'm as afraid to hear what she has to say as she is to speak the words.

"I got the flowers that morning, then I had to meet with Liam, and by the time I checked my phone I had to go." She pauses and looks at me. I give her a reassuring smile, letting her know she can take all the time in the world.

"The note inside the flowers said for me to meet *you* at Drain, and you know that's my favorite place, so I didn't even question it. Since we meet every day for lunch, I just went. I tried to call you on the way, but got your voicemail, so I figured I would see you there. When I parked and didn't see your car, I headed in to order our food. As I was getting out of my car, I noticed someone was behind me and my body froze. Everything happened so quickly. I was in excruciating pain and I realized I was being tasered. That's the last thing I remember before everything went dark."

My breathing catches, thinking of what she must have gone through. The pain had to have been unbearable. Being tasered is no fucking joke. It will drop a beast of a man to his knees in the blink of an eye, much less a hundred and twenty-pound woman. "Then when I came to, he was slapping me, demanding that I wake up. My hands were tied together and he already had me in the motel room."

She looks down at her wrists and I can't bear to bring my eyes to look at them. "I tried to plead with him to let me go. I told him if he ever cared for me he wouldn't do this. There were moments that I thought he might give in. Then he would snap. After you texted me about your cock, he was irate."

"I'm so sorry."

She continues, holding my hand. "He pinned me

down, sitting on top of me, and said *his* cock misses me, and why don't I care about that. The pressure from his body on top of me and me still being tied to the bed is what did this to my wrists. I fought him off the best I could and at that point figured I couldn't convince him to let me go, so I told him I was in love with you.

"You did?" I ask baffled. She nods her head. "Did he say why he did this?"

"Not really. I asked and asked, pleading with him to tell me why. He only said because we were meant for each other. He kept saying how much he loves me. Then he changed and I saw a different side of him. He's a hardcore drug user; I watched it happen right before my eyes. He became a monster getting so spun out of his mind that he could barely function. I watched him lie on that bed, like a fucking zombie, then as he was coming out of it…" She swallows hard, looking at me.

I don't know if I want to hear what's next, but I know that nothing sexual happened so I tell her, "It's okay, baby."

"Are you sure?"

"Yes, if you want to tell me, I want to hear it all." I can make it through this for her. I'm not the one who had to live through it all.

"He wanted to do stuff with me, but he couldn't get hard. I acted like I wanted it, and he started to soften up to me. My plan was when he untied me, to fight, kick, scream, and do anything possible to get out of there, but it never happened. He was so up and down, so he reverted to the drugs, doing more and more. He's nothing but a fucking crackhead, Troy."

"You're so strong and brave. If I haven't told you already, I'm proud of you, more than you'll ever know."

"I honestly don't know if I could have made it through all of this, had I not had you waiting for me. You're all I thought about. You made me fight and stay strong."

Softly, I kiss her lips and neither of us speaks another word regarding David or the events that took place. We finish our food in silence and then cuddle up on the couch. As much as our reasons for being up here are not ideal, it's wonderful to be alone. Right when we drift off to sleep, my cell phone rings. I reach away from her grabbing it and hope she doesn't wake.

She stays in the crook of my arm, comfy and adorable. "Hello," I answer in a bit of a groggy tone.

"Troy?" an unfamiliar voice asks.

"This is him."

"Hey, man, it's Liam. How are you guys doing?"

"Oh, hey, dude, thanks for calling me back. We're good, considering; just making the best of our time."

Bridgette wiggles next to me and I know I've woken her. "No problem. I wanted you to know I talked to my guy at the station, and he knows the officers pretty well that got assigned to the case. He said they have had a few leads. So far they've interviewed David's parents and neither one of them has spoken to him for months. They pulled phone records to confirm that as well."

"What about Bridgette's phone? Has it shown up?"

"Not yet, but it's bound to and it will only lead them closer. It's likely he's holding on to it for some sort of sentimental value."

"God, he's so fucked up."

"I know. I'll keep you updated. Have you guys heard from the investigators at all?"

"Not a peep."

"All right, hang tight, I'll keep you posted and we'll talk soon."

I hang up and look down at my doe-eyed girl. She's calling me to her with those eyes. "What?" I ask.

"You. You're…so perfect."

"Come on, I'm pretty fucked up. You even said so yourself."

"You have your quirks, but I love all of them."

"What do you say we get out of this place for a bit?"

She stares at me questioningly. "I don't know, babe, I feel safe here. I don't want to risk anything."

"Are you sure? Even for a drive?"

"Not yet, maybe tomorrow?"

"What about the hot tub?"

She nods her head. "Yes, please."

I lift her from the couch and carry her out to the deck. The clouds are starting to roll in. It's a perfect day for the hot tub with the cooler temperatures. Thankfully, we left the lid off last night, so I effortlessly walk us up the stairs and set her down on the ledge. Taking our time, we both sit and wade our feet in the fiery water.

I love that since we've been here, neither of us has cared much to put any clothes on. A light breeze rustles through the air causing her nipples to harden. She dips into the water and I laugh at her brazenness. Her breathing ceases as the burning water engulfs her. "What that worth it?" I ask.

"Yeah. Why don't you get in here with me?"

I slide in, sitting across from her, and stretch my long legs out. "How long are we going to stay here?" she asks.

"Until they find him."

"Troy, that could take forever."

Giving her a crooked smile, I think about forever up here, in this house, away from everyone, and I ask, "Is that a problem?"

"What about our jobs?"

"Vincent and Liam said you are *not* to return until they find David. And Abel told me not to worry about things. He's got my back."

She huffs like I'm joking and scrunches her eyebrows at me. "What about money?"

"Oh, uh…Vincent is kinda paying you and I have a shitload of cash saved up from working wild fires this year."

"He's what?!" she snaps.

"Hey, yell at him, not me."

"God, he's as bad as my sister is with babying me."

"They love you, honey, just like I do. Let us take care of you. Don't put a time constraint on this whole situation. Let it be."

"Okay," she whispers, running her hands over her hair and resting her head back. She's so relaxed and comfortable. I love to see her like this. She senses that I'm staring and moves over, clambering onto my lap.

Her tight body awakens my senses. Reaching between us, she grips my dick, causing it to become hard as a rock.

Moving down between us, I take control and rub myself on her clit. The friction causes her to go mad rubbing herself against me, until finally she engulfs me. I sink deep inside of her, taking water with me and I rest my hands on her thighs, letting her take full control.

I want her to do this for us. I need her to do this for us. I can't imagine how she's managed to come out so…strong. Tipping her head back, she begins to move and I follow suit, resting back myself. "Oh God, fuck me, baby."

She moans at my words and moves faster – harder. The water is a barrier, stopping her from really getting going. Regardless of the speed, any time inside of her, I treasure. Her body was made for me, every last detail about it. Right down to these perky ass breasts; watching them bounce drives me crazy. I grab each of them, pulling her down to me and pinch them in between my fingers. "Do you like this?" I ask.

"Mmm-hmm."

"What about this?" I ask sneaking a hand under the water and pinching her clit.

"Yes," she hisses and I know I have her right where I want her.

I continue to torture her clit, watching how my touch affects her body. She has her head hung back and eyes tightly shut. I can see her neck and profile perfectly. With each movement, the tips of her hair hit the water and begin to splash my arm as my hand is now spread across her back. I move my hips under her and suddenly she lets go, out of nowhere she comes fiercely, screaming my name while holding the back of my head.

Of its own accord, my body lets go with her. It has a mind of its own and doesn't care that my brain wants to keep fucking her. My orgasm is as strong as ever, and Bridgette keeps a tight hold on my dick, milking every last drop of cum out of me. We stare at one another as our bodies come back down to earth.

Taking my hand, I brush her hair over her shoulder and hold her body to mine. We sit close together, silent, until she finally speaks. "I don't think I can go back home to the condo."

"Why?" I ask a bit puzzled.

"David told me he watched me there a lot. That's how he knew where I worked…from following me. He said he loved to watch me sleep. God, Troy, what if they don't catch him?"

"They will, baby."

"But if not, we can't stay here forever."

"Move in with me." The words leave my mouth before I realize what I've said, and I couldn't be more sure of them. My only fear is she'll shoot me down, but now's not the time for my self-doubt. I think she knows this is what's right.

"Are you sure?"

"Yes! Absolutely, yes! I want to wake up with you every day, and come home to you every night. Regardless of David or what happens, I want us to live together."

"Okay."

"So it's settled?"

She nods her head, pulling away from me and I grab her, holding both sides of her face as we kiss. I don't need the words, her mouth tells me what I want to hear – it's settled.

Chapter 30

Home

It's been almost a week and she's right…we can't stay here forever. The call came this morning that Alexa wasn't a bone marrow match for Robert, so Bridgette made the decision to go and get tested. I'm not sure how I feel about her going back to the city, considering what happened and with that freak still out there. But we'll get it done. Plus, my gut's telling me he's smart enough to stay away.

I also promised my mother that we would have dinner with her and I really don't feel like letting her down again. I already cancelled over the weekend. As much as I don't want to see my dad, I know he would bathe in the glory of another one-up on me.

"You ready to go, babe?" I ask Bridge after loading the last bag into the Jeep.

"Yeah. I am. I know I have you to get me through whatever is thrown my way."

"Damn straight you do." I open her door and kiss her cheek as she slides in. Her tan legs look gorgeous against the contrast of the black leather. Walking around the car, I take one last look at the house. I know this won't be the last time we'll visit here, but leaving weighs heavy on my heart. Both of us love this place; it's come to be one of our favorite spots.

"What time is your appointment again?" I ask.

"2:15, it's at Cara's hospital. I figured we could stop by and say hi to her if she's not busy, then grab some of my stuff before we go to your place."

"Our place," I promptly correct her.

"Right. Sorry."

She should know I already took care of having all of her stuff moved, but I want to surprise her. I called Alexa after she said she would move in with me and she helped. She said not to worry about a thing and hired a moving company to take care of it all.

She lets out a long yawn and rests her head on my shoulder.

"Take a nap, babe. We have a long drive ahead of us." Slowly she nods her head, closing her eyes. I hold her face as I back out and breathe her in. I love how close she is to me, how close we've become. There's a connection that we share; it's been there since I pressed my lips to her finger the night she cut it at the station.

She didn't know it at the time, but I was a mess. I'd wasted so much time contemplating even talking to her. Self-doubt was my enemy in the beginning. Looking down at her now, I'm grateful beyond any words that I pushed past all of my fears and pursued her.

As the highway rolls by, seconds feel like minutes. It must be because I am lost in my own head thinking over the past. My mind swirls a million miles a minute with absurd thoughts. What if David takes her again? What if us living together is too soon? What if I can't resist tying her up? What if she finds someone else? Then all at once, it hits me…

What if this is all right? What if everything is as it should be? What if all of the trials and tribulations we have been through have had a purpose – a meaning? I hold on to that thought. Carrying positivity with me is way better than the negative. Bridgette has shown me that worrying about the what-ifs isn't going to help anyone. Right now is all that we have and all that matters. I have her next to me, she is safe, and I'll keep her that way –forever – end of story.

As we get close to the hospital, surprisingly it feels good to be home, not scary like I'd imagined. I know Bridgette is ready to get this over with and I want to help her. We found out there's no reason to see Robert. Alexa didn't have to and Bridgette agreed to do the same. I think it's a good decision. He's damn lucky that they are even getting tested. Had it been me, with my dad, I don't know if I would get tested and I know the prick.

If she's a match, they will remove her stem cells and harvest them until he is ready for transplant, which would all happen soon – very soon. Deep down, I hope she's not a match. I don't want her to have to go through any more pain. I want her to look forward to a bright and positive, pain-free future.

Leaning down, I kiss her neck and rub my thumb across her plump lips. "We're here, baby," I say, sitting in the hospital parking lot that I know far too well.

She moans a little and keeps her eyes tightly shut. "Bridge, it's five after, we have to get checked in."

She throws her arm across me and it lands in my lap. *Fuck.* Picking it up, I kiss the top of her hand and she lifts her head. "Come on, you can't be that tired," I tease.

"You have no idea, I am soooooo tired," she grumbles.

"Well, let's get this over with and I'll take you home and put you to bed."

She cocks a brow at me as we get out of the car. "That doesn't sound like sleep at all. That sounds like fun."

"Same difference. I don't care if you're awake or not."

"Gross."

I'm joking with her in hopes she won't be nervous to be back in the city and start looking over her shoulder. "What floor, again?" I ask as we get into the elevator.

"Four."

"Four?" I say questioningly. She catches right on to my game and laughs.

"Yes, four."

"You like that number, huh?"

"Yes."

There's a couple with us stopping me from saying more. Then they exit on the third floor. "Three?" I question, gesturing for her exit.

"Nah, I've had three, I like four. I've never had four."

"Then tonight, you will."

I squeeze her hand as the doors open. Walking out, the waiting area is slow and thankfully that makes check-in a breeze. The clerk asks us to have a seat. Then a nurse, an older female who reminds me of my mom, takes us back. They go through all of the pros and cons of the process and what to expect if she is a match. Personally, I feel like it's a bit too much information considering she's only here to get a simple blood test.

Then I get a death gripping squeeze of my hand, and a few vials of blood later, we're out of there. "Jesus, that was a lot of information," Bridgette gripes.

"I know, but now it's over with and you'll have the results soon."

I pull her to me and she wraps her arm around my waist. "Do you want to go and see Cara?"

She nods her head and I take us over to the ER. Margaret, the usual receptionist, is behind the counter and gives us a toothy smile when she sees me.

She waves to the right and opens the doors so we can go back into the ER. "Troy, what brings you in?" she asks as we approach the counter.

"We're here to see Cara."

"I'll page her," she says and calls Cara over the intercom. I glance at Bridge who is smiling at me and I'm sure it's because of my clear friendship with a fifty-some-year-old woman. "Well, aren't you going to introduce me to your girlfriend?"

I smile at the fact that she knows who Bridgette is. When I was in the hospital last, Margaret would sneak me in snacks, and let's say she got to hear me talk about Bridgette, especially when I was a little loopy on pain medication. After I went on and on, Bridgette showed up and brought me dinner one night. So yeah, Margaret knows exactly who she is.

"Margaret, this is my girlfriend, Bridgette. Bridge, this is Margaret."

The two of them shake hands. "It's nice to meet you. Troy has told me so much about you," Margaret says.

"Really?" she asks with a bit of surprise to her tone.

"Yes, dear, I'm very happy to see that things worked out."

"Thank you!"

"Bridge!" Cara yells from across the ER as she comes running over to us.

"Excuse us," I say to Margaret as we head toward the pregnant woman on speed who is about to pummel down my girlfriend. The girls embrace like they haven't seen one another in years. I can't help but laugh at them. It's only been a little over a week.

"How are you?" Cara asks as they separate.

"Good, you?"

"I'm fucking tired. You look skinny, why aren't you eating? Troy you need to start feeding her."

"I have been, but she eats like a bird."

"Well, now that you two are living together, you can make sure she eats more. Have I told you guys how happy I am for you?"

"Thanks," Bridgette says.

Cara gets called over the intercom. "I'm sorry. I gotta run, but I want you both over for dinner this week. You have to see the house and how nice it looks now that everything's all unpacked. Plus, we have to nail down our Vegas plans."

"I can't wait," Bridgette says.

The girls hug and I wave goodbye to Cara as she runs off. "Let's go home," Bridgette says. It's the first time she has called my house hers, and hearing the words come so freely from her mouth makes me smile. *Thank God, she's mine.*

I don't know why she didn't bring up stopping by her place, but it's a-okay with me. It's empty. "Since Cara said you're not eating enough, what do you want for dinner?"

"Can we order pizza? I would love a big, greasy pizza."

"Sure we can. I got something else that's big, and after I lube it up, it will be greasy for you."

"Hmmm, that too."

We approach the Jeep and she reaches over, rubbing my cock through my pants. I take my hand and grab the back of her hair, guiding her mouth up to mine. It's such a turn on to be doing this in public, everything else washes away as I pin her against my car and claim her mouth. She gives right into me and I pull her hands tightly together as they are between us. Instantly, she panics, ripping them out of my grip and I know I've gone too far. I got lost in the moment and didn't think. What's wrong with me? And why am I kissing her like this, outside, when he's still on the loose?

"I'm sorry, baby. Jesus, I'm sorry. I don't know what I was thinking."

She looks up at me with tears in her eyes and I hold her body tightly to mine. "It's okay. Can we just go?"

"Of course." *What where you thinking, motherfucker?* Quickly I walk her around and help her into the Jeep. As I shut the door, she gives me a small smile and I get into the driver's seat as fast as I can. Neither of us says much on the drive. What can I say? I fucked up. I know that. I need to take this time to figure out how I'm going to convince her that I don't need that, I only need her. The kink and all of that doesn't matter. We'll make it work, whatever *it* turns out to be. I just have to keep myself in check, even in the heat of the moment.

"You okay?" I ask as I park in front of the house.

She nods her head. And her silence hurts me. It's not fair that she can't be herself. The free spirit she was before this shit happened. Leaning over, I kiss her and she doesn't resist. In fact, I even get a light smile when I pull away. I can work with this, so I hop out of my Jeep and jog around to her door, opening it. But before she can step out, I lift her in my arms. She clings to me and I love the feeling of this closeness.

Walking up to our house, I fumble with the lock, determined not to set her down, and then finally get the door open. There are boxes everywhere, and I smile seeing her stuff here. Taking my foot, I kick the door closed, setting her down.

"Is this all of my stuff?" she asks.

I nod my head and ask, "How does it feel?"

"Good," she says and I guide us to sit on the couch.

"Listen, about earlier at the hospital, I'm so sorry. I don't know what I was thinking. It'll never happen again."

"Thank you for saying that, but what if it does? What if I can't give you what you need?"

"Baby, you do. Don't say things like that. You being you *is* enough. I don't need anything else."

"Troy, don't bullshit me. I know what you need."

"I can tell you right now that you getting all worked up has me so hot that it's taking all of my willpower to not bend you over the arm of this couch and fuck you senseless."

"Have I told you how much I love your dirty mouth?"

"No, tell me, what does it do to you?"

"It turns me on, beyond anything imaginable."

"What else? Tell me what else turns you on?"

"Your touch," she says taking my hand in hers and

firmly pressing it to her boobs. I can't stop myself from exposing her and pulling those perky nipples out of her bra. "Troy, the window's open!"

"I don't give a shit, I want to see your nipples."

She lies back laughing at me and I follow suit, pressing my body fully against hers. My erection is anxious, yearning to be inside of her. I grind it against her, showing her how hot she makes me. With the same passion I'm showing her sex, she rips my shirt above my head and connects our lips. She takes control and plunges her tongue into my mouth. I accept it, loving every minute of her crazy escapade.

Reaching between us, she fumbles with my pants. I slide my hand down inside of hers, parting that sweet pussy and rubbing her. My touch stops her right away. She looks at me with heavy lids, loving the attention. "You like this, don't you?"

"God, yes."

"What about this?" I ask as I sink two fingers deep inside of her cunt.

"Fuck," she hisses, bucking her hips towards my hand. I work her and I'm not gentle, slapping my hand on her clit as I do so. My dick pulsates wanting to fuck her just like this. It's an invigorating feeling, watching what you're capable of doing to another person. I know she's close to orgasm, as she bites her bottom lip and squeezes my fingers tightly. My phone begins to ring and she looks at me. I don't falter and say in a demanding tone, "Come for me, baby."

She nods her head, ignoring the noise, and closes her eyes again. Her body quivers in pleasure and as I watch the orgasm roll out of her, I appreciate her, quite possibly more than ever. She's perfect in every motherfucking way imaginable. I want to show her that and can't seem to get my pants down fast enough. She gestures me over to her and I oblige. Gripping my cock, she takes me into her mouth as she lays on the couch.

Those tight lips wrap so securely around the head and slowly I ease myself into her. She works my shaft as she licks and sucks me. A low growl escapes me. Christ, her lips are pure paradise, there's nothing else in this world that compares to them. *Well, maybe her cunt.* "Mmmmmmhhhhh," she moans as I reach down, touching her again.

Then my goddamn phone rings and it angers me that someone's blowing me up. Who in the world could need me so badly that they have to call me back to back? I let it go to voicemail and then it rings again. I pull out of Bridgette's mouth and grab it out of my pocket. The number is unknown and I answer in anger.

"Troy Sorano, please," a male voice asks.

"This is."

"Troy, this is James Ackerman from the Denver police department. I'm a friend of Liam Brown, he asked me to keep an eye on the case and call you first if we made an arrest. I'm happy to report authorities picked up Mr.

Boulge in Texas this morning. He is being transported back to the state as we speak."

"That's great news. Thank you, James."

"I'm happy too. I know how horrible this was for both of you. I'll be in touch."

"Thank you, man."

We hang up and I can tell Bridgette knows what I'm going to say before I can get the words out of my mouth. "They caught him?" she asks.

"Yes, baby. It's over."

She begins to cry and I lay on top of her, holding her firmly to me, gently kissing those sweet lips over and over. She kisses me back and pulls away, looking into my eyes. "It's over," she says and I repeat the words back to her. "Can we never speak of him again?" she asks.

"Of course, I want nothing more. Well, I do want something more." Sitting up on my knees, I remove her pants, adoring the perfection that is her body as she lies below me. Moving down, I open her wide and blow a cool breath of air on her hot sex. She squirms, trying to close her legs, but I stop her. I want her spread open for me. I always want her open for me – she's mine after all.

Diving in, I tease her clit and sink my two fingers back inside of her. As I work her body and watch the pleasure roll out of her like waves of the ocean, she looks different, almost like all of her fears have washed away. This is the girl I first met and fell in love with. I find her spot and suck her swollen clit all at the same time. She screams, gripping the couch, and pushes against me. She's no match though. I smile and push her out of this universe.

"Fuck, Troy," she moans, letting go, twitching beneath my control. I don't stop my movements as her body slows and this only draws out her come that much longer. "Fuck, fuck, fuck," she begins to chant and I know I've pushed her again. Thrashing back and forth, my little sex goddess has turned into a machine.

Quivers of sensation move through me watching her. I can't wait to fuck her. I need to be inside of her pussy again. Finally she pushes my hand away and I know I've pushed my luck.

Heavy breaths travel through her and I know she needs a minute. I'm a gentleman after all, so I wait patiently rather than pummeling inside of her. Gently, I cover her face, neck, chest, stomach, arms, and legs with kisses. I can tell the attention is making her tired.

"Don't get tired on me, baby. You told me four, that was only three."

"I'm not tired," she responds. "I was just enjoying the attention."

"And I love giving it." Slowly I nudge my cock against her sex, only penetrating her in the slightest. Taking my time, I rock myself gently in and out of her, until she stops me by sitting up. We are face to face, and I turn her sitting with my back on the couch. Leaning over, I close the blinds, because the truth is I don't want anyone to see what's mine. Then she pulls her tank top above her head and I unclasp her bra, removing it down those soft arms of hers.

As she begins to move, I grip her thighs guiding her up and down my shaft. She works hard to pleasure us, milking me like I need. She's so good at this that I have to work hard not to come. Each pull and push is a battle. Looking at her as she moans, I'm unbelievably turned on and can't fight it any longer. Taking one of my hands, I grab the back of her hair and pull her to me, taking her mouth in mine.

The moment we connect like this, my cock deep inside of her…I let go. Coming hard and somehow holding onto her even harder. She takes all of me as I am giving it. Then she leans back bracing herself on my knees and readjusts her feet. This is all her, I cannot help her at this angle. Sitting back, I get comfy and do the only thing I can to get her to come a fourth time – I touch the clit. The moment there is friction there, her noises change; she likes this. In fact, I can tell by the spasms of her pussy that she likes this very much.

"Keep your eyes on me."

She nods her head. There are no words, only sounds. She's doing what she likes and I love every minute of it. Watching her causes my balls to tighten and I know she's taking me with her. Right before my release, I hold my breath fighting it stronger than ever, but I fail miserably, letting go and telling her how much I love her as my cum fills her for the second time.

There's something about the connection of coming inside of her. Part of me now lives in her. She moans the words back, letting go. Taking my hands, I hold her sides and help her slam up and down on my cock, working out every last drop. My second orgasm is by far the best, way fiercer than the first.

Bridgette screams madly and I almost want to clamp my hand over her mouth, afraid the neighbors will hear. Then I realize this is a sound they damn well better get used to. I plan to make her come plenty more times in *our* home. I love her boldness, how she can just let go and be wild. I know it's part of knowing that David is no longer free.

As my wild girl calms down, she collapses on me. I hold her tightly against my body, loving the closeness and quite frankly still being nestled inside of her. Fuck it, maybe we'll go for five. I flip her on her back and can see the shock on her face as I begin to move.

Chapter 31

Essential

"I cannot believe we are having this conversation on the way to my parents'."

"What?" she responds nonchalantly.

"I told you, I'm not tying you up. Not ever again."

"Troy, I told you that pisses me off. I'm not going to let what that sicko did to me ruin that part of *us*. I know how much it turns you on. Don't take it away from me."

"Do you think I want to?" I argue back.

"Don't yell at me."

"I'm sorry, baby, I didn't mean to yell, it's…it's just I can't go there with you. Not after seeing you like that on that bed. It freaks me out, okay?"

"But you want to. I know deep down you do. Let it go, I have."

I try to stay calm although my blood is boiling. "I can't, baby. You still have bruises from what that prick did. I know you say you are okay with this, but what if I trigger something and it takes you back to that day? I can't risk it.

I won't risk what we have for my kink. You mean too damn much, Bridge.

"I know you're concerned and I appreciate that. But there's nothing that can trigger within me to make me think of him. I've let it go. I've had to do it my whole life and have gotten really good at it. David's done, he's gone. Yeah, I'll have to see him if he doesn't cop a plea deal and I have to testify. But stressing now or ruining what we have isn't going to help anything."

"I don't know how you do it, baby."

"Do what?" she asks, confused.

"Let it go. Forget about him and what he did."

"It's easy. I focus my mind and energy on the good stuff in life. I've got you and that makes everything so much easier. I couldn't imagine if I had to go at this alone. We just moved in and are having a normal, healthy conversation about our sex life. Things couldn't be better."

"God, I love you. I'm one lucky son of a bitch."

"Hey, don't call yourself that right before we see your mom."

I laugh at her absurd remark and pull down my parents' street. Their home is a new modern ranch style with enough space for them and my sister. "This conversation isn't over," she says.

"Sure it is."

"Troy!" she snaps. "Don't push me or I'll handcuff myself and make you fuck me. Get over this, okay?"

"I might have an idea. Don't go doing anything

brazen, okay?" She nods her head as I put my Jeep in park. "So this is it."

"It's cute. I love the color."

"I don't know how my dad's gonna be as far as drunk or not. So just try and take anything he says lightly and hopefully we won't be here long."

"It'll be fine, baby. Let's do this."

I get out of the Jeep while she waits for me to open her door. As I grab her hand, I notice both of her wrists are covered in bracelets. I know she's trying to hide the bruises; they are faint, but still there. We decided not to tell anyone who didn't need to know about what happened, so I know she doesn't want my parents to see the marks. Hopping out, she looks up at me looking hot as hell, in a pair of dark skinny jeans and a white t-shirt.

I pull her to me and press our lips together knowing it'll be far too long before I can do this again. "Let's go meet your family," she says.

I walk us up to the front door looping our fingers together and as I go to knock, my mom answers it with the biggest smile on her face. "Troy," she exclaims wrapping me in her arms. I have to let go of Bridgette's hand, but for my mom it's worth it. I feel my mom reach away from me to touch Bridgette. As I look to my side she is rubbing her arm. "So this is her? This is the one?"

Instantly I turn ten shades of crimson knowing this is what I am in for tonight. Fuck my big mouth for spouting off. I may or may not have told her that Bridgette was the one…

"Mom, this is Bridgette. Bridge, this is my mom, Krista."

Bridgette goes for a handshake, but my mom engulfs her in a hug like she's known her for years. "Sweetheart, it's so nice to meet you. Troy didn't mention how beautiful you are."

"Thank you, ma'am," she responds.

"Oh Lord, Troy, and she has manners. Wait 'til your father meets her. Come in, come in."

My stomach tightens at the thought of my dad meeting her. I know at first he'll be all nice to try and make me look like an asshole for bad-mouthing him, but it won't be long 'til he has a few drinks and then we're all in trouble.

"Jared, Brittany," my mom calls out as we enter the house following her into the kitchen. "They'll be up soon," she says. "I know Brittany has a big chess tournament they've been preparing for.

"She's still into chess?" I ask as we lean up against the counter.

"Yes, dear. You know how she is, busy-busy."

I thought my sister wasn't playing chess anymore. It was something my dad always wanted her to do. Last I knew she was going to tell him she wasn't interested in it anymore, but I guess not.

"Mmm, it smells great, Krista. What did you cook?" Bridgette asks.

"Pork chops, Troy's favorite."

"No shit. Thanks, Ma."

"Of course, darling. So tell me what you kids have been up to lately."

Both Bridgette and I look at each other. "Not much. We just got back from the cabin; it was nice to get away.

Then I hear my dad and sister walk up from the basement. "Troy, I sure hope you cleared that with your mom, because I sure as hell didn't know about it."

My mom swallows hard and looks at me. I feel bad knowing that she and I didn't talk about it first. Thinking fast, I try and put some shit together to cover my ass, but like usual my mom does it for me. "Of course he cleared it with me, Jared, don't be silly. It just slipped my mind, dear."

The conversation ends with that statement and my sister runs over to me wrapping me in a big hug. "Hey, Brit," I say holding her back.

"Hey. How have you been?"

"I'm good. I have someone I want you to meet." Looking next to me, Bridgette is smiling at us and outstretches her hand to shake Brittany's.

"You must be Brittany."

My sister takes her hand and says, "You must be Bridgette."

"I am. It's nice to meet you. Troy has told me so many great things about you."

"Thanks."

"Bridge, this is my dad, Jared," I interject and introduce the man standing across from me.

"It's a pleasure to meet you, sir," she says, shaking his hand. He looks intently into her eyes, like he's trying to read her then and there as they shake. A wave of nausea takes over when he looks down at her wrists. *Please don't let him notice the marks.* He's the only one who knows about my fetish besides Bridge. He caught me with my high school girlfriend and that's where our relationship went wrong. He was a POW and was held captive for eight months. That shit has fucked with him for years. It's part of the reason he drinks, to dull the pain. I know he was tied while he was held captive and that's why he has such a huge problem. He doesn't accept that side of me and made it very clear then that he never will. Although what happened to him and what I do are two totally different things, to him they are not. I injured someone tying them up, and he'll never let that go.

The oven dings and my mom says, "Why don't you all have a seat at the table and I'll bring the food out."

"I can help," Bridgette offers.

"That's nonsense, dear."

"Are you sure?" she asks again.

"Yes, yes, have a seat." We all go and sit down, well, all of us except my mom and dad. He's in the kitchen making himself a drink and I know it won't be long until the obscenities start.

"So, Brit, Mom said you have a chess match next week, are you excited?"

She nods her head and I call bullshit. "It's the semi-finals. If our team makes it, we go to the division finals."

"So you play chess competitively?" Bridgette asks.

"Uh-huh."

"I thought you did gymnastics?"

"I do that to."

"Wow, how do you have the time to balance everything?"

"I stay up late a lot doing homework. After school is always busy, so I make sacrifices elsewhere. My sleep struggles a little, but I'm used to it."

My dad joins us at the table while my mom follows in after him with her arms full of food. *Asshole.* Why, couldn't he set his drink down to help her?

"Here, Ma, let me get some of this for you." I stand up and take some of the things from her.

"Thanks, honey."

She comes back in, setting the huge pan of pork chops down in front of me. My mouth begins to water. These are my favorite. I had no idea she was making them, but I am about to devour the entire pan. We all begin to serve our plates and before any of us has had our first bite, my dad is making himself another drink.

Bridgette looks at me and I smile at her. I know we don't have long before the monster from within him is released. "So, Bridgette, tell us what you do for a living?" my mom asks sweetly.

"I'm an office manager for a local law firm."

"Oh really, which one?"

"Smith, Brown, and Mileski," she responds.

My dad huffs sitting back down and we all look at him waiting for him to say something. He piles food into his mouth and then to my surprise, Bridgette asks him, "Have you heard of them before, Mr. Sorano?"

He nods his head as he speaks, "Yeah, I have. They have that hot shot attorney from Phoenix, who's," my father air quotes the next statement, "'Never lost a case.' Yeah, right, he's gotta be crooked. No one's that good."

Both Bridgette and I look at each other smiling and I say, "Actually, Dad, that's Bridgette's brother-in-law. Trust me, I know him, he's far from crooked."

"No way. That's awesome," Brittany exclaims. "I've heard about him, he's pretty amazing in the courtroom. I would love to be an attorney one day."

"Really? Well, he's a great guy, and so are C.J. and Liam. If you're serious about a degree in law, let me know. I'm sure I could get you a meeting with the guys."

My mom puts her hand over Bridgette's and before she can speak my dad slams his hand on the table. "Over my dead body. I said he's crooked and so are the rest of them. Plus they're nothing but a bunch of young punks. I don't want my daughter near them, especially if you're vouching for them, Troy."

I glare at him, completely thrown off. All I said was I knew Vincent. "Excuse me?"

"You heard me. I'm sure they are just like you. Look

at what you've already done to this poor girl." Reaching across the table, he lifts Bridgette's wrist and moves her bracelets. She pulls away holding her arm tightly against her chest. I can't help but shoot out of my chair, looking down at him. "You don't know what the fuck you're talking about."

"Really, Troy? I don't? Are you sure you want to do this here?" he questions.

I stand trying to decide if I want my mom and sister to know about that side of me. This is his opportunity to out me. If he does, all of the pieces of the puzzle will click together; everything that has happened over the past ten years will fall into place, and make sense for them. This is why he hates me. This is why I have never and will never live up to his standards.

"I know what you are, Troy, and it disgusts me. You're no better than those pigs who held me captive." I'm speechless, frozen, and ready to take my own father out. However, there's venom in his tone and I know that, mixed with the alcohol, puts me at a great disadvantage. I know if I push this, it'll hurt more for my mom to know the truth. He'll paint me as a monster. Instead of putting her through that and giving him another victory, I grab Bridgette's hand. Right away she stands next to me. "You don't know shit about me," I snarl.

"I don't? Bridgette, who put those marks on your arms?"

"Fuck off, we're leaving. I'm sorry, Ma. I just…I

can't." I can barely look at her as we exit the kitchen and I bolt for the front door. All I hear is the sounds of her sobs. I hate that she had to see this. *Fuck*. Why did he have to take it to this level? If he was really concerned, which I doubt he was, he could have taken me aside and asked.

Rage washes through me as we get into the Jeep. Bridgette doesn't speak and I know it's for the best. I need a few minutes to calm down. On the drive home, I hold her hand tightly. She sits facing me, chewing on her nails. My cell phone rings and I know without answering it, it's my mom. I can't talk to her right now. Pulling into the driveway, I put the car in park and rest my head back. Then I take in a deep breath, hoping it will clear my mind.

"I'm sorry, baby," Bridgette whispers.

"No, no, no. Don't be sorry, Bridge. You didn't do a thing wrong. Thank you for not engaging him and leaving with me."

"Of course. I go where you go. We're a pair and there's nothing I want to tackle in this life without you."

"I feel the same."

"Would it help if we talked about what happened?"

I exhale loudly, letting all of the air escape my lungs shaking my head. "I don't know what to say."

"Why did he accuse you of hurting me and say he knows what you are?"

"God, this happened so long ago, baby. I fucked up. It only happened once and I swear it will never happen again. He caught me with a girl in high school. I was curious and she let me tie her up. I didn't know what I was doing and it left marks, really bad marks, a lot like yours." Taking my hand, I brush her bracelets out of the way and trace the remnants of the bruising. "The thing about my dad is he was a POW and was held captive for eight months. He was tied up and shit like that fucks with him. Because of that he doesn't agree with my lifestyle choices and since that day, he has treated me differently."

"I'm so sorry, baby. I had no idea."

"It's okay. It's not something I talk about, babe. His past is his, not mine. But for me, I didn't know how hard all of this was going to be, then seeing these marks on you took me back. I don't want to ever tie you up again."

"What about what I want?" she asks me point blank. "I trust you and I love you for the man that you are. I fell in love with you because of all the little things, the kinky side of you being one of them. Please don't take that away from me."

I never in a million years thought she would enjoy my kink as much as I do. For years I dreamt of finding someone like Bridge…now I have her and don't know how I got so goddamn lucky. *Please don't take that away from me.* Her words replay in my mind like a broken record.

Instinctively, I know what I have to do; there is something else I can give her. Not her wrists, but I can tie her a million other ways. I get out of the car walking to her side with purpose. Swiftly removing her and tossing her over my shoulder, she giggles as I do. Jesus, I love her laugh.

"Troy," she yells. "Put me down, I can walk."

Ignoring her, I smack her ass, not faltering for one minute. I'm on a mission to get my rope. I never imagined I would find someone like her, someone who completes me and accepts every little fucked up piece of me. She's given me the greatest gift in the world. I know that with her by my side I can survive anything. She is the most essential part of my world and I'm finally seeing the truth in how essential I am to hers. Life may not always be an easy road, but together we can overcome anything.

Epilogue

-Bridgette-

As I stare at Troy, I see nothing but love. I know he won't hurt me – he never has and he never will. My body pulses with endorphins watching his naked frame handle the rope. I hope tonight, he'll finally tie my arms. Since I was taken, he has done everything – except my wrists. And still he won't even touch them.

"How much?" I ask as he doubles the dark gray material.

"One-fifty."

Working with that much line takes skill. Until tonight, the most we have ever used is about a hundred feet.

"So tell me what you want, baby."

I think about all of the scenarios and roles we have played. One in particular sticks out to me. "Karada?" I ask.

"My favorite," he responds. "Maybe I'll tie your feet into it as well."

"Or my wrists?" I ask holding them together in front of him.

"No." He shakes his head and leans down kissing each of them.

I know better than to push the subject. I've tried, and it backfired. I bought a pair of fuzzy handcuffs and cuffed my arms together. Let's just say you don't want to see that side of Troy. Panic and anger is not a good combo.

"Turn around," he requests. I listen and now have my back to his chest. He takes the rope and places it below my breasts. Before he moves any further he pinches each of my nipples, pulling out hard. Then his hands move to my back, creating the first loop and the base to all of this. With his exceptional craftsmanship, he begins to work – over one breast, under the other, and then another loop. Troy knows exactly what I like, how much pressure to use or not use. As he works his way down creating more and more art, he leaves kisses all over my body.

"This is so soft," I say.

"It's silk rope. Only the best for my baby."

I love watching him walk around me. His concentration is on point. I always try to distract him, but it's futile. When we're in this moment and he's in his element, he's in total control. Nothing could take him out of it. As he takes more of the rope behind me, he winds in and out of each of my thighs. Then he pushes his erection into me. The tip is wet and I know it's because of what he just did and he wants me.

"God, you're beautiful," he says into my ear.

I turn to face him, tangling my hands into the back of

his hair and claiming his mouth. As we kiss, I am saddened that this is our last night in Vegas. It's been a blast being here with everyone. Troy begins to walk me backwards to the bed. Once we reach it, he pushes me back letting me fall onto the plush fabric. I can't help but giggle as he clambers over me, straddling my body. I look up at him, ready and willing for anything. Leaning down, he places the blindfold over my eyes. The last thing I see is the gleam of his wedding band.

That ring on his hand is the sexiest thing in the world. Yes, we got married. Did we do it on a whim? Kind of. But Troy and I talked about it many times and this is what *we* wanted. I was a positive stem cell match for Robert and am going forward with the procedure. God forbid anything should happen to me, we wanted to be married. Both of us are certain that we are each other's future. We want to spend the rest of our lives together and if all goes to plan, we can do that.

"Bend over, Mrs. Sorano. Face down and ass up, just like I like."

I comply with his demand. Waiting for what's to come. I'm not sure if he will spank me with his hand or a crop or something else, but I'm wet in expectation.

"Are you going to let me fuck your ass tonight?" he asks.

I shake my head, completely petrified. We might be able to explore every other kinky aspect of sex, but I can't go there. I just can't.

"One day, you'll let me, baby."

An unfamiliar object touches my back. The skin below it tingles and goose bumps form on the surface. Troy moves it down, tracing all around where the rope binds me. It's soft and almost tickles, yet it's so warm.

I shiver in pleasure and have to ask, "What is that?"

"A feather." He moves it between my legs and I shake in excitement. "My wife likes?"

"Mmm-hmm."

"Good. Roll over. Let me get your front."

Troy takes his time moving the feather everywhere. I keep my eyes closed, because everything is black behind the blindfold anyways. He must have sensed I wanted it off and he removes it. When he does, I'm struck by his flawlessness. He is gorgeous and all mine. He moves kneeling next to me and his weight shifts the bed. I lean over, gripping his cock and molding my lips around the end.

Weaving his fingers into my hair, he helps guide me.

"Use your other hand," he requests.

I know he wants to see my ring. Both of us have been admiring how they look on each other's hands. His is a simple titanium band; mine is a thin diamond-encrusted band. Next on our list is the honeymoon.

I move my head meeting his cock as he pushes it into my mouth and I can't help but notice my ring sparkling in the dim light of the room. "I'm gonna come in your sweet mouth."

I adjust myself so I have a good hold and can see him. His hand is still in my hair, while the other one he keeps rested on his hip. I love the expression on his face. But there are so many. I can tell when I push him close and then he slows his movements, holding on to his orgasms. Then there's the one of madness, the one that looks like he's going to explode and fuck me wildly. Then there is him – my Troy – when he concentrates on me, looking into my soul.

Taking my tongue, I swirl it over his shaft with each pull. He begins to moan, then grunts. I never take my eyes off of him and he never closes his. We stay connected like we have been for what seems like so long and how we will be *forever*.

His noises stay even as spurts of warm cum drench my throat. I love his taste. Who am I kidding? I love everything about him. That's how I truly know we are made for each other. It's the little things with Troy – it always has been and it always will be.

"I should make you suck me off again, your mouth feels so fucking good."

"I can…" I offer.

"NO! I want my pussy." He spreads my legs wide. My clit throbs watching him. He takes his time dragging his tongue in between my wet slit, then pulls away and blows on me. I quiver and twist away from him. He grabs the front of the rope, gripping it harshly, and pulls me to him. The force of his hand tightens every cord around my body and this is why I have grown to love what we do just as much as he does. There's something about the control he has over me when I'm bound like this.

"Don't turn away from me, unless I tell you. Understand?"

I nod my head trying to contain the smirk hidden beneath; he acts so tough. Although there's no bite to his bark, he's all talk. Well, almost all talk; he flips me over and swats my ass hard. He does spank me good – really fucking good.

"Is there something funny, Mrs. Sorano?"

"No, absolutely not."

"Good."

He adjusts his grip on the rope to my back and grips his cock holding it against my opening. "I can't wait to fuck you," he says slamming into me. I gasp from the force; it's the best feeling in the world. He satisfies me right away, moving with urgency. His rhythm is fast and hard. I love it when he's not gentle, and tonight…he's not gentle. He pulls me up to him, still pummeling inside of me and holds my breasts.

I'm pinned against him, my back to his front. The only thing separating us is the layer of silk rope. Our noises are in unison, both of us moaning in enjoyment at the same time. I take my hands and reach behind me, holding his head as he sucks on the skin of my neck. With my arms up, my boobs push into his hands even more.

I lock my fingers behind his head, wishing they were

tied as well and enjoy the ride. I try and kiss him, but this angle keeps us separated a bit too much. Troy pulls out of me and flips me over guiding me to lie on my back. "I need to see you," he says.

I nod my head as I sprawl out. He slips back inside of me and lays his weight above me. We move together and he holds my face with each of his hands resting on my cheeks. I plunge my tongue into his mouth. He is *my* husband and I couldn't be happier or ask for anything more.

Troy leans up looking down at me. I have my arms stretched above my head. Each of his movements gets me closer to orgasm and I can't wait. I love how good he makes me come. I can tell as we fuck that he keeps eyeing my wrists, and I wish again he would let go of the past like I have. If he would only tie them together once, I think he could get over his fear and I remember how happy it made him.

All of my worries wash away as my pussy tightens and throbs, pulsating with pure pleasure. Troy works my orgasm out as I start to scream his name. "Fuck yeah, baby. Let me hear you," he encourages me.

I fall out of this world unconscious of anything that is going on. Everything inside of me trembles and ticks. I love being washed away, lost to anything that's important, but us. All I have to do is focus on one thing and one thing only – Troy. Suddenly, the fog I'm in all floats away. I'm a bit caught off guard the moment he takes ahold of my wrists, holding both of them together in a vise. I stare at him surprised, but his eyes are closed. He's in his zone and watching him begin to come, growling loudly, is one of the greatest feelings. His free hand is in a fist on the bed holding him up while his other has a *firm* grip on me, on my arms holding them so tightly together. He hasn't touched me like this since the day at the hospital. I pray this time he is aware of what's he's doing and it's not a mistake.

I know last time when he acted out in the heat of the moment – he regretted it. That day, when he held them together was when everything changed. I don't want another step back for us – we don't need one. My pussy is warm from his cum and my eyes are focused on him.

His breathing is erratic, there's not a calm beat to it. But his movements aren't the same. They are slow, long, and planned. Each is made with accuracy. I can't stop myself from kissing his chest and anywhere my lips can touch as he finishes. Tears prick the back of my eyes when he looks down at me and smiles, still holding my wrists together.

I know then in that exact moment that what he did was on purpose. We've finally made it over our last hurdle. Yes, it took a bit if time, but we got there. Nothing satisfying in life comes easy. Now all that lies ahead is the future – our future. He is essential to my sanity, my well-being, and everything that matters. He is part of me, has been from the day I met him. Our wedding vows ring in my ears. As I close my eyes enjoying the perfection that is my life, I can hear him say the words. *'Til death do us part.*

Acknowledgements

I am seriously speechless to have completed writing my third book. This has been such a whirlwind of a year. I do have to first and foremost thank my wonderful husband, who you all have so graciously named the 'president' for his many talents. Without his constant support, there is no way that I could do what it is that I do. Not only is he behind me one hundred percent, but he has also stepped up by helping me in so many ways with my writing career. I love you, babe, to infinity and beyond.

Miranda, I don't know who in this world to thank for bringing you into my life, but whoever it is, I'm ready to bow down and kiss their feet. I seriously couldn't do all of this without you. You're extremely talented and I'm lucky to have you on my side. Then you add the fact that you're my best friend and I'm…well, I'm the luckiest bitch in the world.

To my amazing editor, Lisa, you rocked my socks with this book. As always working with you is an honor. Your many talents impress me and the laughs we share throughout the process are priceless – there's nothing like rabid children…right? I do have to say, you owe Troy an apology and you know why. I love you, girl.

For my Pimpettes – Adrean, Cheryl, Christina, Karrie,

Keri, Kim, Lindsey, Loca, Mary, Sarah, and Tevy. Each and every one of you brings a smile to my face daily. Sometimes I cannot believe the hard work and dedication you all put into sharing your love of my stories. I honestly couldn't ask for a better group of girls to have my back. Thank you from the bottom of my heart for everything.

To my beta and proofreading team. I'm hands down indebted to each and every one of you always. Leticia, girl, you have some talent. Thank you for making sure my babies are always to perfection. Kate and Michelle, thank you both for dealing with my short deadlines, but most importantly thank you for loving these stories. RL and Christina, thank you both for going above and beyond. I appreciate the hours of time that each of you put into reading and providing feedback for my stories.

And last but not least…there are all of the fans and bloggers. Without all of you, I am nothing. My books would sit idle with unread stories, itching to be free. However that's not that case. You all read them and love them. That motivates me to write and inspires me to make sure I give you nothing less than excellence. Thank you again, for loving these characters.

So what's next for LK? Well, that's for me to know and you to find out. I'm totally joking; I wouldn't do you guys like that. I'm taking a break from the Life. Destiny. Fate. series – for now – to write a standalone novel titled, *Every Soul Has A…* A what, you ask? Well, you'll have to read to find that out. This story came to me after a friend recommended I branch out, and the characters have not stopped talking since. As an author, when that happens – you write. My goal is to deliver *Every Soul Has A…* in the Summer of 2014. Don't worry though, the Life. Destiny. Fate. series isn't over; Liam will be next, ladies.

Lastly to anyone that has left a review for any of my books, thank you. From the ones that are a few sentences, to others that have pushed close to a thousand words, both the president and I read every single one. Please don't forget to leave yours. I want to know exactly what you thought of *Essentialism.* Thank you again for all of the support, and remember to always follow your heart, it will never steer you wrong. XOXO, LK.

www.ingramcontent.com/pod-product-compliance
Lightning Source LLC
Chambersburg PA
CBHW030415180626
46812CB00005B/2010

* 9 7 8 0 5 7 8 1 3 7 4 5 2 *